THE
DROWNING
WORLD

a new novel in the Aquantis Series

by Brenda Peterson
www.BrendaPetersonBooks.com

Note:
The technology of this cosmos is protected
under a pending trademark.

DELPHINIUS
PUBLISHING
SEATTLE
WASHINGTON

Cover design: Betty Watson.
Interior and paperback design: Sherry Wachter
Cover photo: "Whirlpool in France," © James A. Sugar
National Geographic Stock. Image 43967
Mermaid art: original photo by Mehgan Heaney-Grier,
"Mermaid, 2010" wickimedia commons license

A note on the cover: Meghan Heaney-Grier is a U.S. Free Dive
Champion who has dived to a depth of 165 feet and can hold her
breath for 4 and ½ minutes. For more on her ocean advocacy, acting,
and diving: www.freediver.com/

Praise for Brenda Peterson's Books

DUCK AND COVER
A *New York Times* "Notable Book of the Year"

"A wicked black comedy ...
Peterson would seem to hold out just about as much hope
for the family as she does the planet."
New York Times

"Bittersweet and utterly beguiling novel."
Publishers Weekly

"A hauntingly funny writer ...
the balance she strikes is almost hypnotic."
Los Angeles Times

I WANT TO BE LEFT BEHIND:
Finding Rapture Here on Earth

"Top Ten Best Non-Fiction Books of the Year"
by *The Christian Science Monitor*

"An unusually affecting and radiant spiritual memoir ...
a witty, enrapturing account of a spiritual journey of
great relevance to us all."
Booklist, starred review

"Outstanding memoir ... her vivid imagination combined with
a lilting writing style makes this book a pleasure to read."
Miami Herald

ANIMAL HEART

"One can hardly imagine a more heartfelt work or a more unusual
love story than this one. Highly recommended."
Library Journal

"Brenda Peterson weaves a haunting love story
into a fast-moving plot.
Please read it."
Jane Goodall, author *Reason for Hope*

PRAISE FOR THE DROWNING WORLD

"This underwater world is so believable and vivid and fascinating.
It's a page-turner. Irresistible!"

Sy Montgomery,
The Good, Good Pig

"The merpeople and their resplendent undersea setting are so full
and rich ... truly a water world. Amazing and haunting, *The Drowning World* exceeds the grasp of *The Golden Compass* in its themes and
imaginative reach. A wonderful novel."

Marion Copeland
Nature in Legend and Story

"*The Drowning World* is a rollicking good tale of shape-shifting,
time travel, mermaids, sound tattoos, the secret world of Aquantis,
and other dreams of Peterson's glorious imagination—
all set against the backdrop of powerful forces—
the fate of the seas, human turmoil, young love, and
what everyone feels at some point in their life:
The sense of being an alien in an alien land.
Its pull is oceanic—it quickly lures you deep beneath its waves
while time evaporates."

Diane Ackerman
The Zookeeper's Wife

www.BrendaPetersonBooks.com

TABLE OF CONTENTS

For my dear friend and visionary,
Rebecca Romanelli,
who read, advised, and
took this journey with me every week
at the Salish Sea Spa

Author's Note

Since 2003, I've been building this underwater cosmos. *The Drowning World* is part of my Aquantis Series. Its characters and technologies are fully imagined and fictional. May this novel help us adapt to our amphibious future. Shift!

PART ONE

CHAPTER 1
Shape-Shifting

MARINA

Our Aquantan Masters always taught us: "Never try to Shift into your land legs if you're hungry, tired, or scared."

I was all of those things as my dolphin, Dao, and I floated in the warm waves off the empty shores of SkyeWorld.

"Where are we?"

"Gulf of Mexico, circa 2020, according to my acoustic map," Dao replied anxiously. He was also hungry and exhausted from the long journey up through the WaveHole. But we were under strict orders not to eat any fish in SkyeWorld waters. Spinning around in the waves, his sonar clicking, Dao telepathed, "We're right off Siesta Key ... in a place called Florida."

"Think I can pass for human?" I asked Dao. My mind-talk trembled with self-doubt.

"Guess you'll find out, Marina," was all Dao would say. His brown, unblinking eyes mirrored my anxiety.

It was the first time in our sixteen years that Dao and I would be separated, though this mission was not our first Diplomat-Spy assignment to SkyeWorld. Once before, Dao and I had taken an advanced class field trip here. We witnessed a terrible tsunami. But we never ventured on land to see the humans' ruined shelters and drenched earth. The Sound Masters kept us far offshore, barely riding the gigantic wall of water that threatened to drown even us sea creatures. I would never forget the sinking humans—their eyes open wide in terror. Their arms flailed upward like useless wings as they floated, their quiet lungs at last liquid. Unlike us, they couldn't breathe underwater.

We couldn't save them all. This time our mission was to save our underwater civilization. We were here to discover why so many adult Aquantan ambassadors and spies were returning very ill from Skye-World.

"Time to Sound Shift," Dao advised, his eyes troubled. "Do it, before the humans wake up."

I sang and was suddenly naked. Visible. Vulnerable. Not even my acoustic *lanugo* cloak with its protective second skin could hide me now. Above us in the vast sky, a few sleek silver blimps sailed. "Solar dirigibles," they called them. It was SkyeWorld's main form of transportation, since the humans had all but drained the oil supply from their earth.

"This is the beach where the Blue Beings told us we'd find Elder Turtle *Honu-wahi*," Dao told me. "She'll nest again onshore tonight. You have just this one day on land to find out what's going wrong here ... before we meet the Elder."

"Got it," I nodded quickly, but my webbed hands were shaking.

I shifted my breathing from gills to mouth. At first the air was heavy, burning my throat and lungs. But after a few minutes, the breeze off the earth tasted like the sweetest ambrosial Aquantan *manna*—golden liquid with a honeyed perfume. Intoxicating. I felt a weird hunger as I breathed in the delicious air.

"Don't be a show-off on shore, Marina," Dao warned. "That would be dangerous."

Then he telepathed a few vivid images to me: Aquantan ambassadors imprisoned in medical labs as human conducted secret, mostly military experiments on them. Elegant tail flukes painfully explored with electric probes and primitive ultrasound. The last image Dao sent me was the worst: an Aquantan Diplomat-Spy, Master Loo, one of my favorite teachers, laid out on a cold, metal table, his once mighty tail flukes still, his torso sliced open and stitched with coarse, black thread. Dead, dissected.

I shivered, though the water was even warmer with the heat of the morning sun. "Seeeeeeeooooooohhhh," I trilled all twelve octaves of my Signature Song, rising and falling.

Birds overhead practically fell from the sky, startled by my ultrasonic song. It was too high for humans to hear. My whole body shuddered. It was painful. Shifting is always painful. My tail flukes glittered and shook free from the thousands of tinkling silver scales. My backbone hummed as my dorsal fin folded neatly, hidden against my spine. Heat lightning slashed like a laser up through my flukes and ripped my lovely tail in two.

My fins unfurled into feet with ten wobbly toes. I wiggled them to make sure the blood was flowing. Without my tail flukes to steady me, I sank beneath the waves, sputtering. I didn't like how slow and limited I was without my powerful flukes.

"Do you think you can walk on them?" Dao asked, scanning my legs for any flaws, his sonar pinging off muscles and femur bones that were usually fused.

I lifted my long legs to study them as I floated. Only a few scales still shone on my calves, which were a shade lighter than my bronzed torso. I would need some time in the sun to balance my skin tones. Toenails always intrigued me. They were so transparent and weirdly pretty. When I'd studied this world in our Sound Mural training documentaries, I'd noted that some girls painted their toenails bright colors. Maybe I could do that, too.

"I'm ready."

"Go," Dao said softly, "and come back to me soon." His dark eyes held mine.

I was facing a test unlike any other I'd ever aced. This mission was real and the consequences deadly if I failed. But it was strangely exciting to walk on the earth, to try to fit in, to finally find out who I really was.

"I'll meet you back here tonight at low tide," I told Dao, feeling less brave than I sounded.

Born together, we would die together. Dao was my Constant, my dolphin companion and twin soul. How could I leave him?

Stretching my legs tentatively, my feet landed on the soft, sinking sand. I bounced a few times. At least this felt familiar. The beach was blazing white and looked hot to the touch. A shiver ran along my new legs. I wriggled my toes in the sand, scattering a few tiny crabs. The sight of them made my stomach growl again with hunger. But I knew better than to devour them.

I sloshed out of the surf. First one wobbly leg. Then the other. Standing upright on the beach, I glanced both ways to make sure no one saw me. In the surf, Dao leapt and pirouetted, scouting for any signs of trouble. "Don't trust anyone!" he whistled. Fear darkened his tones.

I took each step with some effort. Gravity felt like a hand pushing my body down into the earth. No wonder humans sometimes seemed burdened. The air they breathed was so dense, heavy. It didn't float or carry them up like the waves.

Once out of the sea, the sand was surprisingly cool. Stealthily, I sprinted toward the shade of a palm tree. My first task was to find some proper clothes. As I strode toward a clothesline outside a beach cottage, I was surprised to feel my legs gain strength with each step. My toes gripped the sand with authority. I had the weird sensation that I belonged here. And this frightened me more than anything else so far on the mission.

I quickly snatched a soggy swimsuit from a clothesline that was hung with T-shirts and shorts. The material was tight and uncomfortable. It didn't breathe and was hot to the touch. Zigzag patterns on the swimsuit made me wince. It was too noisy. I studied the T-shirts. Which one was right to give me the most camouflage? I chose one with a cute human baby swimming naked in a turquoise pool. People would know by this T-shirt that I meant them no harm. The T-shirt read:

NIRVANA
Nevermind

What did that mean? I tried to recall my Cross-Cultural Skye-World studies for the word: Wasn't nirvana heaven for humans? Was this really a paradise? I wasn't sure I should wear a shirt whose message I didn't quite understand. It might even be a secret code, but I didn't have much choice. Quickly, I pulled it on over my loud swimsuit. When I saw rubber flip-flops and leather sandals lining someone's beach deck, my mood lightened. First I tried on the flip-flops, which made a spongy, slapping sound when I walked. But then I decided on the more practical sandals because they made less noise. Most of all, I needed to be quiet to avoid attracting any attention.

Walking the deserted beach at dawn, I didn't realize that I had already dropped into what humans would call a "stroll." My arms moved casually in synch with my legs. It felt free and easy, even though I was still getting the hang of the gravity thing.

It was good I'd stolen sandals because the street was black, scalding even through the leather soles. As I walked, I heard the clinking sound from the coins inside the small satchel strung across my chest. I'd never heard the sound of money before, since the tinkling of silver and gold coins was always muted underwater. The noise was intriguing, a metal music. I kind of liked its rhythm.

Other Aquantan visitors to the SkyeWorld always returned with lots of money for the next diplomatic missions. We also had storehouses of Spanish doubloons, precious gems, and pearls from shipwrecks at the bottom of the sea.

Seeing the small shops dotting the beach boulevard, I wished I'd paid more attention to my Foreign Currency Exchange classes. The tedious financial lessons had always bored me. In Aquantis, we used a barter system instead of money. I hoped that humans would help me figure out their coins. But Sound Master Lioli had warned us that in SkyeWorld wealth and power here were what dominated every exchange.

Most of the cottages in Siesta Key were still dark this early in the morning. While I got my bearings, it was nice to walk the crooked and curving sidewalks without meeting anybody else, though I did see some gardeners already at work, speaking a language I hadn't studied much.

"Hola!" one of the workmen called out pleasantly as he tipped his battered hat to me.

I knew enough to respond, "Buenos dias," and hurry away.

But this human's cheerful greeting gave me some confidence. At least one human believed I belonged here. But perhaps he knew better than to question anyone strolling this obviously wealthy neighborhood.

Exploring this community, I was surprised by its extremes. Some people lived in huge, red-tiled mansions with many attached outbuildings; others lived in modest cottages hidden by trees draped with hanging moss. Just as I was turning a corner, a rickety bicycle zoomed past, almost knocking me down.

"Watch where you're going!" a man yelled.

Soon I found myself on a street jammed with fusion and electric motorcycles, a few very old model cars that probably still ran on gas. The once chic boutiques and restaurants seemed washed out, some even boarded up. It looked like this place had seen better days. Neon flickered and there was a disturbing hum from electricity. It was all so loud and chaotic. Suddenly I felt light-headed. My stomach twisted.

I had to find some nourishment—even if it was only liquid. When I pinched my skin it wrinkled, a sure sign of dehydration. I was no longer getting liquid oxygen and nutrients from the sea through my gills. Air didn't feed my body. A nasty headache pounded in both my temples.

Scanning the street for a restaurant that was open, I finally saw a sign before a ramshackle shop called, "Sid's Fish Shack."

I slipped inside and the smell was dazzling. Clams, shrimp, even lobster were sizzling over a small fire. I'd never had fried fish but heard from other Aquantans that it was quite tasty. My stomach gurgled with hunger. Why hadn't I eaten more from our stash of seaweed and kelp before I came ashore?

There were only a few customers, mostly fishermen at the bar bent over their morning coffee or foaming beers. They'd probably been out at sea all night and were too tired to notice me. At least, that's what I hoped.

"What'ya having?" a waitress with startling frizzy red hair demanded. She seemed to be chewing something over and over that she never swallowed.

"Water, please," I said. My voice was a little hoarse and sounded too loud for my sensitive ears. It was a shame humans hadn't yet evolved telepathy.

"Strange accent," the waitress commented and looked me up and down. "You from South Africa or something?"

I shook my head, trying to remember my geography class. Where was that country?

"So ... what else?"

I didn't know what to say. "That's all, please."

The waitress scowled at me. "You gotta order more than water, honey, if you're going to take up a whole table for yourself. That's the rule."

I glanced anxiously around the fish shack, which was adorned with tattered driftnets and a huge, glazed trophy of a Bluefin tuna. Fear and hunger swirled in my stomach. What if I was captured and mounted up on someone's wall like a trophy?

"I'll have your special," I said, repeating a phrase I'd learned in Language Studies; it was to be used when visiting all foreign worlds.

The waitress chomped and gave me a suspicious look. "So you're ordering peeled shrimp and fried oysters ... for breakfast?"

"Yes ... yes," I said too quickly. It was obvious the waitress was beginning to think I was strange. "Thank you!"

Shrugging her shoulders and rolling her eyes, the waitress ambled off. "Peeled shrimp special, Sid!" she yelled.

A bleary-eyed man leaned out from the kitchen counter and stared intently at me. Bad sign. Would they arrest me now? "Well, ain't you the brave one?" the man laughed. "You sober?"

What did he mean? There was no one to ask. I slid lower in my chair. When the waitress brought me a tall glass of water with little cubes in it that clinked oddly, I drank it in one, thirsty gulp, even though it was much too cold.

I was just about to pay for the water and bolt from the place, when the waitress returned with a red plastic basket of steaming, boiled shrimp and succulent breaded oysters.

The spicy smell of seafood made me almost gasp with hunger. Before I could stop myself, I grabbed a handful of shrimp and devoured them. The shrimp were delicate with a salty tang and rich seasoning. I had never tasted anything so delicious. No wonder so many people in SkyeWorld were overweight!

I ploughed through the entire pile of shrimp before I noticed the waitress was staring at me in dismay. What was I doing wrong? Eating was something all species did.

"Ya know, most folks peel 'em first, honey," she said brusquely. "That's why they call it 'peeled' shrimp."

I heard laughter from a table behind me and turned to see several girls. I'd been eating so heartily I hadn't noticed them come in.

"Not from around here, is she?" one of the girls giggled, nodding toward me.

"Ya think?" one of the others smirked.

I imagine there were bullies in any world. But those human girls were really a threat. One call to the authorities could be the end of me. I summoned all my courage and smiled, though it felt quite false. I ignored them and turned back to eating.

"Nirvana?" one of the girls sniffed and nodded at my T-shirt. "Who's into grunge anymore? That's a blast from the past."

So was there time travel here, too? I wondered. I didn't think the SkyeWorld had evolved that far. Scanning the girls with my sonar, I heard churning stomach gases. They were just as starved as I was. But none of them ate a thing. Why not? Maybe they seemed so irritated watching me eat because they were hungry.

Frightened, I did what the Masters had taught me in Diplomat-Spy training: Keep your enemy close. That's what I'd learned to do with the snobbery and many slights from my younger sister, Pandora.

My sister always acted like we were highborn Aquantans, with all the rights and privileges our advanced civilization offered. Pandora never admitted that our family was mixed-blood human-Aquantan hybrids. We were just a controversial experiment, yet another new species created by the Blue Beings to act as ambassadors and diplomats to keep the peace between the worlds. Pandora had chosen the Warrior Way and was well known for her dangerous beauty. Already she had suitors, even from the Aquantan aristocracy, who were not officially allowed to mate with hybrids like us.

If Pandora had been selected for this mission to SkyeWorld instead of me, she'd be plotting how to conquer these snotty human girls, not befriend them.

I could never understand why my sister was always so angry and envious of me — ever since we were little. And it was not my fault that I was also chosen as High Priestess. I didn't even want that honorary title. It seemed more like a burden and a responsibility than an opportunity. Why hadn't the Blue Beings given Pandora the role? She was the Warrior who craved power in Aquantan society. I just wanted to travel and explore many other worlds.

"War is what will save us from SkyeWorld's sickness," Pandora always said. "It's the only thing that changes humans."

But my training was in clandestine diplomacy. And for that, I had to engage in cross-cultural courtesy.

"Would you ... would you like to join me?" I offered the girls in the fish shack.

Eyes rolling, hair flipping, they turned away as if I had some kind of disease. But dismissing me was better than discovering I was an alien.

Though I didn't look directly at the girls, I expanded my sonar range to study them secretly. The three girls were about my age, dressed in stylish tanktops and shorts. Their blonde or bleached hair was coiffed perfectly in complicated braids; their feet were tantalizingly bright in different nail polish shades—from hot pink to dark blue to coral. Their colorful toenails were what I admired most. Maybe I could return to Dao that night with painted toenails of my own.

Though the girls were pretty, they lacked any electromagnetic fields or acoustic tattoos that might reveal their family heritage or life stories they wanted to share with the world. One of the girls had a black butterfly etched right into her thin ankle. It was a new tattoo and still scabbed over. That must have been painful; and it seemed quite primitive. Our Aquantan acoustic tattoos were layers of sound and pictures just humming in our fields; they never pierced the skin. I assumed the girls also had no acoustic *lanugo* cloaks so they could be invisible and hide from predators.

My sonar picked up very little light beaming within their hearts. Not like in Aquantis, where every heart made its own light; collectively, all our bioluminescence makes our undersea city shine.

One of the girls, who acted like the leader, had an ulcer and seemed quite troubled. What was gnawing at her from the inside? On the outside, their splendor was visible. One girl had a small diamond stud in her nose and another girl wore stylish white-gold hoop earrings. I guessed that these girls were popular and valuable in their culture. The weary fishermen at the bar swiveled around in their chairs to admire the girls. One even whistled.

The girls acted as if the fishermen didn't exist. Again, they turned their critical focus on me.

"That's some tan you got there," one of the girls commented drily.

My skin was the color of the coffee and cream the fishermen were drinking. I tried to pull the T-shirt down over my legs. Pale with dark patches, my legs were still too new to match my upper torso. I was two-toned. Perhaps that was unacceptable in their world? And, unlike the other girls, my dark, unruly hair was braided with seed pearls.

"Mulatta," another girl whispered, her tone soft and menacing.

Whatever that meant, it was not good. It was perhaps a crime.

"Mixed blood," another girl sniggered.

And then, they all glared at me.

I had to get out of here and fast! Obviously I had failed to fit in. How had they recognized that I was of mixed blood—a human and Aquantan hybrid? I realized I was in great danger. But how could I ease myself out of the situation before someone called the authorities?

Images of my body strapped to a metal lab table flashed through my brain. Heart pounding, I ducked my head. How I wished I hadn't eaten all those shrimp because my stomach was cramping, tight.

Everybody, even the fishermen, stared at me. "You Creole, from New Orleans?" one demanded suspiciously.

"Uh, no," I said. "I'm from ..." my mind scrambled for something they might accept. "South Africa," I finished, with a glance at the waitress.

"Good. We got enough of that Cajun riff raff here. Ever since Hurricane Zora drowned New Orleans for good, we got nothing but trouble. Not enough fish. No jobs."

I felt pure panic rising and my invisible gills fluttered for air. But then I remembered I was out of the water and must steady my breath through my nose and mouth. I wondered how fast my strange new legs could carry me out of here? If I bolted, would they realize I was alien and attack?

I was surprised when the waitress came to my defense. "Rich white girls," she leaned down and whispered to me. "Pay them no mind. Eat your oysters now, sister," she winked. "They'll make you sexy."

I was so grateful for such generosity from the waitress whose skin tones were even darker than my own. Nodding dutifully, I quickly ate all the oysters, as instructed. I knew I was violating orders not to eat in SkyeWorld, but what else could I do? I couldn't make any more mistakes with these suspicious humans.

"You girls ever goin' to school?" the waitress asked, ambling over to their table and handing them a white slip of paper. Perhaps it was a secret note. "Best git!"

The girls pointedly ignored the waitress and me. But they did finish their coffee quickly before sauntering past my table.

"See you in school ..." one of the girls snipped. "New girl."

The last girl out slammed the screen door behind her so hard, even the waitress winced at the noise.

"Good riddance to bad rubbish," the waitress laughed. "Seconds, sister?" she asked.

I felt I should eat more to show proper courtesy to the waitress. "Uh, yes ... if you have enough."

"All you can eat, honey," the waitress laughed.

The fishermen at the bar turned away to hunker again over their coffee. The waitress snapped on a flat, square screen and it came alive with sounds and moving pictures. It was just like the Sound Murals in Aquantis, except it was much smaller, and only three-dimensional. I doubted these screens could depict shifts in time, like our Sound Murals could.

The screen showed a 3-D hologram of a black, serpentine stain seeping out over the turquoise waves. It looked ominous. A voice-over said: "Florida's Gulf Coast is facing its worst catastrophe in nine years, since the 2011 Deep Horizon oil spill."

Nobody was paying any attention to me now as the fishermen and the waitress, and all of the other few customers stared up at the screen in dismay. A reporter there was speaking in somber tones.

"North of Sarasota, Panama City beaches are already covered in tar balls," the reporter continued. Images shifted to scenes of people scooping toxic blobs of blackened sand into plastic robots that shuffled along the beach. "Many beaches are officially closed. The government has expanded the "No Fishing Zone" ...""

One of the fishermen exploded. "If that damned oil gets into the food chain like last time, our shrimp's ruined."

"We're on a death watch," another added.

I felt my intestines cramp and nausea rise up in my throat. Why had I eaten the food here against all of my orders? Now I knew why other Aquantans were returning home with strange stomach and respiratory maladies. It was oil tainting their food. My mission was over before it had begun. I was surprisingly disappointed.

"Change the channel," the waitress snapped. "I just can't watch it one more minute."

Before a fisherman could oblige, the screen shifted to a scene that so galvanized me I couldn't move. There was a stranded sea turtle dead and oil-soaked in the black sand. The desiccated carcass of a bottlenose dolphin mother and calf floated in the surf.

I bolted up from my table. I must warn Dao—and the turtles! My chair fell backwards as I ran toward the door.

"No one eats for free here," the waitress said, blocking my exit. She was not mean. She actually seemed a little sympathetic now. "I know you're down on your luck, honey, but pay me something, or Sid'll take it out of my paycheck."

I hesitated. I had no idea how much money my ill-considered consumption had cost me.

Hurriedly, I reached into my small satchel and brought out a Spanish doubloon. I knew it was precious and only to be spent wisely. But this waitress had rescued me from the girls. She looked so sad and beaten down. I hoped the doubloon might also in some way save this woman.

"Thank you for your kindness to strangers," I said with my best diplomatic formality. I placed the burnished gold coin in the waitress's outstretched hand. Then I ran as fast as my new legs could carry me toward the beach.

As I glanced back, I saw the waitress's face expand in astonishment and the fishermen in awe as she held up the golden doubloon for everyone to see.

Sprinting toward the surf, I had to navigate around a multitude of bodies now lying transfixed on the white sand. Were they also victims of the tainted food? Their skin seemed to be covered in a thin sheen of light-colored oil. I had to bounce my sonar off their listless bodies to make sure they weren't all dead.

No, they were sleeping. But during the day? I noticed that many of the sun worshippers had noisy acoustic fields around their ears. I clearly heard a cacophony of song: rap, country-western, oldies, and rock n' roll. I'd studied some of these fascinating musical traditions with Master Lioli in the Sound Temples. Master Lioli always said human music was melodic but primitive. Maybe there was some hope for a species that still spent so much time listening to music.

I had no time to do any more spying. At the moment, I knew enough. I had to go protect Dao and tell him this terrible news. Stashing my T-Shirt and sandals under a beach rock, I ran toward the surf in my bathing suit. Splashing into the waves, I couldn't shift back into my tail flukes without being seen. So I swam as far and as fast as my legs would allow. Far, far out into the warm waves. All the while I whistled and called out over the ultrasonic frequency I alone shared with my dolphin.

Mid-ocean, treading water with my weary legs, my breath was ragged. At last, I opened my gills and gratefully breathed in the saltwater's nourishing oxygen. Only when I heard Dao answer in his familiar clicks and bleeps, did I allow myself a few, quick tears of relief. And then, I promptly heaved up the two baskets of peeled shrimp. ˜

CHAPTER 2
Thieves

idnight. The Siesta Key beach was again empty as we waited for the Elder Turtle, *Honu-wahi,* to nest on the beach where she was born. Invisible, Dao and I floated offshore hidden inside my *lanugo.* We couldn't take any more chances at being seen or captured. The oil spill was moving ominously closer. We could hear the cries of far-off dying birds and dolphins suffocating on the Black Death. It was terrifying.

A few fishing boats rocked and creaked in the distance. Even the fishermen were sleeping below decks. But somewhere, a man was singing a plaintive song called "Yesterday," his voice full of longing and a gruff passion.

Who was he singing for? Would someone ever sing with such tender pain for me? And in what world would I fall in love?

As a Diplomat-Spy, my destiny was to travel many dimensions. I might discover a mate in my wanderings, someone very different from me. Or I might simply be used to make an alliance with another world—with someone I didn't even love. As a hybrid, who knew if the Blue Beings would even allow me to mate? Maybe I really was what some Aquantan aristocrats called "an evolutionary mistake."

Many Diplomat-Spies before me had found romantic intrigue in their travels, but rarely loyalty or love. Most of all, we were taught to distrust. Diplomat-Spies know that few people are what they seem. There's always a secret, an ulterior motive. I'd had enough training to recognize at least this lesson in Emotional Espionage.

Dao let go of me suddenly and faced me head-on. "One more night to find *Honu-wahi*," he said in a measured tone. "Then you promise to return to Aquantis with me?"

"I promise," I said solemnly. And I meant it. I rarely lied to my Constant.

"Go back, then." He dismissed me, but I could hear his turmoil.

Shifting was a little easier this time, but still uncomfortable. My flukes shed their scales and with an audible crack, my tail split into two legs. Quickly, I propelled myself through the warm waves and back to the shore.

The sand was soft and brilliantly white in the moonlight. When my legs touched the beach again, I felt an unsettling rush of adrenalin and attraction. Why did my body suddenly crave the touch and resonance of land?

I ran to the boulder under which I'd stashed my sandals and clothes, hurriedly slipped them on, and strode down the beach. Siesta Key crackled and shone like a nearby constellation. It was almost beautiful, this terrestrial town. I could hear the buzz of even more electric wires and had to adjust my ears to tune down the noise of this civilization so I could navigate by the stars and the sea.

I heard Dao's distant voice, "Tell *Honu-wahi* she must not lay her eggs here because of the oil."

I walked carefully but quickly down the beach toward the city lights. Soon I was running, my feet slapping the wet sand with a percussive rhythm. It was wonderful to discover that my land legs were almost as fast as my tail flukes. Locomotion, that's what they called it in this world. Freedom, I called it.

"Hey, you!" someone shouted, so loud that I had to cover my ears. "Stop!"

I froze. Exposed already! Glancing at the waves, I calculated if I was speedy enough to run straight back into the sea.

"Don't move one more step!" The voice was young, but quite authoritative. He had a slight, musical tone that was not unpleasant.

I couldn't see my attacker because his light was blaring. It had very few colors, except white. But I was able to echolocate him and spot his exact location. He was too close for me to escape without a chase. And his legs might just be faster than mine.

"Are you blind or something? You almost tripped over one."

"I didn't trip!" I exclaimed.

"Yes, you did!" The boy sounded impatient. "Are you so tuned into your iPod that you can't see there are turtles nesting here? Besides, this beach is closed tonight."

"Then why are you here?" I didn't like this boy's imperious tone. My anger at being so misunderstood by this human momentarily eclipsed my concern for the turtles.

Scanning the human in the dark I saw he wasn't much taller than me and his bone structure told me he was about 16, my same age. "I don't have to tell you anything!" I said.

He seemed surprised by my protest. Or perhaps the bedraggled T-shirt clinging to my knees tipped him off that I was alien. Maybe my legs weren't quite right, either. The girls this morning in the fish shack seemed to think being two-toned was suspicious.

His light moved up and down my body, and I flinched uncomfortably. Too bad my acoustic cloak didn't work on land. Well, I could always stun him with my song, but that would be a last resort; it would reveal my powers and I must try harder to pass as human, at least for now.

From the nearby waves, I heard Dao's caution: "Remember, you must be a diplomat or they'll see you're a spy."

I shifted tactics. "I would never harm a turtle," I explained to the boy in my most harmonious voice. "They are my father's ancestors."

"Yeah, right," the boy snorted, letting out a belly laugh. It was quite an ugly sound. "Look, you're trespassing."

"But I am here for the turtles, too," I insisted.

"I'm with the scientists," the boy declared with a pomposity recognizable in any world. "My father is the team leader."

His tone reminded me a little of Master Lioli, self-assured and self-important. "And so you're the team follower?" I snapped.

For a moment the boy seemed stunned, not by my sonar, but by my words. It was a revelation to me that spoken words could also be weapons of self-defense.

The boy cleared his throat and said in a steady voice, "My name is Lukas Barrios Rodriguez, and I'm turning you into the feds for harassing an endangered species. Your parents will have to pay a penalty."

"I didn't step on any nests!" I shouted. It was the first time I'd ever heard my own voice rise so loudly. It was not very diplomatic or pretty, but I kind of liked the strong sound of it. "I'm here to save turtles, too."

"You are?" Lukas asked doubtfully. "Who are you with—NOAA or the university? My father's with the University of Florida. We have jurisdiction here."

I scanned my memory for that word, jurisdiction. It was not an Aquantan concept and for a moment, I was at a loss to understand.

"Jurisdiction," Dao telepathed from the nearby surf. "It means they claim this beach for their own. Be careful, Marina, and watch your temper! You have to make this boy trust you."

I forced myself to smile, which the boy took this for an apology.

"Okay, just leave," he said. "And I won't report you for trespassing."

"Thank you, Lukas Barrios Rodriguez," I replied, transforming my voice into a sweet song.

Summoning all of my courtesy, I scanned the boy with a subsonic frequency that was beneath his hearing. But I knew he felt it subconsciously. I'd been taught humans would experience my acoustic hum as a slight tingling pleasure.

"What did you say?" His tone was softer as he succumbed to my voice.

Why had my sound spell worked with this boy and not the girls in the fish shack? Scanning his stomach gases, I noticed Lukas was experiencing the emotion of contentment. My fears ebbed. Since I was having more success handling the male of the species than the girls my age, I concluded maybe I wasn't so bad looking —at least to this human. But it was difficult to make out his face in the glare of his light. I wondered if his bad manners meant that he must be quite ugly. Though that wasn't true of the girls in the restaurant. They were both mean and beautiful.

Again, he rudely ran his light up and down my body. "Where'd you get that lame T-shirt?" he laughed.

"Please ..." I made my voice smooth, almost a purr, "May I stay with you, Lukas Barrios Rodriguez? Would you allow me to watch your scientific work with the turtles?" I secretly scanned his heart, which now pounded with pride. "You could be my teacher and I could tell my whole class about you."

"Are you taking marine science or something? Which high school?"

"Oh," I faltered a moment. "I'm ... not from around here."

"Out of state?" he asked. His tone was both confused and a little suspicious.

"Uh, yes," I stalled, "from there ... out of the state."

The boy was about to question me further when someone in the darkness distracted him by calling out, "Hurry up, Lukas!"

So there were more humans out here on the beach! My pulse quickened. I'd better be very careful.

"Okay!" Lukas shouted back, and then turned to me with a shrug. "You can observe and go back to ... wherever you're from ... and tell everybody what's happening here in our Gulf." His voice lost its bravado and fell. "It's the worst ... ever."

For a moment I almost liked this bossy boy. There was a melancholy shadow echoing inside his heart. A birth defect or a secret. And that made him much more intriguing.

Sensing that I heard his sorrow, Lukas abruptly turned away, as if he could ever hide from me. "C'mon," he said roughly. "We've got so much work to do. You can help out. The turtles need all the hands we can get."

"Thank you, Lukas Barrios Rodriguez," I said and again sent him that low humming. But this time it was with good intentions, and not just to manipulate him. Any boy who was helping the endangered turtles deserved some respect.

"Just call me Lukas," he said.

"I am seeking a Great Elder turtle called *Honuwahi*." I took a risk and revealed my mission. I might as well tell the boy some truth.

Near in the surf, I heard Dao's cautionary whistles. "Don't tell him too much!" my dolphin warned. "Don't trust him ..."

"Are you from the islands?" Lukas asked. "Honu means 'turtle' in Hawaiian."

"Uh, yes," I answered. "My father's people."

"So, you're Native, " he said in a more conversational tone. There was even a hint of respect in his voice. "Then you must know these are migrating green turtles nesting on our beach. We don't name them like you do. We just tag them."

Careful to avoid the square turtle nest barriers, we both followed the beam of the boy's light scanning the sand. Only then did I realize, with some pity, that Lukas did not make his own light. It was some kind of tool he wielded. Though his light was strong, it was artificial. That meant his light could be stolen or stopped. Perhaps this was why humans so often lost their way?

Lukas stopped suddenly, grabbing me by the arm and holding me tightly. "Shhhhhh," he said in a voice that again was much too loud. "Look!"

I heard the short, hard panting and felt the sand gritty and flying against my skin. A turtle nesting!

"This is the third night she's nested here." Lukas whispered so fiercely that for a moment the green sea turtle stopped furiously digging in the sand. "See her?"

"Of course."

"Tell the old turtle not to lay her eggs here!" Dao telepathed frantically from the surf. "Is it *Honu-wahi*?"

How was I supposed to warn this turtle about the oil without revealing my true nature to this boy? I sent out a sub-sonic greeting to the turtle, as was proper etiquette. No answer.

Lukas had me firmly by the elbow. I was torn between my duty to protect the turtle and my hesitation over stunning the boy so he'd release me. Why did I feel so paralyzed? With one basic Marine Arts move, I could've taken Lukas down. Pandora would never have had a moment's pause. Any human was her enemy. But this boy was different. I didn't want to hurt him.

Lukas shut off his light to give the turtle privacy and safety. And then I saw the boy's face silhouetted in the moonlight. His brow was generous, his cheekbones high, and his jawline strong. A tiny scar was etched on his temple and he had a dolphin tattoo on his neck. His thick, black hair was curly, tousled. He smelled of salt and warm sand. My gills fluttered and I caught my breath. He seemed so familiar.

There was a glint of intelligence in his dark eyes as Lukas caught me studying him. "What?" he shrugged. "You've never seen a turtle before?" Then he laughed harshly and I dropped my gaze.

But it had been enough. That second of recognition disorient-ed me. For a moment, my land legs trembled and hummed. I was afraid I might shift. It's what our Aquantan bodies naturally did when alarmed. Or aroused.

"Turtles follow moonlight to navigate the beach," he said. Lukas's know-it-all lecture tone snapped me back to my mission. The turtle was still digging in the sand near us. "Sometimes they mistake car or hotel lights for the moon and end up getting run over."

"Is it *Honu-wahi*?" Dao called anxiously from the waves. "Why don't you warn her?"

"Can't!" I told Dao. "She doesn't hear me."

To a trained Aquantan or any skillful observer, the elaborate mark-ings on a turtle's shell gave their name, their rank, their clan, and their heritage. Not quite as ornate as the vivid video stories of an Aquan-tan's acoustic tattoos, but clear identification. I focused my sonar to sight exactly on the turtle's shell. Was she the one? The Great Elder?

Lukas suddenly leaned so close to me that I felt his breath. It was strangely sweet and moist.

I bolted out of Lukas's grip. "I've got to introduce myself to this Elder."

"Elder?" Lukas glanced around the beach. "I told you, nobody's allowed on this beach tonight."

Lukas ran after me and wrapped his arms around my waist. Easily he hoisted me up midair. My land legs hung helplessly. Oh, for my tail flukes to attack him!

"Stop!" Lukas held me fast. "We have to stay 100 yards away—it's the law!"

The law? What kind of law was it that I couldn't make a courteous introduction to such a revered elder? These humans had no manners at all. No wonder their world was falling apart.

"Put me down!" I yelled.

"No," Lukas snapped. "You're trespassing!"

Lukas gripped me so tightly I could hear his heart pounding against my backbone. Though his heart made no light, its sound stunned me — strong and so steady. And again somehow familiar. Suddenly, without my song, without any signal from me, my legs vibrated and began fusing back into my tail flukes. My body had never shifted without my command. What was happening to me?

"What the hell ...?" Lukas shouted as my tail flukes unfurled, silver scales tinkling out a musical trill.

Whipping around the back of the boy's legs, my flukes squeezed him tightly and he fell, with me on top of him. Facing him.

"You're ... you're ... " Lukas sputtered.

"Not from around here," I said firmly and held his face close to mine. He smelled spicy, like the delicious food I'd devoured in Sid's Fish Shack.

Lukas's body went rigid, completely still. I scanned his stomach. Fear, yes, but also curiosity. "You're ... you're ... beautiful."

His eyes scanned my body, taking in the silver tail now pinning him down in the wet sand. He seemed to be carrying on a conversation with himself that I couldn't read. At last his eyes met mine in the moonlight. And then I knew, he also somehow recognized me.

His warmth was in the tone of his voice now. "Mermaids don't kill people," was all he said. "At least, not according to most of our legends." He held my gaze.

"Stun him, Marina!" it was Dao in the surf. He had practically beached himself in his panic to be closer to me.

Dao was right, of course. I couldn't let this boy know who I was. He was such a braggart—he'd tell everybody who'd listen. And we'd be exposed.

"Liiiiiiiiiiiiiiiiiii!" I sang out my ultrasonic song and surrounded the boy in my powerful acoustic embrace.

Lukas's body rose up once and then fell limp, unconscious.

With a sigh, I held his face between my hands, my webbed fingers touching each eyelid, his surprisingly long lashes, and his salt-tinged, chapped lips. His features were too broad-boned to be really handsome. But there was still sunlight in his warm skin. And we were the same bronzed color. For just a moment, I felt some regret. Because I'd stunned him, Lukas wouldn't remember who I really was. Not just some ordinary human girl.

As soon as I eased myself off him, my tail flukes shifted back into legs with an agonizing and audible crack. Again without my command. Why had I lost control of my body? Maybe I wasn't ready for this world, after all.

With a groan, I stood up and tested my land legs. Solid. But still trembling.

Lukas also moaned and shuddered into consciousness. "Oh, " he said, looking up at me. "It's you ..."

For a split second, he seemed to be remembering something. Perhaps a shimmer of flukes in the moonlight. Or my cool touch on his face. Then he fell back into unconsciousness. He would be completely awake in a few more minutes.

I ran over near the old turtle, careful not to disturb her as she covered her nest. Tears streamed from her eyes with the effort of burying her multitude of eggs. They shone in the dark like huge pearls.

Desperately I called out in the turtle's frequency far below the boy's hearing, "Great Elder, *Honu-wahi*, we have come all the way from the Sound Temples of Aquantis with greetings and a plea for your wisdom."

No response. I focused all of my acoustic attention on the ancient turtle's shell. I scanned for her ancestry. Elegant swirls of gold reflected that this turtle was of the highest rank, Elder Diplomat. The reddish-brown pyramid pattern raised at the pinnacle of her carapace revealed she was more than 150 years old. And most exciting of all, the turtle's acoustic field at last echoed her name: *Honu-wahi*!

The elder turtle slowly pulled her huge body down the beach to plunge back into the surf. She did not even pause in her sashaying slide toward the water. In her wake, her back flippers left squiggles in the sand like hieroglyphics. For a second, I scanned the flipper prints to see if there was any message for me. But there was none.

Fiercely concentrating, I tuned to a lower frequency of telepathy. "Please, Wise One, the Blue Beings need your counsel."

Inches from the surf, *Honu-wahi* looked back, as if she'd finally heard me. For a moment, time slowed down to the turtle's dimension. And in that expanded second, I scanned something marvelous, but also bewildering.

Flickering on *Honu-wahi*'s shell were sound pictures of family clans dancing on the turtle's back, singing. At the very edge of *Honu-wahi*'s shell were images of my father, with his mother and sisters.

I recognized these pictures from years of scanning my father's acoustic tattoos to learn more about my Hawaiian human family. My father's tattoos were more primitive sound images because he was born human and he had trained to learn to Shift in Aquantis. But the pictures were familiar. I ran toward the Elder Turtle, but she was already slipping into the surf. Was my image there etched in her ancient shell? Was my future foretold? I had to know.

"Great-great-great-Grandmother!" I called out to *Honu-wahi* on all acoustic channels. "Wait! It's me, Marina!"

No answer. For a moment, the old turtle turned in the waves and gave me the most mournful look I'd ever seen. Then, with a sigh and a great gasp of air, she dove into the surf. Her leathery wings stretched out and she flew fast underwater. I couldn't shift fast enough to follow her.

"Dao, stay with *Honu-wahi*!" I screamed out loud. "There's something wrong. I think she's ... she's deaf." It was certain death for any marine mammal to lose their hearing, their navigational skills.

"Who're you talking to?" Lukas demanded. He was standing right behind me. But this time, he didn't grab my arm. He even seemed somewhat concerned for me, as I stood knee-high in the surf. "You know, this beach is closed to swimming at night. It's dangerous. Riptides."

"I'll be fine," I said.

I needed to shift and get off this beach to find Dao and *Honu-Wahi*. But instead, I lingered. Why?

"Hey, you still want to do your science report on our turtle work?" he offered. Obviously he remembered nothing from my shifting. He probably just thought he'd tripped and fell in the sand.

"No," I said. And my regret was real. "I've got to get back ... home."

"Okay," he said lightly.

But his eyes held mine. Again, that spark of intelligence and now something else: connection. As if we'd been through something together. Even if I was the only one to really remember it.

I was just about to dive when I glanced up the beach and saw a terrible thing. Sacrilege. "Oh, no ..." I gasped.

On the beach, a man and several women were digging up *Honu-Wahi's* nest while it was still warm. Though they dug down very carefully when they discovered the fragile turtle eggs, they gingerly lifted each one up from the safety of the nest and into a Styrofoam box full of sand.

"Careful ..." a woman warned the others. "Don't jiggle the eggs, or the embryos might detach from the shell wall and die."

"They feel like heavy Ping-Pong balls," someone said and in slow motion removed a turtle egg from the nest.

"Solid, surprisingly firm," a woman commented and held an egg up to see it better with her tool light. "Not squishy."

"I guess an egg is an egg, whatever species," another said.

They all wore white gloves. Someone with a clipboard was scrawling notes as each egg was very delicately removed from the nest and placed in the white box full of sand.

"That's all of them," the woman said. "The nest is empty."

The people had not left a single one of the Great Elder's eggs to survive. They were stealing an entire generation of turtle royalty. My ancient family history—broken.

"You can't steal those eggs!" I screamed and pushed Lukas down in the surf. "They belong in my family."

"Who's she?" an older man demanded. The man also had the same rather disheveled look as Lukas. "What's she doing here?"

Lukas's manner was suddenly so polite and submissive that I didn't recognize him. "Nada, Papi. Some girl wandering the beach. I told her it was closed tonight, but she won't listen to me."

"I don't have time to deal with you, young lady," Lukas's father snapped. He and a heavy woman hoisted up the box of stolen turtle eggs. "We've got to get these to my lab." He commanded another man. "Mark this nest No. 23. We've counted 156 eggs."

"Stop!" I shouted at Lukas's father. "I forbid you to take those eggs away from their beach!" Frightening images of lab experiments on Aquantans swirled in my mind. What were they going to do with these precious eggs?

"Get that girl outta here, Lukas," his father muttered.

Lukas obediently pulled me along with him.

"Marina!" It was Dao's panic-stricken voice from the surf. "Come back to the sea! *Honu-wahi* tells me the Council of Elders will meet. We must attend her."

"I've got to stay with her eggs," I told Dao, hoping he would not hear my panic. "You follow *Honu-wahi*. I'll see you here tomorrow morning."

"Cannot leave you!" Dao's mind-talk was broken and full of static. "Go! Please ..."

A sleek, silver body leapt and pirouetted high out of the waves, then dove deep and disappeared. Dao was so fast I couldn't hear him anymore. For a moment, tears streamed down my cheeks. Good thing it was dark.

"We've got much more work to do tonight," Lukas's father ordered the other people. I could see where his son got his bad manners. "There are ten other nests we've got to empty, before it's too late."

Ten other nests? I despaired.

"You really think it's going to hit our shores?" Lukas asked his father.

"Tomorrow sometime," he replied grimly. "That's what they predict."

Some tone in their voices caught me. It was a frequency I'd rarely heard, but recognized. Grief. Pure grief. And fear.

Lukas's voice fell into a low pitch, almost like a song. "The oil will destroy our beaches ... " he turned to me. "Everything we love ..."

I scanned Lukas's heart and saw it was more resonant than I'd expected. More expansive. And for the first time I thought the boy might have some goodness in him—even if he and his father were thieves. ˜

CHAPTER 3
Night Lab

In the lab, it was just as Dao warned me: long, metal tables with dead sea turtles, their fore flippers splayed out in bloody dissections. If they did this to creatures who belonged in SkyeWorld, what would they do to aliens like me?

I thought I could save the sea turtle eggs. But, then I realized I might have a hard time saving myself. How could I get out of here without attracting any more attention?

Sensing my distress, Lukas muttered, "That's the worst of it. They bring all the turtles here." He took my arm again, lightly. "Sorry it's so grisly ..."

I shuddered and calculated how far I'd have to run to bolt out of this lab and back to the sea. Problem was, I'd begged Lukas and his father to let me come along to the lab. They might wonder why I was in such a hurry to get out of here.

"Got to leave now," I said politely, shrugging off Lukas. The last thing I needed was his mistrust.

"I thought you wanted to see our work here at Turtle Lab?"

"I do, but ..."

Where was my spy training when I really needed it? We'd been taught many ways to extricate ourselves from dangerous situations. I couldn't think of any of them. Every instinct in me just wanted to flat out run. My land legs twitched with anxiety and my stomach roiled. I realized I was terribly hungry, even though cannibals surrounded me. I was sure they were going to cook up these dead turtles in some disgusting soup. And who knew what horror they had planned for the eggs? And me?

"Hey, are you some kind of immigrant?" Lukas asked.

Spy strategy: When asked a question—respond with a question. At least I remembered that much of my training. "Where're you from?"

"My father came here from Cuba in a boat trying to escape Castro."

"What about your mother?"

He scowled. "Drowned. Papi's boat capsized and he could only save me."

Why was the boy trying to contain the emotions that I could so clearly hear rumbling in his belly? I couldn't read his thoughts. But his face was frozen with the effort of hiding his sorrow from me. If he was working this hard to disguise himself, I decided to pretend not to notice. "Oh," was all I said. "Sorry."

"No time to chat, Lukas!" his father called, his voice hoarse. "We need your help with these eggs."

I snapped back to attention. Maybe if I could get away from Lukas and do some menial task, I could rescue *Honuwahi*'s eggs and return to Dao. "What can I do, sir?" I asked in my most courteous tone.

"You can stay out of the way," Lukas's father muttered. "Or just go home to your parents."

"Yes," I said, "it's time for me to go."

Here was my chance to get out of here and return to the sea. In formal Aquantan style, I touched my forehead and heart. Then I bowed with my palms placed together to take my leave of these savages.

"What are you ... Buddhist?" Lukas asked.

His father stared at me as if suddenly noticing me for the very first time. He seemed to be in physical shock. Pulse rapid, eyes dilated, hands clenched.

"Are you here ... alone?" he said.

His voice was so intense, yet suddenly tender that it shocked me. How I wished these humans had developed their telepathy. It was limiting to only be able to listen what they said out loud.

"Yes, alone," I lied. Of course, I must protect Dao. Where was he? Had he found *Honuwahi* again? I needed to get out of there fast and join him for the turtle Council of Elders.

"Are you ... lost?" Lukas's father asked me. His tone was full of longing as if he were really the lost one. He was a tall, angular man with glasses too big for his face and a shock of salt-and-pepper hair. He did have remarkable eyes, dark and dense. "Are you looking for someone? For me?"

I couldn't tell him our real mission. For a moment, I hesitated, and then said, "Yes, I am seeking a sea turtle named —"

"She's Native, Papi," Lukas rudely interrupted, as if to explain my foreignness. It was obvious he was trying to impress his father. "Do any of these turtles in the lab have a Hawaiian tag?"

"*Honu-wahi*," I finished, ignoring Lukas. "The Elder." His father had the power here. Maybe he could help me.

"Who?" Lukas's father demanded. His heart was thudding so loudly I thought he might be ill. He bent down and took me by the shoulders. What was it about humans? They were always grabbing each other.

"The great Elder *Honu-wahi*," I repeated loudly. Maybe everybody in this world was hard of hearing.

The man let out a great breath of air that I realized he'd been holding too long. His soulful black eyes opened wide and his tanned brow furrowed into deep lines. Intently, Lukas's father scanned me foot to head. "Her eggs are safe," he said very slowly, as if I would have trouble understanding him. As if he recognized I wasn't from this world. But how? What gave me away? My two-toned skin?

I should have felt danger, exposed. But I felt strangely seen and somehow important. "But you stole them," I began.

"Tell your Elder that ..." Lukas's father seemed to choke on his words. Why was his voice so charged with emotion? Did Lukas's father also know *Honu-wahi*? "Tell her that I ... that I've kept my promises ... that we both—"

"Talking to turtles now, Papi?" Lukas laughed. He seemed embarrassed by his father's sudden intensity. Then he turned to me quickly and said, "When you've spent as much time at sea with turtles as my father has, you think you know them personally."

"They are family," I ignored Lukas and fixed my gaze on his father.

"Do you have ... any ... message ... for me?" Lukas's father continued, his eyes riveted on me. Each word was a struggle for him to get out. His demeanor had so drastically changed from his attitude on the beach when he had treated me as just a silly girl, a nuisance.

29

This was the type of diplomatic exchange I'd hoped to experience in SkyeWorld. Lukas's father knew something about me—of that I was now sure. But what exactly did he know? I was just about to engage in the delicate dueling of diplomacy, when a heavy-set woman ran up and tapped Lukas's father on the shoulder.

"We need you in the infirmary, Manuel ... now!"

Reluctantly the man stood up. He still kept his eyes riveted on me. "Please ... don't leave. There is something I have to tell you ... " he said, glancing at Lukas and then me. "Tell you both ..."

Studying his son, his father let slip an expression of concern and fierce love. It looked the same in any culture: Eyebrows raised, lips contemplative, and eyes alive with hope.

"Help out with the eggs, mi hijo," Lukas's father said. He turned to me, "Thank you ... for coming back. I've waited a long time." And then, he was gone.

I had no time to wonder about Lukas's father's strange reaction to me or his confusing words.

"Just make yourself at home," Lukas said. "Check things out for your science project."

Finally free of Lukas and his inscrutable father, I could do some spying. Lukas's father didn't seem to have any plans to dissect me. He actually seemed to need me here. In the artificial light above, I watched Lukas, who was now running from table to table and box-to-box of precious turtle eggs.

For the first time, I could study Lukas from a distance. He was not as unpleasant as his voice, or as aggressive here in his father's lab. Tall and dark-haired with a strained and crooked smile, Lukas just seemed like any anxious boy trying to please his very busy and moody father.

"Can you help us secure these eggs?" a woman asked Lukas. "The Fed Ex truck is due at dawn."

"Sure," he replied.

Unfortunately, the boy ran back over to me. "Stay with me and you won't get in any more trouble," he said.

"OK," I agreed.

There was much to record in my acoustic memory: People in white coats scrambling around with masks over their faces. Was the air here as toxic as their oceans?

As I walked into the laboratory's outer office, I heard something that stopped me cold. What was that soaring, ultrasonic song shimmering around me? Like fractals of prismatic light, the music vibrated inside my bones, echoing along my jaw.

Closing my eyes, I let the wondrous human music resonate through my whole body. "What ... is ... that song?" I managed to ask.

"Oh," a woman said. "They play Mozart in the lab. It seems to calm the turtles."

"I've never heard—" I began and then had to stop because tears were streaming down my face. I couldn't help it. The woven strings and singers were almost unbearably beautiful. I was embarrassed to be so moved by this music, since it didn't seem to even register in Lukas.

"I don't really like classical," he explained with another shrug.

Again he took my arm and pulled me back into the lab. Still dazed by the music, I followed him like a sleepwalker. I resolved to return to SkyeWorld someday when I was not on a spy mission—simply to memorize Mozart. I would share it with Dao and explain that this music was a human treasure. It was a reason to keep the WaveHole open to any world. Why had Master Lioli never played Mozart for me? Maybe he was worried I'd fall in love with any world that had such music in it.

On the wall hung inside the laboratory hung a sign that read:

Health Complaint: If you are experiencing health effects
Related to the spill, call Florida Poison Center.

So humans were also getting sick from this oil, I noted, trying to tune out the music so I could focus on spying. On another wall was a big screen with a complicated map of the Gulf of Mexico and its shores that I recognized from the little sound murals this morning at the fish shack.

"It's a 3-D flat screen hologram TV," Lukas boasted, noting my scrutiny. "Someone donated it to the rehab center. Cool, isn't it?"

I scanned the sleek box with my sonar to gauge its temperature. "No, it's actually quite hot."

Lukas gave me a funny look. Knowing that he'd be pleased if I asked him a question he could easily answer, I said, "Do you see the past, present, and future in your ... primitive sound murals?"

Lukas was dumbstruck. "What?" he asked. "What are you talking about? No one can see the future ..."

Instantly, I knew I'd made a grave mistake. I tried to distract Lukas with another simpler question. "Where's the oil spill now?"

Lukas stared at me in confusion. At last he shook his head. "Geez, don't you ever watch the news? Last time in the Deep Horizon spill, Siesta Key was spared. But this spill is heading right toward us." Lukas grabbed another little black box and raised the volume. "Tune in!" he told me.

"Lukas!" someone suddenly shouted from across the lab. "They need you. Now!"

"Come on," Lukas again grabbed my arm and again pulled me toward a back room.

These humans were so physical, always latching on. Maybe this way of locomotion in tandem was another survival skill for dealing with the weight of gravity. Were two bodies stronger that way?

Lukas opened the door to reveal a terrible sight: A dozen sea turtles were lying helplessly on metal tables, their flippers useless as they flailed about in only air. At least these turtles were still alive. Workers with big blue gloves were scrubbing their shells. Was this some kind of kitchen?

"They're so ... dirty," I marveled.

Each turtle shell was streaked with black goo that obscured their markings and all hope of hearing their names or histories.

"We're saving them," Lukas said, his voice soft.

Then I noticed that the workers had green shirts on with the words SHARE THE BEACH: SEA TURTLE VOLUNTEER PROJECT and a sea turtle sketched beneath it. What did this mean? Could these savages actually be allies?

Lukas let go of me and strode over to help a worker hold down a struggling sea turtle's flippers. While Lukas was busy, I scanned the turtles and let out a low-frequency greeting. With their shells so disfigured, it was the only way to connect with them. Most turtles were in too much pain and confusion to respond. But one voice came back weakly.

"Priestess ..." the ancient turtle said, seeming to bow her head toward me. "Help us!"

"I'm trying to save your eggs," I assured the Elder.

"Priestess, we have been waiting for you ... for a very long time." The turtle fixed me with her square yellow eyes. "It is a fulfillment of ... of the Prophecy," the turtle choked.

No one had said anything to me about a Prophecy. In fact, even as a High Priestess, very little was revealed to me of my fate. Maybe Dao knew more about our destiny and was keeping it from me.

"You must save us and warn *Honuwahi* ..." the turtle's voice faded.

"She is at sea," I telepathed. "Safe."

"None of us is safe at sea anymore." The turtle fell into another choking fit and the workers shook their heads. They seemed truly sad.

The turtle fell unconscious. I scanned her vital organs and heard her heart beating way too fast. Her intestines were twisted and full of little black blobs.

I had to wonder if my own belly was also infiltrated with oil from the shrimp I'd eaten this morning. Maybe I'd vomited enough of it up so that it wouldn't poison me, too. I held a hand over my belly, which was still cramping.

A worker listening to the turtle with a metal snake of some kind pronounced, "She's suffocating on the tar balls ... we're losing her!"

The worker leaned over the turtle, his expression anxious. "No!" he cried. "C'mon, old turtle—keep breathing. You can make it!"

The turtle seemed to hear him, reviving long enough to reach out a foreflipper to me. "Bless me, Priestess."

There was a shimmer in the air as I watched the ancient turtle's spirit rise up and leave her shell. Empty now, except for the brief music of her passing like golden gongs.

I bowed my head and hummed, the death elegy. "In another world ... See you in another world."

"Don't take it so hard, honey," one of the women workers said and laid a hand across my shoulders. Her touch startled me. It was warm and kind.

I noticed that Lukas, too, had ducked his head. When the woman also placed a hand on his back, Lukas roused himself and threw her off. For a boy who was always grabbing other people, he seemed not to respond well to anyone else's touch. "Forget it, Lyla, I'm fine," he muttered. But his voice said otherwise.

In that moment, I felt myself strangely drawn to Lukas. He truly seemed as sad as I was over this turtle's death, though he didn't even know her name, family, or history. His gloom convinced me that Lukas really was trying to help the turtles. They all were. But how?

I glanced around at the white-clad volunteers with new eyes. Maybe they weren't so primitive after all. On another TV screen in the room, a woman announced, "The great sea turtle egg rescue is underway in the Gulf."

The screen flashed with a series of pictures of other people digging up sea turtle nests and removing eggs.

"It's a last-ditch attempt to save a generation of these endangered marine mammals. Scientists are afraid that hatchlings will swim straight out into the oil and die."

"That's us!" Lukas said proudly. "Us and all the other volunteers."

I had to ask Lukas, "Do you really know how to save all these eggs?"

"Well, it's only been done once and that was almost a decade ago," Lukas began. For the first time there was a hint of hesitation undercutting his usual bravado. "But we gotta try."

"You know," one of the women scrubbing another turtle's neck and mouth with something sudsy told me. "The turtle populations were just recovering in the Gulf after the last big spill, and now ... now this." The woman tenderly placed a gloved hand over the turtle's blackened head.

I was really confused. Their world was so upside down. Natural laws and rules were out of synch. Perhaps the turtles and their eggs really were safer in the lab than back at the beach. And what did this oil spill mean for Dao? He had no option to shift form and come onshore for safety. The sea was his element, forever. Was it possible that I might have to stay on land to survive? I couldn't fathom how I could ever live alone without my constant. I'd rather die at sea with Dao.

A bolt of panic ran through me. Forget the mission. I only wanted to get back to my Dao. Save us.

"Is it morning yet?" I asked, my heart pounding.

"Almost 4 a.m.," said Lukas wearily. "You need to go home and sleep?"

"Sleep here, Lukas," the woman worker offered. "We have cots in the back room. Can't you hear all the snoring?"

I tuned in and did, indeed, hear strange, guttural noises coming from the sleeping rooms. I also heard the woman whisper to a worker alongside her, "Poor boy, if he had a mother, he'd have someone to go home to, instead of always hanging around here."

"Run along, you two," the woman called Lyla said. "Most of these turtles aren't going to make it. No reason for you to have to watch this … tragedy."

"I'm staying," Lukas said resolutely. "I'll sleep in the back with the others. She's going home." He gave me a strange look. "Wherever that is."

It was time. I had to get back to the beach and Dao by dawn. I knew that I should have been glad to leave this boy and all the sad, dying turtles, and their stolen eggs. But I wasn't. Why?

I shocked myself by asking, "May I return, Lukas Barrios Rodriguez?"

Lukas sighed and ran a hand through his curly black hair. He almost smiled, but instead just shrugged. "Sure, come back tomorrow if you like. If you need more interviews for your science project."

I smiled. This seemed to have quite an effect on the boy. Lukas's eyes widened, his stomach gases swirled and even grumbled. Blood rushed to his head. Strange symptoms. Fight or flight? Or something else. Attraction?

Lukas turned to go. Then he stopped suddenly and called back, "Hey, I don't even know your name."

"Marina," I pronounced clearly.

Of course, Lukas couldn't hear all the acoustic harmonies that accompanied my Sound Signature. He couldn't scan my acoustic tattoos that came to life in my magnetic field whenever I spoke my name aloud. No need to really cloak myself with these humans. Everything that was so revealed in Aquantis was hidden in their world. This spying might be a lot easier than I'd ever imagined. But it was also unexpectedly sad and complicated by feelings I didn't quite understand.

"That's a pretty name," Lukas said sleepily. He seemed to be slipping already into his dreamtime. "In Spanish, it means 'sea.'" The boy grinned. There was a gap between his front teeth. It was strangely endearing.

"Good to meet you, Marina. Thanks for helping out tonight." He reached out to take my hand. His fingers were tapered and strong.

Now it was my turn to blush. "Tomorrow, then?" I turned to leave. Why was I ambivalent? I didn't belong here. It was just like my mother said, "beautiful, but very dangerous." Kind of like my sister, Pandora.

"Hey, take a Turtle Lab T-shirt," Lukas called out and tossed me an official shirt of the Turtle Volunteers. "That way they'll let you back into the lab."

"Thanks." I took off the Nirvana t-shirt and slipped the smaller Turtle Lab one over my bathing suit.

At the entrance to the warehouse, I glanced back, wondering if Lukas's dark eyes were following me. But the boy had already disappeared into his dreams. ~

PART TWO

CHAPTER 4
The Burning

LUKAS

Dreams of a girl with strange green eyes. They spin somehow. She is lean and kind of muscular. Just when I am about to kiss her, I feel something wet and warm wrapping around me. A silver tail. And then an old turtle is staring right into my face. I always have weird dreams when I spend the night on Papi's old cot at the Turtle Lab.

I know better than to tell my father about my dream. He already thinks I'm strange.

"If your madre was still here," Papi always says, "she'd know what to do with you, mi hijo. I mean, teach you ... things."

I don't need a mother. Dad and I are okay on our own. Papi has his wildlife rehab work and I've got my science studies. Best student in my class and a good singer and martial artist. I'm not popular, but I hold my own with girls at least smart ones like Jenny. She's my lab partner and kind of my girlfriend. Still, there are times when I wish we had a real family. But then I look around at my friends and realize family life is mostly a mess. Rules, curfews, nosy parents, and siblings who stab you in the back every chance they get.

No thank you. Just my Papi and me. That's the way it's always been.

The cot squeaks when I jump out of it and pull on a fresh Turtle Lab T-shirt. No time to go home and change. I can hear turtles screaming on the lab tables as the volunteers try to save them. I've always been able to hear animal vocalizations, sub or ultra-sonic.

"Born that way," Papi tells me. "Or maybe a side effect of almost drowning."

My good hearing comes in handy when we're out at sea searching for an injured sea turtle or dolphin. Once they even tested my hearing at an acoustics lab and the doctor discovered I could hear "the suggestion of sound." I think that's pretty cool—my own private super power. I don't tell people about it, so I can eavesdrop on their conversations from far away. You'd be surprised what I overhear. It's almost like telepathy. And sometimes it's pretty depressing. I think in the future our species will have to go telepathic, if just to survive. All our high-tech communications are just training us to take the leap into mind reading. "Where's my father?" I ask the volunteers. They look sleepless and exhausted.

Papi's assistant, Lyla, gives me the once over with her bloodshot eye. "Why don't you go home, sweetie, and get some real sleep?"

"Why don't you?" I snap and notice Lyla looks hurt.

I don't like Lyla. Nobody calls me "sweetie." She thinks because sometimes Papi sleeps over with her that she can act like my mother. I know Papi needs women, just like he needs to get drunk with his fishermen buddies sometimes. He'd probably go a little crazy without his work, and women like Lyla who adore him. If my mother hadn't drowned on his raft, Papi wouldn't have to keep rescuing women—and turtles. I don't really blame Papi. That's because he already blames himself.

I scan the lab. No sign of Papi. "Is he out on the boat already?" I demand.

Lyla takes her time answering. She's slow and methodical about everything. Her red hair is frizzy and her blue eyes dead serious as she scrubs the turtles clean. Lyla always gets every bit of oil off the birds and turtles who come in here half-dead, suffocating. When Lyla turns her attention to me, her expression is troubled. "Your dad got a report that oil company cleanup crews are trapping turtles while they burn off the oil."

"Idiots!" I say and bolt out of the lab before Lyla can ask me what I want for breakfast. She's a rotten cook. Gluten-free. Everything tastes like cardboard.

40

"Wait, sweetie," Lyla runs after me. Her hands are all soapy and dripping foam like some kind of horror movie. "You father wants you to stay here with me in the lab." She can't catch up with me and I hear her voice fading. "Too ... dangerous ... out ... there!" Then I hear a drop in her voice. "Manuel will never forgive me."

Good. Maybe they'll break up. My bare feet slap the dock in a rhythm that makes me grin. My feet can play this old wood like my own drum set.

"Papi!" I catch him just as he's firing up the rubber orange Zodiac.

"No," my father shouts, "Stay in the lab with Lyla!"

I know what he's thinking. Papi can't risk losing me, too. I always have to beg him to take me out in his boat for turtle patrol. The only time he brings me along is if the seas are boring and the weather report is perfectly clear.

If Papi thinks he's going to leave me behind with all those dying turtles and his sappy girlfriend, forget it! I leap off the dock and land with a plop on the hard, rubber bow.

"Lukas Barrios Rodriguez!" For just a moment my father glares at me.

He never calls me by my full name unless he's trying not to blow up. I can almost hear his thoughts: What am I going to do with that boy? Then he sets his jaw and I see he's grinding his teeth with frustration. No time to turn back!

Shaking his head, Papi jerks the tiller so hard I fall forward into the boat. We zoom off faster than my father has ever driven—at least with me.

"Make yourself useful," Papi growls. "Get the nets ready."

"Sure thing."

I don't let Papi see my grin. It's not usually this easy to win with him. But he's distracted by wildlife in such danger. Ever since a pod of dolphins rescued my father with me in his arms off the coast of Key West, Papi has been paying back. By helping marine mammals.

"A life for lives saved" he always says.

He doesn't like to talk about what happened out there in the open ocean. All I know is this: For three days, Papi and my mother clung to me. There was nothing much left of their stolen research boat. Sharks were everywhere. My mother at last slipped down under the waves. Papi couldn't save us both. And then the dolphins showed up and towed us to land. I was six months old so I don't really remember much, except drifting on the sea. Sometimes I have floating dreams.

"Where we going, Papi?"

"Those damned cleanup crews!" Again he's grinding his teeth. "All they think about is burning the oil before it reaches shore. Nothing else matters. Wildlife workers spotted a whole lot of turtles near MacLain Point. They're in trouble."

The engine is so loud there's no point in talking anymore. I start preparing the turtle rescue nets. But I'm distracted. Images of that foreign girl last night cross my mind. What was her name? Marina.

Now she was really weird. Where did she say she was from? Cute but kind of pushy. And she was way too opinionated. She even talked back to Papi on the beach. Something about the girl stays with me. Her smell? No, every girl on the beach smells of salt and sand, sometimes even spicy shellfish. It was her voice. That was the best part of her. Her voice was low and kind of musical like my choir director, Mrs. Shvets. We all listen up when she talks—or sings.

As I secure the ropes and pad the metal kennels we use to carry turtles, I remember that Papi wanted to tell me something in the lab. And Marina, too. He seemed agitated, like it was really important. Why would Papi have anything to tell a stranger? Maybe just facts about turtles? Papi loves to lecture. And he notices pretty girls, especially if they listen to him.

"Almost there, Lukas! Ready?"

"Yup."

Papi drives his boat so fast I have to hold onto the ropes so I won't fly off the Zodiac. Fun—if not for all the turtles in danger. So far we've lost more than 1,500 turtles in this terrible spill. Worse than the Deep Horizon—probably because the shrimpers are out desperately trying to catch their share before the oil hits. And most of those greedy buggers don't bother using the turtle extender safety door to help sea creatures escape their big nets.

"There!" Papi yells as we roar toward the point.

I can't believe it. Must be a hundred turtles huddled together in the floating gulfweed. Never seen such a sight. It looks like some kind of turtle convention. All kinds—loggerheads, Kemp's Ridleys, hawks-bills, and green sea turtles.

"Everything seems okay, Papi ... well, except there are too many of them."

"Too many ..." he frowns as he scans with his binoculars. "They're trapped."

Then I see the long red booms encircling the turtles, penning them in like they're some kind of livestock ready for slaughter. Booms can't stop the oil from spreading. So the cleanup crews just set the ocean on fire.

And there it is, far-off, but moving fast. The first licks of red flames rising from the sea. Fire racing across on the waves. It's so unnatural that it's frightening.

"Listen, Papi, can you hear them?"

"No, Lukas, you know turtles only vocalize when they're mating."

"They're ... screaming, Papi," I feel sick to my stomach as the eerie subsonic cries echo inside my head.

Then a crackling and roaring noise. Near us, all of the turtles form what seems to be a protective circle around one very ancient-looking green sea turtle.

Everywhere around us turtles flail in a pool of fiery, black sheen that coats the waves. I cover my nose with a rag to escape the noxious scent. Burning flesh and sizzling shells. Never in my worst nightmares did I imagine that waves could blaze and lick its creatures with such scalding heat. Fire should never burn water.

"Stay down in the boat," Papi orders me. "Cover yourself with this wet blanket."

But how can I hide when turtles are dying? Their flippers are so saturated with oil they can't flee from the flames. Papi is scooping for turtles with his huge net, but they're heavy and he can't lift them all himself. We can only do it together.

One, two, three, four, we lift a struggling loggerhead and a Kemp's Ridley to the surface and into the boat. The turtles are so panicked they almost capsize us.

"That's all we can save," Papi yells. "We gotta get out of here right now!"

"There's one more turtle ..."

All the turtles are swimming around one turtle as if they're trying to protect her. Then they all dive down under our boat. I close my eyes and listen for their screams. But all I can hear is a haunting low tone, like a song. Leaning way over the edge of the Zodiac, my arm blindly searches below for a turtle I can haul up into the boat. I grab hold of a out-flung flipper and pull up with all my might.

But it is the turtle who somehow latches onto me. And before I can catch hold of any rope, I'm plunged into the fiery water with her. No time to catch my breath.

"Dios, mi hijo!"

I hear my father's shouts from above. They sound watery, distant. For an instant I see his life preserver floating like a white doughnut on the surface. I reach for it. But no matter how hard I swim upward with one arm, the turtle somehow blocks my ascent. Then she wraps her fore flipper around me my waist and dives deeper with me in tow. I'm running out of breath. And I know she can hold her breath longer than two hours.

"Noooooooooo!" I scream. "Let me go!"

Too much of my air comes out in bubbles. I can't drown. I can't leave Papi alone! He will never survive losing his whole family. He'll just drink himself to death.

Focus. Slow down your breath. That's what I tell myself as the turtle drags me down through the gulfweed. The surface light above dims and I hear a splash.

No, Papi. Stay in the boat! He must not drown with me.

My lungs burn, aching for air. My head feels too light, my legs heavy. No more strength to fight off the old turtle. For a moment, she stops swimming and actually seems to be looking directly at me. Her amber eyes are ancient. Like in my dream, she's trying to communicate. But I can't focus on anything except my need for more fresh air.

With both flippers now, the turtle holds me to her belly and we are face-to-face. That wrinkled alien face, those yellow-green eyes. She seems to be telling me to give up. At least I'm not alone. My chest heaves once. Even though I try to keep my mouth shut—my body, at last, desperately gasps for air.

To my shock, I can breathe! How is this possible? Instinctively I draw in all the H2O in the water and somehow my lungs can filter it.

The turtle seems to be almost smiling. She nods, but doesn't let me go.

I float there for one more minute, my mind racing. At least my lungs are full, functioning. Far above I hear Papi's voice. He's screaming. Is he also burning alive with all the turtles?

Stronger now, I pump my legs and struggle to get free from this turtle. I'm no match for her strength. She must weigh half a ton. "Don't kill Papi!" I shout. Underwater my voice warbles. "He's saving all of you!"

"Lukas!"

It's not my father's voice. It's familiar, female. The old turtle suddenly lets me go. But before I can swim upward, someone else grabs me by the shoulders. I see green eyes and long, curly hair floating out.

"Marina?"

Firmly, she fits her lips to mine. Twooooosh. A blast of pure, liquid oxygen deep into my lungs. I can't even tell her I don't need her air because somehow I can breathe on my own underwater. But she's holding onto me so tightly. And I have to admit—I've never had a kiss quite like this. Not just like artificial respiration, but full and sensual. She tastes spicy and sweet. A warm, tingling sensation runs all the way down to my toes.

And then I see her silver tail. Just like in my dream. Or nightmare. "We have to get you to safety," Marina tells me, but her mouth isn't moving because it's still glued to mine.

How can I hear her? Telepathy? At last, Marina lifts her lips from mine and holds my face between her hands. They're webbed with almost invisible blue-tinged skin. Luminous.

"Listen, Lukas, the sea is still on fire up there. I've got you safely inside my acoustic cloak. But now we have to dive down."

"No, my father is drowning ... we've got to save him, too!" I struggle to push the girl away. But she's stronger than I am—at least underwater.

45

"My dolphin lifted your father safely back up into his boat and led him away from the flames."

"Take me back up to him!" I shout. "Papi'll never get over losing me."

"Times flows differently in your world," Marina reassures me "We can move backward and forward in time. You won't be gone too long."

"But Papi will search for me everywhere!" Again I struggle to get free of the mergirl and the old turtle. "It'll break his heart! Why are you stealing me?"

It is the old turtle who answers, "It is time, Young Ones."

Then there is a strange whistling and a bottlenose dolphin speeds down to join us.

"Good, Dao," Marina nods with relief. The dolphin may have his ever-present smile, but he doesn't seem too pleased to see me. Not one bit. He lets out a string of very loud whistles and shakes his head sideways. Giving me the evil eye.

"Time for what?" I demand.

"For you to begin your training," the old turtle says in that weird accent echoing inside my head. "Now, dive!" ~

CHAPTER 5
WaveHole

"Am I dead?" I ask Marina. She's got me tucked under her arm, dragging me down through the sea.

"No."

I realize that along with her tail flukes she's got a sleek dorsal fin ridging her backbone. No wonder she can swim so fast.

"Let go of me!" I shout.

No use struggling. She's got a fierce grip on my waist. My heart is beating wildly. But my breathing is better. Why was I able to breathe by myself underwater right before Marina grabbed me? Did I just imagine it? Why aren't my ears popping as we dive like torpedoes? Is it the big air bubble Marina spun around me?

"Am I dreaming?"

"No," Marina answers.

She tows me along as if we're doing some crazy man-overboard drill, except I'm so far under the sea I don't know if I'll ever get back up to Papi and the boat. And we're still swimming in the wrong direction. Down.

"Why are you doing this to me?" I demand.

"Because it's the only way to save you."

"If you really want to save me, take me back up to find my father's boat!"

"Sorry," Marina says. "We've got our orders."

"From whom?"

Marina doesn't answer. She somehow shoots out some kind of bioluminescence like a high-powered strobe to light our way. Marina calls it an ultrasonic beam of light. Like seeing with sound. I look

47

around at the humming walls of a complex tunnel with many chambers. I don't know whether to be astonished or horrified. Maybe both.

I have no choice but to let her pull me down through this weird portal. This undersea tunnel reminds me of diving the Great Blue Hole off Belize with my father. Except this portal is spinning like a whirlpool and the pressure is like an undertow.

"Are we in Belize?" I demand.

I wrote a science project about that famous underwater cave system—how rising sea levels triggered a sinkhole in the middle of the ocean. Same kind of eerie stalactites and dangerous caverns here.

"No," Marina says.

Just like in the Blue Hole of Belize, I see perfectly preserved fossils lodged in the hanging stalactites — skeletons of crocodiles, tortoises, and a shark. Papi and I descended 125 feet on that Belize dive. How far down are we now? I can't help thinking about that old movie, *Abyss*, when divers discover extraterrestrials and their spaceship at the bottom of the ocean. Used to be my favorite movie. Until now.

"I knew you were an alien the first minute I saw you!" I shout and try again to break free of Marina's grasp. "Where are you taking me?"

Marina just holds a webbed finger up to her lips. "Save your air," she says firmly. Like she's in charge of me, though the turtle and dolphin are swimming alongside. "It's a long journey through the WaveHole."

"What?" Does she mean a spinning, black hole—but underwater? Black holes in the stratosphere suck in everything. Nothing comes out of them. Does that mean I'll never get back home? With all my strength, I again fight to get free. But her grip around my waist only tightens. It's even a little hard to breathe. My ribs feel bruised.

"Hey, give me some slack," I gasp.

She does. But just a little.

I'm sure no human being has ever dived this far down without a submersible. Even those new underwater glider planes the military is using don't go this deep. We're almost out of the sunlight zone and any heat. Why am I not freezing to death? Why isn't the pressure collapsing my lungs? Marina says I'm safe inside her acoustic cloak. But will it break as we keep descending?

Zooming past us in the WaveHole are all sorts of deep-ocean fish. Jellyfish and mackerel swirl around us. A hammerhead shark zigzags by, glancing my way. I know he can smell me.

I've only read about these submarine depths in my marine research books. Some of these underwater trenches are deeper than Mt. Everest is high. What would my science teacher, Mr. Meeker, say if I told him I'd actually dived down to the mesopelagic layer? The Twilight Zone under the sea where, when sunlight fades, creatures make their own light called bioluminescence.

A dragon fish flickers near. Bolts of light shoot out of his mouth. I almost laugh. But then I remember, I'm in trouble. Deep trouble. Trouble in the Deep. I worry about my brain and hypoxia. Even if I ever got back up to the surface, I'd probably have the bends so bad I'd die. Or I'd be brain dead.

Will I ever get home? Above me I see only fading sunlight. Below me is blue-black. The Midnight Zone. The Dark Zone. There's no coming back from this. I've got to get out of here! Or die trying.

"No way! Not going down anymore!" I punch Marina hard in her flanks and hear a pop from her sound bubble. For a moment I'm free. I kick off against a mossy wall and swim up frantically toward a faint ray of sunlight far above.

Whooosh! Before I can make any progress, I'm sucked back down through the spiraling WaveHole even faster without anyone to hold onto me. It's like going down a whirlpool drain. I gasp. Water suddenly fills my lungs. Everything goes black.

When I come to, I'm on the shores of a vast underwater crater filled with turquoise waters. Mountains rise up from coral gardens. Nearby volcanic vents belch fiery red lava. It's like being in Hawaii when Haleakala erupts—except we're under the sea. I'm breathing very hard. The pressure must be tons down here. It's cold. But I'm not frozen, like I should be. Who knows how or why this fathoms deep, I'm still alive?

How deep I am, I don't know. Maybe we're in the Abyss Zone. Bottomless. They used to believe nothing could live here, that the bottom of the ocean was completely empty, except for white sand. That's until diving bells and deep-sea cameras discovered a whole world of starfish and tubeworms and creatures who look like monsters—all of whom shoot out bioluminescence as a warning or a weapon. I've seen videos on the National Geographic program, "Monsters of the Deep." I never thought I'd see this for real.

"I've got you inside my *lanugo* cloak again," Marina leans over me. Her lips cover mine, salty and warm. So I realize we're back to telepathy. "Breathe slow and steady, Lukas."

I do. What else can I do? Even if I wanted to stop breathing, my body gulps the cool, liquid air. It reminds me of those divers who learn to use re-breathers. They train themselves to put on huge scuba helmets that slowly fill up with liquid oxygen. They breathe water again, like babies in the womb.

"Please don't try to escape," Marina stops her artificial respiration, which feels more like a kiss. "*Honu-wahi* says you're here for a reason. You're part of a Prophecy." She hesitates. "I'm part of it, too."

"So what are we supposed to do?" I demand.

She smiles faintly and shrugs. "I don't know, either."

This is not the time to notice how lovely this mergirl is. How her coral necklaces and curly red-highlighted hair cover her torso. But I can still see the curve of her small breasts. If she weren't kidnapping me, I'd be attracted to her. It's obvious that I need her help if I'm ever going to get back to the surface. So I try to play along.

"Who's *Honu-wahi?*" I ask, sitting up on the sand.

"The turtle Elder who invited you to —"

"Invited me? That turtle pulled Papi and me into the water. And all we were doing was trying to save her!"

The old turtle floats alongside me now. I can see her fore flippers are still singed from the burning oil. And one of her eyes is swollen shut. She's in bad shape. If she were in our Turtle Lab, Papi would help her heal. It occurs to me for the first time that maybe it's because of Papi and his turtle work that I've been dragged down here. And it might not be so bad if only I could get word to my father that I'm not dead.

"I'm sorry, Lukas. We can't let your father know you are with us ... yet," the old turtle tells me. Obviously, everybody here can read minds.

So I better try to keep my thoughts to myself. "First, you must fulfill the Prophecy."

"What Prophecy?" I shout.

"A promise was made. You are here to fulfill it and the Prophecy."

Somebody has made them a promise. Not me! Not Papi, I'm sure. He would never let me go. Not after losing my mother. Maybe this Prophecy and promise are some ancestral magic or mumbo jumbo from a Cuban ancestor I've never met. Papi hardly ever talks about the family we left behind on that godforsaken island. I do know there were some medicine people in his family, curanderas. Crazy old wise women. Maybe they made the promise, but to sea turtles? I know some people talk to animals. But who makes promises to them? Who fulfills them?

Honu-wahi opens her mouth to say something more. Maybe she'll explain it all to me now. But then, she clamps shut her beak and shakes her head. "Lukas Barrios Rodriguez, you are welcome to study with us in the Sound Temples. You must complete the first stages of your training."

"Training? For what? Why should I study anything with you?"

"Because it is the only way you will ever return home."

"I know it's scary." Marina is floating beside me.

She doesn't hold onto me now. Maybe she should, because my whole body starts to shake. I'm shocked that it's not that cold. It should be. Maybe I'm hallucinating from lack of oxygen?

"I'm not scared," I lie. "I'm ... my father ... he's ..."

"He will understand." *Honu-wahi* reaches out a fore flipper to touch my arm.

"You don't know Papi ..." I begin. But then a weird thought whirls around my brain. "Do you?"

She says softly, "Your father is a friend to all sea turtles."

They're talking in riddles. They're not going to reveal the truth. So I might as well do what they say. "Okay, I'll study with you. Whatever." The sooner we begin the sooner I'll get back home.

"Will you please hold onto Dao's dorsal fin, so we can finish the journey?" Marina asks. There is a politeness now in her tone. A detachment. Will she be part of this training? Will she be my teacher? I wouldn't mind. She's much prettier than my on-again-off-again girlfriend. Jenny would love it down here, though. She's always talking about running away from home. And this is about as far away from home as you can get.

"Okay."

I grab onto Dao's dorsal fin. Always wanted to get a tow from a wild dolphin. But this one is still eyeing me with disapproval. Maybe he and I are the only ones who think this Prophecy or promise is a really bad plan.

We're off, zooming around the lake and gliding through a huge sandstone gate. It looks like the Pillars of Hercules, but sunken. Huge kelp forests sway as we veer through them so fast my eyes blur.

"Don't tuck your knees," the dolphin tells me. In his tone is a not-so-subtle criticism. "You're slowing us down. Stretch out like you're flying."

"So you talk, too," I say. "Shoulda known."

Of all the marine mammals I've studied, dolphins are the most likely to break the interspecies communication barrier. Usually they're chatty. Always whistling and bleeping to one another and even to us humans. But not this one. Dao seems downright determined to ignore me, except I'm gripping his dorsal fin with all my strength. Just to hang on.

As we glide through another cavern studded with volcanic vents and wiggling tubeworms, I can't help but think how cool it will be to tell all my friends about this place. They probably won't believe me. I'll have to bring some evidence back to convince them. Papi might understand; but Jenny would demand scientific proof. So would Mr. Meeker.

Maybe I'll learn something that will be proof enough. Like how to shift from legs into those fast tail flukes. Swimming behind Marina I see how powerful the thrust of those flukes can be. They make my own legs seems kind of spindly and pathetic. Is that what I'm going be trained to do? Shift? I think I'd like that. With tail flukes, maybe I could escape.

Before I can ask anybody, Dao suddenly twists and spins down into a narrow cave opening. Sharp ledges scrape my arms and face. For a few seconds everything closes in on me. Claustrophobia. This is my worst fear. Panic seizes me. My heart thuds so loud I can hear it. My lungs freeze and my legs tremble. If there were any space, I'd just curl up into a fetal position and freak out.

But I've trained for this. Papi and I have scuba dived through caves almost as tight as this one. Count each breath and stay focused, that's what Papi always told me. Every bit of air is precious. You're not trapped. You're exploring. And I'm here with you.

But my father is not here now. I'm lost with only these alien creatures as guides. I thought they were from my world. They're not. What am I doing here? I'll die down here!

"Let me tell you a story ..." the old turtle's voice reaches me, even though she's not far ahead, I can't even see her in this darkness. Marina is the one who makes the light. Where is she? I grasp Dao's fin for dear life. The cave passage seems to be closing in on me. I can feel it cutting into my thighs.

"Listen, Lukas." The turtle's tone is low, like a lullaby. I feel my breathing calm down. "Do you know about the lost city of Atlantis?"

"Uh, yeah ..." I say, my eyes still clamped shut tightly. "The city that supposedly sank into the sea."

"In one day and one night," Dao murmurs, "the whole city was destroyed by an earthquake and huge tsunami."

"Yes," the turtle continues. "Atlantis was a great and highly advanced metropolis and a major seaport of the ancient world. Atlantis was full of extraordinary teachers, artists, and scientists. They were already experimenting with crystals like your computers; their gold-inlay art and murals were world-renowned." *Honu-wahi's* voice softens. "Atlantis Masters apprenticed themselves to communicating with and imitating dolphins. These people were experimenting with Sound Shifting, so they were truly amphibious."

"You mean, some of our human ancestors had tail flukes, too?"

"Yes, it was quite an evolutionary adaptation—and an advantage. As you will see."

In that instant, we slip out of the terrible, tight darkness of the cave into a vast panorama. I gasp in astonishment. No one would believe this. It's beyond mesmerizing. Below us is a swirling constellation of lights. It looks like a spinning underwater galaxy.

"Home," Marina says with satisfaction. She smiles back at me. "Welcome to Aquantis, Lukas Barrios Rodriguez."

I don't have any words to describe this city. It's not a spaceship like in that old movie. It's more like those drawings of ancient Greece from our world history class. The city is laid out in three concentric circles with waterways like moats inside each round sand bar. Ornate and towering temples dominate each layered circle of the city.

"The Rings of Atlantis," Honu-wai tells me. "Those Atlantean Sound Shifters who survived the tsunami in your SkyeWorld recreated their drowned city here at the bottom of the ocean. Aquantis is safe from tsunamis and earthquakes."

"But not from volcanoes," Dao adds with a dark look at me.

I'm not so afraid anymore, not of the dolphin, not of this place. It's amazing. I wish Papi could see it.

"Our Master builders have continued in the Atlantean traditions," *Honu-wahi* explains. We soar above the bright underwater city. "That's Poseidon's temple." She points to a coral island and a temple with coral and jet black columns, all alive with living reefs. Nothing bleached or dying down here. Not like in our oceans.

"It's like ... like the beginning of the world," I say. "Awesome."

"There's the acropolis, the center of Aquantis," *Honu-wahi* points out with her fore flipper.

Below us are beautiful, busy passages and sophisticated dwellings like the shining white sandstone homes on Greek islands. Murals everywhere are etched in gold with stylized blue and white dolphins swimming alongside half-human, half-dolphin merpeople. Some of the ornate murals and inlaid tiles have mermaids who look a lot like Marina, except she's much prettier.

Before we zoom down into the city, I glimpse just outside the acropolis vast coral gardens and kelp forests, some kind of aquaculture. Zipping between neat rows of sea veggies are workers and strange animals. The small sandstone cottages near the undersea gardens are modest, even a little run-down. It reminds me of the migrant workers' quarters in Florida orchards.

"The Outer Reefs," Marina informs me. There's a hint of sadness in her tone. "Working the fields is a rough life."

"Where do your workers come from?"

"Here ... and many other worlds," Marina explains as we swim down near the city's huge moats. Are they constructed to keep out strangers? Couldn't outsiders just swim right in?

"Do you ever deport your workers back to their own worlds?" I ask.

When Papi and I straggled onshore in the Florida Keys, we were allowed to stay as Cuban exiles and apply for citizenship. But Papi has always seemed a little uneasy. Florida never quite felt like home to him. And he always feared we might get deported back to Cuba.

"You never know when life can turn upside down and you find yourself suddenly in a different world," Papi would always tell me.

"Sometimes immigrants in Aquantis are ... dismissed," Marina answered. "Forbidden to work here."

"Are they slaves then here in the Outer Reefs?"

"No, it is their destiny."

"I don't believe in destiny," I say boldly.

Marina looks at me strangely. She frowns and then nods very slowly. "Me, neither."

"And what are those weird creatures?" I see prehistoric-looking fish with tusks and what look like tiny legs; and some workers swimming through the kelp forests, are half-human and half-shark. Scary-looking.

"They're ... experiments in cross-species that ... didn't work out so well."

Marina seems quite agitated and hesitant to say more. At last she adds one word that is supposed to explain it all to me, but doesn't. Hybrids.

I don't know what to say. Suddenly I feel an instinct to reassure her, even though obviously I'm not in control here. "You can change your own life, Marina," I tell her. "You can escape your fate and even leave your homeland. My Papi did."

Marina seems deeply troubled by my words and glances quickly at Honu-wahi, as if for advice. We sail down into the acropolis and join the rush hour of Aquantans speeding through narrow passages.

"We'll have to leave you at the Students' Quarters," Dao informs me, "They're expecting you in the Sound Temples."

"But I want to stay with Marina," I say, hoping I don't sound like a whiny kid. I really do want to stay near her. "Can't you be ... my guide, Marina? My teacher?"

"Master Lioli would never allow ..." Dao begins.

"It's okay, Dao," Marina soothes. "Go easy on Lukas. He helped me in his world. We can help him here. Besides, he's our guest."

With an easy move, Marina slips her own dorsal fin under my arm. Dao seems glad to let go of me. He zips ahead without looking back. But he doesn't leave us completely behind.

"Your dolphin hates me," I say.

"He's not my dolphin," Marina explains with a laugh. "We belong to each other. He's my Constant. We were born together."

"Twins?"

"Twin souls," she says happily.

Her expression is so benevolent; I don't say anything else bad about Dao. I do wonder what she means by "twin souls." Did dolphins and humans interbreed at some point in evolution? How did they do that? I've seen dolphins mate underwater. Quick flicks of their tails together, a brief swim belly-to-belly, a stroke and clasp of their pectoral fins, and they're done. More like play than sex. And they do it over and over. Must be fun.

Are Marina and Dao also mates? If so, that might explain why her dolphin is so jealous of me. I'll keep my eyes out for him. One thwack of his tail and I'd be knocked out for good.

Dao leads the way through very busy thoroughfares in this city. He's speeding, except everybody else is swimming just as fast. Some are dolphins, others merpeople. There are lots of other sea creatures—sharks, octopus, barracuda, and swordfish—all swimming in synch. How do they do that?

"What do you call yourselves?"

"Aquantans, of course." Marina nods. She waves to a few passersby. They glance at me but don't seem surprised that I've got legs. Does that mean other humans have visited here before me?

"Do you each have a twin soul ... a sea creature? Do you stay together for your whole lives?"

"Oh, yes," Marina tells me.

Her green eyes hold mine and I feel warmth circling in my belly. But I'm thinking this is bad news for me. Dao will never disappear or let me be alone with Marina. "Cool," I say and hope Marina isn't reading my disappointment.

"And if your training goes well, Lukas, you may ask for an animal ally to accompany you, too."

I glance over at the old sea turtle they call *Honu-wahi* flying alongside. Her fore flippers flap like great wings. I'm surprised she can keep up with us. I would choose her, if she'd let me.

"Forget it," Dao snaps. "Sea turtles are Elders. They never make the animal alliance with ... anybody. Especially humans."

Suddenly Marina darts into a narrow alleyway that opens into a huge stone gate. It is a market thoroughfare thronged with glass booths full of buyers and sellers. It reminds me of Ybor City, the Cuban quarters in Tampa, where Papi takes me some Sundays to shop for everything from hand-rolled cigars to Cuban sandwiches, espresso, and the best mango flan I've ever tasted.

As we speed by a stand of fresh oysters and sea vegetables, I shout, "Hey, I'm hungry. Can't we eat?" I'm starving. "Oysters are my favorite," I plead. "I can eat them raw, if I have a little hot sauce."

Honu-wahi doesn't slow down one bit. "There will be food for you in your quarters," she assures me.

I look back regretfully, watching an Aquantan hold up a huge oyster, tip his head back, and nod with satisfaction. My stomach growls. The market opens up into a wide passage that is adorned with black and red coral pillars. A gargantuan circular shrine looms on a mossy hill just above the Acropolis.

"The Sound Temples," *Honu-wahi* says with a respectful nod.

Marina smiles at me and touches my arm. "You'll do really well here, Lukas," she says. "I know you will."

The Sound Temples gleam with light and I can hear a hum that seems to rise up from its carved columns. More elaborate gold and blazing blue murals with curling wave patterns and chambered Nautilus shells. It's the most beautiful and natural architecture I've ever seen.

"That's where I study?" I ask in astonishment. "Looks more like some sort of museum."

"Yes, dear boy," *Honu-wahi* says. There is a note of tenderness in her tone. At least I know the old turtle cares for me. Marina is probably just being kind because it's her duty. "Good luck, Lukas Barrios Rodriguez." The turtle touches my arm with her foreflipper. "Your father will be proud of you."

"My father?" I ask. "Does he know I'm here?"

"Not yet," *Honu-wahi* says. "But we will try to get word to him in a dream that you are … with us."

Before I can ask her anything more about Papi, *Honu-wahi* flaps her fore flippers and glides away gracefully.

Marina suddenly seems a little shy. Maybe she doesn't want to leave me either? "Yes, good luck, Lukas." She hesitates, and then quickly gives me a little peck on the cheek.

I blush, remembering all the times her lips pressed mine deeply; and I breathed her in. Marina seems to remember, too, and she pushes away gently. For just one more moment, she floats near me. Her reddish curls glow in the light that seems to emanate from inside her somehow.

"Will I see you again?" I ask.

"I don't know, Lukas." She gazes at me, as if she'll say more.

But then her dolphin swishes between us and effortlessly hooks Marina's elbow under his dorsal fin. Her acoustic cloak pops open and I somersault out on my own. Free of her hold. In a nanosecond, they are gone.

Turning back to float before the imposing Sound Temples, I realize I can again breathe without her. But I have never felt so alone. ˜

CHAPTER 6
Aquantis

Why am I here? No one will give me a straight answer. The Masters only say that until I pass my Lower School tests, I can't go back home. But why do these Aquantans want a human like me to learn their skills? I've heard rumors in my training classes about Marina and me and some Prophecy. But it's a big state secret—no one will tell me anything. Why would their High Priestess be linked to me, a SkyeWorlder? I do know that there's a controversy swirling around Aquantis about Marina rescuing me from the burning oil. That's probably why they keep us so separate. I've hardly seen her at all.

I haven't told anybody that I wasn't rescued or that I was stolen from my world and dragged down here. That *Honu-wahi* pulled me down into the sea on purpose. Why? Until I can figure out this mystery, I'll learn their Aquantan skills. But I'll also keep my eyes and ears open to find out the whole truth.

No idea how long I've been down here. There is no night and day. Only tides. And nobody sleeps, except me. Like dolphins, these merpeople just rest one side of their brain at a time, and keep going, wide-awake.

I wish I didn't have to sleep—or dream. I don't really get much rest because of nightmares: the ocean on fire, sea turtles screaming, and my father calling out to me from the boat. Don't like to think about my father and what he must be going through. He must be devastated, if he's even conscious.

Every year on the anniversary of my mother's death, Papi gets shit-faced drunk. I don't want to imagine what he's doing now with me drowned, too. *Honu-wahi* says that no more Aquantans, even young ones, are allowed to travel to SkyeWorld now because of the terrible pollution. So Papi doesn't know I'm safe, unless *Honu-wahi* got through to his dreams. This is the first time I am actually glad that Lyla's always hanging around Papi. Someone has to keep him sane and alive. Maybe the injured turtles in his lab will also keep him busy—rescue him.

Everything here is so bizarre and mind-blowing. Nobody back home would ever believe me if I told them there's a civilization at the bottom of our ocean, hidden in these undersea trenches. My goal is to ace my Temple tests, figure out what they really want from me, and then get back up to SkyeWorld. I'm determined to succeed here. There's no other way to escape.

Here, you make your own light, which means I'm left in the dark a lot. That's why they gave me a string of glowing seed pearls for a head-band, which befits an apprentice Navigator. The Masters are teaching me mind-talk. I pick it up pretty easy. This surprises everybody, but not me. With my super-hearing, I've been eavesdropping on people's conversations for a long time. Why not their thoughts? Or their private protests:

Why did the Priestess bring him here? Was that wise?

Send him back to his polluted world. He shouldn't know any of our secrets.

But how else are we going to change SkyeWorld if we don't teach them how to survive their future?

A gong sounds twice. It's high tide.

"Time for your Sound Shifting lessons," my keeper, a Sound Temple teaching assistant named Trill tells me, as she swims by. She glances into my little cell of sandstone and spun glass. No doors here. So nobody knocks.

"Is there anybody here who understands the concept of privacy?" I ask her. But then it occurs to me I'm using mind-talk. "Oh, forget it!" I shrug.

What's the point? Until I learn to cloak my thoughts like other Aquantans, I'll just be a wide, open door. Anybody can walk right into me. At home Papi never invades my room. I've never had to put up a sign, "Keep Out: Hazardous Waste," like my friend Romanelli with his huge Italian family. Papi gives me all the time alone I need. Sometimes too much.

"Lukas," Trill says sternly. Her black, kinky hair is disciplined in a tight topknot encircled with sharp razor clams and black abalone. She would be pretty if she weren't so bossy. "You need to eat more to keep up your strength. Training is very hard, even on Aquantans."

"Not hungry," I lie.

The truth is the sea veggies and kelp they feed me are awful. Slimy and bland. Why can't they give me oysters when I ask for them? Apparently, those are a delicacy reserved for the aristocracy. Right now, I'd even be grateful for gluten-free anything. So I swim around all the time half-starved.

With a frown, Twill offers me her dorsal fin. This is the way I get towed to class. Twill scowls as she notices that I refused to put on those lame Aquantan student outfits—coral and black pearl necklaces over a bare chest and armbands of abalone. I'm still wearing my shorts and Turtle Lab T-shirt. No doubt she'll report me to Sound Master Lioli for breaking the dress code and not eating. He already thinks I'm hopeless.

"Why did they send me such an unevolved species?" was how Master Lioli first greeted me, like I was retarded or something. Then the Sound Master turned away, muttering to himself, "The Blue Beings choose him, but Marina deserves so much more."

Before I could get excited about any connection to Marina, Master Lioli sent me to the back of the class with a bunch of Aquantan kids who snickered. One even swatted me with his tail flukes. I'm not exactly popular here.

"We're late, Lukas," Trill chides me as she speeds us along toward the Sound Temples. "It's really important you do well in your studies."

"Why?" I demand. Though I know Trill is probably as clueless as I am about why I'm here. Still, I ask, "Why do I have to learn all this Aquantan stuff? I'm never going to really use it—am I?"

For just a moment, Trill veers off course in our race to class. My questions have thrown her off track. She almost drops me, but then her tail twitches like a strong rudder, and we straighten out in our fast glide through the Aquantan passages. They are carved of spun glass and limestone with high arches that glow with reflected light from the rush hour of speeding students.

"I don't know why the Masters think you're so ... special, Lukas," Trill tells me. Her tone is irritated but also confused. "All I know is that if you don't learn our skills, everyone will suffer."

"Aquantans, you mean?"

"Everyone. " Trill turns and looks at me strangely. "Didn't they teach you in your schools that all worlds are connected? That what happens in your SkyeWorld echoes and affects all other realms?"

I don't mean to laugh, but I do. "Uh, nooooo ... we don't believe in other realms?"

"Your physicists do," Trill corrects me. She is a master student in string theory, parallel universes, and multidimensional exploration.

I tell her a sad truth. "But nobody in my world really listens to scientists anymore. If they did, we would try to stop global warming."

"Well," Trill bristles. Her gills flutter and her tail twitches. I'm sure she'd like to whack me with it. "Many worlds exist, even if you don't believe in them. And you've got to study with us, even if you don't want to be here or we don't want you here."

Her words hurt me more than I let on. I say nothing, just grab onto Trill's dorsal fin more tightly as she zooms sideways to avoid on-coming swimmers. Something in my expression must have signaled that she hurt my feelings. She slows down long enough to turn and face me.

"Sorry, Lukas, I didn't mean to be rude," she says. "Are you coming to the party at high tide?"

"What party?" I retort. "Aquantans have fun? I thought you're too evolved for that."

Trill frowns and speeds up again. She's obviously made a mistake in thinking I would be invited to any Aquantan party.

"Are you asking me out, Trill?"

"Uh, no," she says quickly. "It's ... it's kind of a secret ... just a few kids," she glances at my land legs. "I don't think you could keep up with us."

End of subject. I hate being towed around by Trill. But as hard as I've studied, I still can't Sound Shift. Humans are supposed to be adaptive enough to remember how to do this. After all, we once crawled out of the primal ooze with flukes and flippers. Creatures from the Black Lagoon.

But my body seems stuck with legs. So I have to hitch a ride whenever I want to go anywhere in this huge city. It's a sprawling metropolis like Miami with people of all colors: from bronze like Marina to skin like white pearls. And no cars and no energy crisis. Just glass tunnels and sandstone pillars with Aquantans speeding around using their own fluke power.

The crowded thoroughfares pass by in a blur, as Trill zooms us toward the Sound Temples. "Hold on tight," Trill warns as we turn to glide past a gigantic cavern guarded by bioluminescent creatures with fangs and flukes that are studded with sharp, pointed scales like Tyrannosaurus rex tails. They glow and glare at me.

"That's where we bury our dead," Trill tells me in a softer tone than usual. "Don't ever go in there. No one comes out alive."

It's spooky staring into the twisting cavern with mossy walls and skeletons wedged in the crevices. Looks like those old pictures of catacombs under cities. "Don't worry," I assure Trill. "I'm not planning on spelunking those caves."

"Some creatures ... hide there," Trill says.

"Hide from what?"

This world seems pretty peaceful, so why would Aquantans need to escape or hide out? Maybe they have criminals here, like in any world, or prisoners from other dimensions. A dark thought occurs to me: What if you tried to change your destiny, like Papi, and the catacombs were your punishment? Do their graveyards double as a prison?

Trill is obviously wary and frightened as we cruise past the cavern. I can feel it in her trembling body. But she will tell me no more. Instead she abruptly turns us sideways to slip through the Great Gate.

I grasp her dorsal fin with both hands and flatten my body for better aerodynamic speed. So many other students are swimming through the gate that it's like rush hour. Silver tails flashing, making that eerie, ultrasonic music. It's hypnotic, like a flash forward video. I wish I had my own pair of fast flukes so I could keep up with everybody.

"Lukas," I hear her voice before I can see her. And my heart almost makes its own light. But not quite.

Marina swims up alongside us. She tries not to show her disappointment that I don't yet have my own flukes and I still have to be towed by Trill.

"It'll happen ... when you're ready," Marina says, reading my mind like everybody else. It's like being naked, but on the inside. Her bright green eyes do that spinning thing again. It's mesmerizing and disorienting, like staring into twin green whirlpools. Marina nods to Trill. "I'll take him from here."

Trill seems eager to get rid of me. She speeds off to her advanced classes. Marina offers me her small dorsal fin. It's sleek and silver and fast and when she's passing for human, it folds into her spine. Freaking amazing. Marina can almost beat her own dolphin at races. Having a dorsal fin seems pretty cool when you see Marina navigate so expertly with it, slicing through the water.

"Good tide," Dao says, nodding to me tersely.

He's never far from Marina. I guess that's why they call their animal twin souls "Constants." Of course, I don't have a Constant and nobody's volunteered. That's part of the final exams. And who knows if I'll ever advance that far or if any animal will ever agree to make an alliance with me. So far, none of the sea creatures have treated me like I'm special at all. Most of the dolphins and sea turtles and octopi just avoid me.

As Marina tows me along I remember all the times I struggled against her grip in the WaveHole. Now it feels surprisingly natural: Me holding onto her dorsal fin as we speed through the spun-glass passageways.

"How are you?" I ask. I really want to know. Of everybody here in Aquantis, she's the only one I'll miss when I return home.

"Good, Lukas ... and you?"

It's a formula, this exchange. But somehow when Marina's mind-talk echoes inside me I also feel her warmth. And I see colors—blues and deep purples. It's a pleasure to hear her.

"Great!" I say. "I'm making progress."

"Do you like it here in Aquantis?"

I try to hide my thoughts. What I want to say is that I like her, but I wish we were still in my world together. Maybe she gets my telepathy because I feel a slight twitch of her tail against my legs.

"It's okay here," I tell her. "But I'd rather be home."

We speed along in silence. For the first time in many tides, I feel less anxious. Being near Marina reassures me. It also excites me. Why do I want to please her so much, even after she stole me away from my own world?

"Lukas," her voice is so low I can hardly hear her. "I've been meaning to ask you something ..."

"What?"

"Remember in your Turtle Lab that night?"

"Yes." I wonder if that night meant anything to her. Or if she was just being a spy and I was her mission.

"Your father said he wanted to tell us something. Both of us."

"Oh, right, I remember that."

"What do you think he meant? He'd never met me before. What could he have to tell us ... together?"

We slow down a little and let Dao zip ahead. I have a clear image of Papi's face as he looked at Marina and me. When she bowed to him in the formal Aquantan style, he seemed suddenly so focused on her. It's not like Papi to pay that much attention to anyone in his lab but turtles. What did he mean?

"I have no idea," I have to tell Marina. "I wish I did." I shrug. "Maybe Papi liked you ... he likes pretty women. Maybe he wanted to impress you with all he knows about turtles."

Marina smiles, but seems dubious. "That's sweet, Lukas. But I don't think it was about turtles."

"Did you read his mind, too?"

"No, that doesn't happen much with humans," she says. Again, we speed up.

"It does with me."

"You're the exception," Marina laughs.

Even her laughter is musical and exhilarating. Her openness gives me a chance to ask, "And can you tell me something, Marina?"

"What?"

"What's the Prophecy ... you know, about us?"

Marina actually blushes red like an octopus whose skin changes colors with its many moods. "I told you the truth: I don't know my part in it ... or yours, Lukas. Honesty, I don't." She pauses, "I've heard the Masters say that you must do well in your studies ..." Again she glances at my legs, my obvious lack of my tail flukes. "Will you do that, Lukas. For me?"

"Yes," I promise her. And I mean it. "I'll do it for us ..."

Again, she blushes.

Because I can feel my own face flushing a little, too, I quickly add: "And because it's the only way I'll ever get to go home."

"Thank you, Lukas." Marina eyes me with a steady curiosity.

"Are we in the same class today?" I ask Marina, trying to sound casual, not like I want to be with her or anything.

"No," Marina says and there is some real regret in her voice. "Not this tide."

She doesn't have to say it: I'm remedial compared to her advanced studies. This is really hard for me. I'm used to being a super student. Marina would be slumming to hang out with someone who's still trying to figure out how to shift. Baby stuff. And then there's that High Priestess thing. Though she's a new species, and an experiment, she's still way out of my league. Humans are ranked even lower here in Aquantis than hybrids. Maybe if I fail my Sound Shifting I'll end up in the Outer Reefs with the other mistakes. Or the catacombs. The thought frightens me more than I will ever admit.

"But perhaps after class," Marina adds. "You and I could meet and—"

"No, you've got Clandestine Communications," Dao reminds her with a rather triumphant look at me. If he could, her dolphin would make sure I never saw Marina again for as long as I'm here.

"Oh, that's right," Marina shrugs, but she also flashes a smile at me.

Her dark face lights up and for one second I feel a shimmering in my legs. My muscles ache as if I've been running for days. Like I might suddenly shift for the first time. Though I try to cloak my thoughts I can't help wondering: How do Aquantans have sex? Nobody has bothered to teach me the "facts of life" here. Are merpeople like dolphins—who do it dozens of times a day? That would be pretty cool. But if Marina ever wanted me, would I even know what to do?

Besides kissing? Could I keep up with her if we had to swim and make love at the same time?

"Well," Marina says, gently easing her dorsal fin out from under my hand, "See you ... soon, I hope."

She drops me in front of the Lower Class school steps. For a moment she floats near me, her eyes cool and assessing. What does she really think about me? Am I just a creep or a curiosity or something more? How are our fates linked?

"Thanks ... for the lift," I say, adjusting my kelp satchel full of miniature Sound Murals. They're like electronic tablets, except they're acoustic holograms. And only voice-activated. Good thing I can sing.

"Best of luck with your Temple Tests," Marina says, lightly touching my arm. The delicate filaments between her webbed fingers are a silken blue. They seem to hum into my skin.

Her touch both unsettles and arouses me. My body stirs like it's just waking up for the first time. You'd think I'd never met a girl before Marina. My body glows with a strange heat and my pulse throbs. Hard to breathe. It's like I've been running, but I'm just floating helplessly in front of this girl. Her green eyes spin and hold mine and I have no desire to move. Never felt like this with Jenny or any other girlfriend. They all seem so boring next to Marina's elegance and poise. Even silly. Marina is the most advanced and yet accessible girl. Why is she so open to me, a mere human? Maybe I'm picking up the Aquantan prejudice against SkyeWorlders. How weird is it to look down on my own kind?

"See you there?" I hate myself for asking. But it's not like a date. It's a graduation. And surely as High Priestess Marina will be expected to attend the Temple Tests.

"I wouldn't miss it ... miss you," Marina adds. She almost looks shy for a second and then tosses her curls and turns away.

I can't help but think about our journey through the WaveHole. When I finally got the hang of breathing easily underwater, I sometimes still pretended I was choking—just so Marina would kiss my lips firmly and breathe into me. The Aquantan healers here stitched some invisible little gills at each side of my neck so I could breathe more deeply at these depths. They flutter and filter oxygen from the seawater. No more need for the kiss of life.

"See you, Lukas," Marina sings out as she swims off with her dolphin. Dao seems to be scolding her with a stream of really loud whistles.

Marina glances back at me as she speeds away toward the Upper School. But then I see Dylan pull alongside her and swim in easy synch with Marina. They're both so fast. Dylan is probably going with her to the high tide party that I'm not invited to attend.

Marina smiles warmly at Dylan. Everybody smiles at him. He's the most popular boy in the Sound Temples. A scholar-athlete and aristocrat from the best family—all the boys want to be just like Dylan. And all the girls want to be with him. Dylan only wants to be with Marina. And no one really wants to be with me. ˜

CHAPTER 7
Cave Dancing

Since I'm the only one who sleeps in this underwater world, Aquantans don't really understand the etiquette for waking a human being. No alarm clocks or cell phone music alarms, just a shout.

"Lukas, get up!"

It's Trill again outside my door and she's giggling, holding onto a guy I vaguely recognize as Finn, a stuck-up Aquantan aristocrat and Upper School tutor.

"Am I late for class?" I leap up from my cozy sea moss bed. I've slept in my Turtle Lab T-shirt and cut-offs.

"Not class, you goof," Trill laughs. "You're coming with us to that party I told you about."

I don't know whether I'm more shocked to see Trill out of school uniform and hanging onto Finn's muscled shoulder or that they're here for me. Trill looks very hot with her hair unbraided, her clingy moss blouse barely revealing a pale and distracting cleavage.

"Back off, buddy," Finn says, his tone menacing. "She's with me."

Suddenly, Finn zooms close to me and grips my arm until it hurts. He has polished, high-born Aquantan features—slanting silver-gray eyes, chiseled cheekbones, pale almost blue-tinged skin, and magnificent silver tail flukes. His raven-colored hair is pulled back tightly from his face in an elaborate top-knot studded with coral and bright abalone. He's no one to mess with, not in this world where there are such strict class divisions.

"Hey, dude," I begin, but Finn cuts me off with a scowl.

"Dude? I'm not a rancher. I don't work the fields. You're the human scum we've been trying to quarantine ..."

"Oh, Finn, don't be so jealous," Trill laughs, dismissing me with the same condescension I've seen aristocratic Aquantans show some of their lower classes — those Outer Reef laborers in the kelp forests and sea vegetable fields. "And don't be such a snob. Lukas is just a foreign exchange student. C'mon, the party will be over by the time we get there."

Trill seems like a different person now, flirtatious and—is it possible—a little tipsy? I've heard that some of the wilder students get high off fumes from the geo-thermal vents. Others prefer swilling Noki, a fermented seaweed brew that is hallucinogenic and illegal. I imagine it's like moonshine or that new drug Xcess, that some of the kids in my high school are scoring; but I've never tried Noki.

"The cave dancing party is beyond the Outer Reef," Trill says, winking at Finn.

"But the Outer Reef is off limits, especially to students," I say.

If I'm caught, who knows what the Masters would do to punish me? Throw me into one of those spooky catacombs where I'd be at the mercy of criminals and runaways. Maybe I'd never be allowed to see Marina again. After all, the Blue Beings' decision to elevate a new species hybrid like Marina to High Priestess has shocked everyone— and outraged many. There are not-so-quiet protests in the Acropolis assembly and secret petitions being circled to strip Marina of this honor. No one but an aristocrat has ever been allowed to serve as High Priestess.

"You always follow the rules?" Trill asks, grinning wickedly. And then she offers me her dorsal fin.

I gratefully grab on to Trill's dorsal. She zips me through the glass hallways of the students' quarters. I guess she really does feel sorry for me. Doesn't matter, I'll take whatever she's offering.

Finn doesn't seem too keen on a Lower School kid, especially a human, tagging along. Many Aquantan aristocrats don't think too highly of SkyeWorld and its "primitive" humans.

Again, Finn glances sideways at me to size me up. I know what he sees: a skinny, human boy with no tail flukes, dark, curly hair that sticks straight up from his head, crooked teeth, and someone who thinks he's smart—but really isn't anymore in this world. No, I'm not advanced enough to be a rival for Trill's affections. I must be her pet project or pupil. The guy shrugs and dismisses me with a wry grin.

If we were still in my world, I could probably run circles around this guy. I haven't been practicing aikido all my life for nothing. Or I could make him look stupid by talking with Trill about physics. But all I can do here is nod at him politely. I guess I should be thankful that Trill and her boyfriend are taking me someplace besides class. But I'm a little anxious. It's one thing to be considered a loser in class, another to be uncool at a party.

I wasn't very popular in my high school, but I wasn't an untouchable, either. I could hang with the science geeks, the musicians, and sometimes even the bad boys. But I've never done anything illegal, because I know better than to attract attention from the police. It would be my father they'd punish more than me. He might lose his university grant for the Turtle Lab, or even our small stipend from the Cuban Education Fund. Papi's dream has always been to take me back to Cuba to continue his research on marine mammals in those more pristine waters.

Once out of the student quarters, Trill tows me even faster—past the grave yard catacombs, way past the Acropolis with its impressive towers of sandstone and spun glass, past the vast kelp forests and sea vegetable gardens—farther than I've ever been before here in Aquantis.

"Hold on tight, kid." Finn grins again, his expression taunting. "Wouldn't want you to get lost."

"Where are we going?"

"Scared?" Finn asks.

"No!" But I'm sure they can both hear my heart beating faster.

"Sea caves," is all that Trill will say.

Again, she giggles and removes a glass flask from her backpack that's filled with some glowing, amber liquid. Trill hands the Noki to Finn, who makes a point of not offering me a drop.

"Oh, give him a swig, Finn," Trill says. "Lukas might need it!"

Reluctantly, Finn offers me the glass flask. Without hesitation and with what I hope is a bit of bravado, I take a big gulp. An evil-tasting fire shoots down my throat and swirls in my belly. How can Noki be so hot and cold at the same time? Gagging on the vile brew, my stomach cramps and my throat burns.

"Yuuuuuuuuck!" is all I can say.

"You'll get used to it," Finn laughs. "It's worth it. Dare you to take another drink."

It's the last thing on earth I want to do. But we're not on Earth. So I take Finn's dare and swill the foul stuff again. This time, not such a big swallow. And this time, it doesn't scald my throat. The liquid is cooler. But it still tastes just as hideous. Like rotten shrimp and some weird spice, like old garlic.

Trill and Finn think my reaction is hilarious. As we zoom alongside a dark abyss toward the Outer Reefs, I notice that the coral reefs and flickering fish start to look a little too bright, yet unfocused. Everything is haloed with electric shadows and a kind of white noise. I feel a rush of dizziness and disorientation.

But then an inner glow begins at my toes and rises up through my body like a slow little tsunami of pleasure. My heart flutters, my Aqua-Lungs expand, and I'm giddy with excitement—and power. With this Noki swirling through my system, I feel like I could even take on that arrogant Finn.

"Whoa!" I say to Trill. "How 'bout some more Noki?"

"You've had enough," Trill laughs.

Do I detect a note of fondness, even indulgence, in her voice? It's really weird to see Trill, my taskmaster tutor, so playful and undisciplined. I wonder if Marina is ever so unguarded.

"Will Marina be at the cave dancing party?"

For a moment Trill is uptight again. "Of course not! Our High Priestess doesn't break the rules."

"Not like us." Finn makes a show of taking a long gulp of the Noki. Then he leans over and kisses Trill full on the mouth while we all zoom along, without missing a beat. He acts like I'm not even there.

Such high-speed kissing is pretty cool. Maybe there will be an Aquantan girl at this party who actually likes me. As we veer down into a deep cavern, I'm psyched and up for anything.

"We're here," Trill announces.

"What do you mean here?" I ask. I don't see a thing except coral reefs and small blue sinkholes.

Finn nods down at a very narrow slit in the sea bottom, like a thermal vent. I expect hot lava to flow up and burn my feet. I'm shocked when Trill turns sideways, squeezes herself into the vent, and disappears. Finn follows her, and then grabs me by the arm and pulls me into the rocky passage. Claustrophobic, I close my eyes. Rocks scrape my arms and there's a strange, sulfurous heat swirling.

Choking, I fight off Finn's grip. It occurs to me that maybe Finn and Trill aren't taking me to a party at all. Maybe they're just going to bury me alive down here. There's hardly any space to fight with Finn, but I manage to twist his arm backward.

"Ouch!" Finn yells. He lets go of me and swims ahead.

I'm trying to feel my way back along the slit of stone when a blast of hot air shoots me through the vent into a gigantic cavern. It's the most spectacular sea cave I've ever seen: Tall limestone chimneys belch smoke and fire, spooky stalactites hang down draped with emerald moss, and the smooth stone walls are alive with cave paintings. They flicker like 3-D movies or holograms, echoing pictures of Aquantans from long ago. Dancing.

"It's always been a pretty popular place," Finn comments drily as he notes my amazement. "Considering that it's supposed to be a big secret. Have fun."

He shoots up into the cavern to join what looks like a formal waltz of Aquantan couples. Not all aristocrats. I see some of the outliers and laborer classes also dancing. And a few Constants are lounging around the reefs watching the dance or guarding the cavern entrance. Everyone is dressed in lush green blouses and a few rare black sea moss gowns. The girls have studded their coiled hair and elegant tails with shipwreck pearls, blue sapphires, and rubies. Boys wear strands of carved abalone shells and turquoise across their chest and their hair is all tied up in the Aquantan topknot.

I look pretty silly with just my legs, my cutoffs and my Turtle Lab T-shirt. No one gives me a second glance. Stuck on the white sand sea bottom, I perch on a round brain coral ledge and watch.

Acrobatic, the couples sway and leap and pirouette together in an underwater waltz. There are no musicians. The couples each sing variations on a melody shared by everyone dancing. Ultrasonic arpeggios, baritone beats, and husky textures all blend in harmonies that would make my choir director weep with happiness. Each sound radiates the most astonishing colors: warm rose, silver flares, and golden flickers.

Then the music and the beat shifts into a wild, pulsing rhythm. Now the singing is more like some kind of urgent chant. Some of the singer-dancers make percussive pops and shimmering rhythms like snare drums or cymbals.

Even my land legs keep the beat in the shifting sand, while above couples gyrate and even make a noise like a growling purr. I notice that Trill and Finn are dancing so close together their tails are entwined. It looks sexy and fun and fast. A few of the couples, their tails slapping and twisting around each other, their mouths glued together, streak away from the dance. They disappear into side caverns to hook up, I assume. Drunk on Noki, my own body throbs with an urgent desire. Maybe I can get some Aquantan girl to notice me. But what would I do if she did? No one's really taught me the facts of life here. I use my land legs to propel up into the wild dance. But Finn just thwacks me with his tail and on purpose and sends me somersaulting back down to the white-sand sea bottom.

"So you're the new boy." I hear a voice that's smooth and sexy, like raw honey.

My whole body is suddenly alert. I spin toward that voice and trip, almost falling into a geothermal vent. With a casual but expert hand, a gorgeous blonde girl catches me. Laughing, the girl pulls me toward her as if I was just dancing, not stumbling.

"Hey, thanks," I say, keenly aware that this girl is all curves and armor. She must be one of the Warrior students I've heard so much about. They say the girls are even more dangerous with their weapons than the boys. The closer you get to them, the more intimate their attack.

Underneath her shell mesh breastplate, this beautiful girl is wearing a mossy gown inlaid with shark's teeth and star coral. When she smiles she seems friendly enough, but her pale blue eyes are calculating. They almost make a slight clicking sound as she scans me. Unlike Marina, her eyes don't spin with colors. No one needs to tell me she's a worthy, even intimidating, opponent. Or partner. And she's sizing me up. I can't imagine she likes what she sees.

"Pandora," another Warrior student sings out, swimming toward us. "Come back!"

So this is Marina's famous younger sister. I've heard rumors about Pandora: her exquisite beauty, her bad-girl reputation, and her rivalry with Marina. Pandora is the greatly sought-after prize in her family. She has secret admirers from the Aquantan aristocracy—even though she's only fifteen and a hybrid. Soon she'll have her pick of suitors. I hear the sisters don't get along. I'm not going to like this girl. I hope.

"Why don't you try a real dance partner, Pandora?" the boy teases her. He floats nearby us, his splendid tail flukes unfurled. He eyes me with scorn. "Someone who can keep up with you."

Pandora tosses her head and her blonde curls trill. "Like you?" she shoots back. "The one I just beat in a race? Swim along, Lars, and find another girl ... someone ... slower."

With a scowl and a shrug, the boy zooms back up to join the other swirling dancers. Their music is now loud and percussive; the chants a little more like rap—guttural and rapid-fire. More couples sneak off into secret side caverns. My own heart is pounding, my breathing quick and a little ragged. I clench my fists to stop my body from getting too turned on.

Pandora notices my arousal and laughs. Suddenly, her Constant, a swordfish with mean eyes, darts out from a nearby ledge and slashes a small cut in my arm.

"Stop, Lak!" Pandora says, her tone both annoyed and amused. "He's mine. Go play with the others."

Lak casts me a baleful look and disappears. Pandora twirls me around like I'm some kind of plaything. A boy bauble. Then she shocks me by pulling me closer. Her body is shapely, her breasts full and her arms toned. She moves with all the strength and grace of a trained athlete. But there's something wild and wary about her. Like she could strike or kiss me on a whim. Of course, I can't keep up with her. But I try.

I plant my feet in the sand and try to twirl her. Her tail thwacks me smartly across my legs. It doesn't really hurt. But all my senses are heightened, vigilant. What is Pandora playing at? What does she want with me?

As I dance with this dangerous beauty, my body fits perfectly into Pandora's generous curves. Heat stirs in my spine, and my heart is thudding so loud I'm sure Pandora can hear it. Now I'm getting the hang of this music because it's shifted from rap-like rhythms to a fast, bright beat like salsa. I know how to move to hints of conga drums and fluttering high-octave flutes.

"You're a good dancer," Pandora says in surprise as we sway together, our hips locked in the quick rhythms.

"Of course," I grin. "I'm Cuban!"

Pandora throws her head back and laughs, exposing the vulnerable hollow of her neck, the delicious curve of her jaw. I want to kiss her pale skin, but I don't dare. Instead, I reach up to twirl a delicate, blonde curl in my finger and playfully pull it tight. Even tug a little. Pandora's body responds with a slight tremble and then impulsively she pulls me even closer to her. In spite of her silvery mesh armor, I can feel her breasts, soft and full against my chest. Her heart quickens in synch with mine. I run my hand down the curve of Pandora's spine and she sways into me, her hipbones sharp against mine.

I feel a little guilty, as if I'm betraying Marina. But Marina is way off-limits to me, especially here. And her sister is not bound by the destiny and duties of a High Priestess. From what I've heard, Pandora makes her own decisions and her own conquests. After all, she's a Warrior, not a Diplomat.

"Not bad, Lukas," Pandora says, her voice a husky whisper in my ear. "For a human." Abruptly, she twirls me far out from her body and then lets me go. Drifting. "Even if you're just as forbidden as this Outer Reef."

Suddenly, I know two things about this girl: Pandora is reckless. And she is brave. She'll do and she'll take whatever she wants. Could she ever really want me? One thing for sure, this girl is trouble. Why is that so attractive? I never felt this way about my girlfriend, Jenny. She was so sensible and predictable.

Pandora's tail flukes slap perilously close to my face as she zooms up to rejoin the other dancers. Nothing more than a discarded suitor.

I'm left to rock in her wake. I sigh and sink my feet back into the sand. Everybody is coupled or dancing, ignoring me. What's the point of being at a party if you can't —well, party?

I plop down on a slick ledge and watch the dancers sing and carry on above me. Now I know what girls at school dances feel like when they're called wall flowers. I wish someone would at least offer me some Noki, so I could just drown my misery. Oh, I forgot. I already drowned.

"Hey, Lukas, you gamble?" It's Finn, his face flushed from Noki. Several other guys, arrogant aristocrats all, flank him.

"No money," I shrug.

"Leave the kid alone, Finn," a low voice behind me says. "We'll take you on."

I turn to see one of the boys from Marine Arts class, Rip, and some of his buddies. They're scholarship kids from the laborer classes and live near these Outer Reefs. With their wide and strong shoulders and their shabbier shirts, they remind me of the so-called "disadvantaged" kids back home. The ones who never have lunch money.

"What d'you got to gamble?" Finn snorts.

"We'll gamble for Noki," Rip says, his gold-flecked brown eyes narrowed. "We got plenty of that. We brew it."

This kid means business. I've seen him throw guys twice his size in Marine Arts. Rip and his friends have never really included me in their games. Who knows why he's stepping up for me? Maybe it's just a chance to take Finn and his conceited friends down a peg or two.

The gambling starts in earnest, with both sides eyeing each other threateningly. I can't help but laugh when I see it's an elaborate shell game. Conch shells hiding shipwreck doubloons.

"What's so funny?" Finn glares at me.

"Nothing." But I can't wipe the grin off my face.

Rip's attention is riveted on Finn's fast hands as he shifts the shell from one golden coin to another. Maybe it's just because I'm the least drunk of them all, but I can see that Finn is cheating. In one move, he palms the doubloon in his hand. When Rip tries to choose which conch shell is hiding the gold, all will be empty. There's no winning with a cheat.

I don't want to see Rip lose, but I also don't want to call out Finn on his cheating. After all, Finn and Trill are my tow home. But game after game, when I see Finn lording it over Rip, I can't just sit by and let the humiliation continue.

"Hey, dude," I say, "I saw you hide the doubloon."

"You little creep!" Finn grabs my arm and punches me in the face so fast I can't escape. My nose feels like it's been rearranged and my jaw pounds with pain.

Suddenly Rip spins and thwacks Finn hard with his tail flukes. They all fall in, tails slapping and thrusting. Finn somersaults backward to escape Rip's powerful attack, and then regroups. Finn swims straight toward me, his shoulders hunched, head lowered to ram me.

I stand my ground, but just before Finn can slam into me, someone grabs my arm and jerks me out of the way. Shocked, I turn and see it's Rip. He tows me away from the fight so fast my eyes blur. Then with a nod, he deposits me in a nearby cavern that is hidden and narrow.

"Here he is," Rip says, and then turns and bows his head.

"Thank you, Rip." I recognize the melodic voice before I see her. "Thanks for watching out for Lukas—and me."

With a thrust of his tail flukes, Rip jets up to rejoin the brawl. I hope he wins. But how unprecedented for a High Priestess to make an alliance with someone from the lower classes. Word of this will make Marina even more unpopular among the Aquantis aristocrats.

In the cavern, Marina is almost hidden behind a moss-covered stalagtite. Dao is nowhere in sight. Maybe she sneaked out and left him behind. "Lukas, why are you here!"

"Me? What about you? Is this any place for a High Priestess?"

My impudence makes Marina smile. But I wonder: Has she assigned Rip the undercover job of being my bodyguard? Maybe Marina really does care about me. Or maybe I'm just her responsibility.

"I've come to fetch my sister before she gets into any more trouble." Marina glances around at the couples swirling above us, as if to find Pandora. "Have you seen her?"

"Uh ... no," I say. Why am I lying? Did Marina see me dancing with Pandora?

Nothing really happened with her sister—or did it? It's risky lying to Marina, but for some reason I don't quite understand, it's my first impulse. "But I'm really glad you're here, Marina. You wanna dance?"

"Thanks, Lukas, but ..." Discreetly, Marina glances down at my land legs.

"Try me." I offer my hand to Marina, the memory of her sister still echoing in my body. "I might surprise you."

Marina looks at me, her eyes very still, not spinning. She's not as hot as Pandora, but Marina is easier to be around. I can talk to her and I feel more like myself with her. Suddenly, I remember how Marina transported me safely here in her *lanugo* cloak so tenderly, kissed me to help me breathe. Then I think about Pandora's body pressed against mine, the seductive curve of her hips as they swayed beneath my hands.

Marina suddenly blushes. Did she somehow read my unguarded mind? Did she see images dancing there of me partnered with Pandora? I don't have any acoustic tattoos yet to cloak and hide—do I?

"Well, we could try, Lukas ... you and I." Marina smiles and there is so much warmth in her eyes, I feel another rush of adrenaline. It's deeper than what I felt dancing with Pandora. And more soulful. Serious. Real.

In the narrow cavern, I take Marina in my arms and spin her around. With a delighted laugh, Marina lets me lead. I do watery waltz steps on the sand, holding Marina tightly as she floats, her tail furled.

As Marina and I slow dance, my legs suddenly shudder and ache to shift. I want to sing out my Sound Signature and wrap a strong, protective tail around Marina's. When dancing with Pandora, I never felt the urge to protect her. If anything, I would need protection from that Warrior girl.

"Sing with me, Lukas," Marina says and begins humming a delicious melody, her rich soprano riffing with each note like jazzy scat singing. There's a sensual humor to her improvisations.

I love jazz and can easily join in her runs with my tenor. Our singing actually lights up the stalactites and hanging moss in the cavern. Marina's heart pulses in exact rhythm to mine and her small breasts are firm. She wears no armor, just a woven moss-green blouse that matches her eyes. Marina moves with me as if she can anticipate each twirl.

Maybe it's singing together, our voices again and again finding the most erotic harmonies. Or maybe it's the way Marina floats in my arms as if she's always belonged there. A flash of heat rises up in my body. Before can I stop myself, I kiss her. Marina's trembling lips feel strangely cool.

She's so surprised she stops singing. But I don't. I hum and my lips vibrate against hers. This makes Marina laugh. Yet she doesn't break away from me. She returns my kiss with a passion I never expected. And ever so slowly, Marina's tail flukes unfurl and wrap around my legs, lifting me up higher and higher. Out of the hidden cavern and back into the larger cave with all the other dancing couples.

"Break it up, you two!" Trill demands, looking quite upset.

Out of nowhere, Marina's Constant, Dao, slips between us and eases her away from my embrace. I've never seen a dolphin who didn't have a natural smile, but Dao seems to frown. He doesn't have to say a word of reproach. His narrowed eyes are a reprimand to both Marina and me.

Trill is still tipsy, but now reverting to her bossy tutor mode. I note with satisfaction that behind her, Finn's refined face is bruised, his perfect nose is broken, and his tail flukes are bloodied and some silver scales raked off.

"Priestess," Trill says, bowing her head slightly to Marina. "It's best you not be seen here."

"You're right. I was just ... trying to find Pandora." Marina holds onto Dao firmly and won't meet my eyes.

Finn snarls. "Good luck. Last time I saw your sister she was outracing some other Warrior student."

"Party's over," Trill says in her no-nonsense voice. Then she and Finn drag me away from the cave and Marina. Trill gives me a sidelong glance, "Did you really have to start a fight, Lukas?"

I don't bother trying to explain. I don't even get to properly say goodbye to Marina. The last thing I see Marina and Dao are obviously arguing as they slip back into her hiding place amidst the hanging moss and kelp forest. But just before Marina disappears, I scan her.

With my new acoustic training, I can hear Marina's rapid heartbeat and her blood still pulsing in exact rhythm to mine. I scan the subtle curve of her flushed, high cheekbones; her shapely lips are still rosy and a little swollen from our kiss. Marina's expression is undeniable. I feel the thrill of dancing with Marina still echoing in every zinging inch of my body. And there's something else there, too—the surprise of longing. ~

CHAPTER 8
Marine Arts

I barely slept after the cave party. My body is still glowing from the excitement of dancing—first with Pandora and then Marina. I can still feel the sharp, silver mesh armor sculpted to fit Pandora's breasts as she pressed herself against me. I can still taste her sister, Marina's, soft, salt-tinged lips, and I can't stop thinking about the way she lifted me with her tail flukes wrapped around my legs. It's the first class of the day, and I should be paying attention, but I'm still pretty dazed and dreamy.

"Wake up!" Master Lioli flounces in with a twoosh of his tail and a stern eye on me. He turns to the rest of the class and explains in a condescending tone. "Isn't it a shame humans spend most of their lives asleep."

The other students giggle and glance my way. Of course, everyone else floats gracefully at their desks, while I have to sit cross-legged on a nob of red brain coral like a dunce.

As Master Lioli begins to sing his Signature Song, I have to admit it's impressive. His scales echo twelve octaves and he can sing from sub-sonic baritone to lyric ultrasonic soprano. I'd swear the Master was gay, except that he delights in attracting both male and female attention. His upper torso is muscular, streamlined and strong. I can count his abs beneath his scarlet Scholar robes. But something about his face makes him seem feminine—it's too pretty. A perfect nose and high cheekbones. Braided black hair circling his head like a crown, beaded with turquoise and black pearls. He's majestic and very mysterious like some kind of wizard. Everyone's terrified of him. Master Lioli can silence a student with one raised eyebrow or those spinning prismatic eyes. Something in his expression reminds me of Marina. Proud, but still vulnerable.

"Now, let me hear you." Master Lioli sings several octaves to warm us up.

We imitate him as best we can. My voice breaks on both the lower and upper registers. But I'm holding my own. At least all those years in choir count for something here. And I'm good at rhythm from my banging away at my drum set in the basement at home. But Aquantan singing is extraordinary; each note not only creates intense sounds, but vibrant colors, too. Their voices are their instruments. Still, some of the younger Aquantan boys can't stay on pitch because their voices are changing. And that means they can't always shift from flukes to land legs. So I'm not the only one flunking.

Except for Sound Shifting and finding my own tail flukes, I'm picking things up in this world quickly. All those years of Papi moving us from town to town and my being the new boy in school comes in handy here.

My class is small and most of the Aquantan kids are younger than me. I float around a lot between the cliques. Right now, I'm kind of in no-man's land—on the edge of every group. No one's invited me in. They're trying to figure out if I'm an asset or a liability. And there are some real bullies who've got their eye on me. If the powers-that-be here ever decide I'm more of a disappointment than an honored guest, I'm screwed. So much for being "special."

I've mapped out the class into groups. I guess it's kind of the same in any school. There are the losers goofing off in the back, and the smart kids in front who raise their hand high for every question. Then in the middle are the jocks and popular girls who are so busy flirting, they only tune in to take the tests. And they're smart enough sometimes to ace them. The popular kids preen just like primates in my world. So much for their "evolved civilization."

Except for the fact that Aquantans are so far ahead of humans technologically, live underwater, can shift from tail flukes to legs, and travel backward and forward in time—these merpeople seem more like us than aliens. I mean, they have problems, prejudices, and even poor people. Outliers live way out past the Outer Reefs in submarine trenches not even Aquantans dare explore. Sometimes they raid the city just like undersea pirates. There are also invaders from other worlds who use the WaveHole passages as a secret tunnel to hide their treasures and conquer other realms. I've heard stories of Aquantan Warriors fiercely defending their city from otherworld armies.

"How about a solo from our new student?" Master Lioli startles me out of my rote singing of scales.

"Uh, I'm not ..."

"Of course, you're not ... anything, " Master Lioli says, scowling at me. "You can't shift, and you can barely reach two octaves." He shakes his head. "I don't know why you're even here."

"So they don't tell you anything either!" I shoot back. I'm just fed up with all of this Aquantan arrogance. For a so-called "advanced" civilization, they're just as prejudiced as my world. I'm hoping Master Lioli will be too vain to back down from my challenge.

Sure enough, Master Lioli snaps, "I don't question the wisdom of the Blue Beings in bringing you here. They have their ... logic. But I do know what will happen to you, Lukas, if you don't succeed in your studies."

"What?" I dare him. "What're you going to do—kill me?"

Master Lioli glares at me and opens his mouth to speak. Maybe he will finally tell me what's going on. But then he abruptly turns away, twitching his tail in fury. With his back to the class, the Master struggles to contain his emotions.

I have to wonder why he's so upset. He obviously despises me. I disappoint him every time I open my mouth to sing and fail to shift. I'm sick of everybody here having such big expectations of me and never telling me why I have to learn their ways. All I want is to just get the hell out of here.

"Look," I say, pointing out the obvious. "I'll never be as good as even the worst Aquantan student." Everyone in class laughs. "So just flunk me and send me back home."

Master Lioli turns to me again. With one raised eyebrow, he silences the giggling class. I can't quite read his expression. It's something between frustration and real regret. Why does it matter so much to him if I fail?

"Is it so hard for you to believe that we ... that Aquantans actually care about SkyeWorld?" Master Lioli asks. "The skills we are teaching you are vital to your survival and your work."

"You mean, saving sea life?" I ask. "Why take me away from Papi, then? I'm sure it's killing him to think he's lost me, too. Just like he lost my mother."

When I mention her, Master Lioli's face falls open. He appears strangely unguarded and exposed. Why? He couldn't possibly have known my mother. She died a long time ago. Master Lioli looks as if he might tell me something more. With a scowl, Master Lioli beckons me to follow him outside the classroom. In the curving glass corridor, he leans near me.

"Your mother," he says very softly. "She was ..." He stops and his brows knit together in anguish.

"You knew my mother?" I practically leap up and grab the Master by his braids. "How?"

My gills flutter. I'm so upset I can hardly breathe seawater. Did Master Lioli meet my mother somehow when she drowned? When she sank beneath the waves, leaving my father holding onto only me—was she somehow taken down here to Aquantis? Could she still be alive?

"Tell me!" I shout out loud.

"Your mother drowned ..." Master Lioli, pronouncing each word as if it costs him some effort. "Or, so I've heard."

The Master is hiding something from me. He knows much more than he's telling. Then a series of terrible thoughts hit me all at once: What if my mother didn't really drown, but, like me, was stolen? What if she was imprisoned? Or, what if she preferred to stay in Aquantis and chose to abandon my Papi and me? What if Master Lioli broke Aquantan law and seduced her, so she never wanted to be with mere humans again?

Maybe that's the big secret. That I'm here because my mother was imprisoned here, too! Or maybe she was forced to mate with Master Lioli. I've heard vague rumors of forbidden, interspecies love affairs. But the History Masters never teach us about outlaw lineages or impure bloodlines. If these rogue hybrids exist, they must be hidden in some secret archive.

"Is my mother here in Aquantis?" I yell. "Did you steal her, too?"

I swim dangerously close to Master Lioli. I figure I know enough Marine Arts to get at least a few blows in before he can stun me with his sonar.

Master Lioli holds up a tapered hand and lets out a single ultrasonic note that paralyzes me. "No, Lukas," he says. His tone is softer, somehow indulgent, as if to reprimand a misbehaving pet. "Your mother is not here."

"Is she still ... alive?" I ask. "Are you teaching me these skills so I can ... can find her again?"

Master Lioli sighs. "Every skill we are teaching you, Lukas Barrios Rodriguez, is one you will need to survive—not just here, but also in your own SkyeWorld ."

So he's not going to say anything more about my mother. That's clear. His face, which had opened for just a moment now clenches again in the cold formality of a Master.

Then another question tumbles out, one that shocks even me: "Are you going to declare war on my world?" I demand.

Maybe the Blue Beings are planning on taking over Earth. Was I being trained to lead Aquantan Warriors against my own kind? If so, I would refuse.

Dismissing me, Master Lioli quickly returns to the classroom and snaps, "Now, who wants to shift and show this human how it's done?"

That's it—conversation over. I don't know whether it's a good thing or a bad thing that he didn't answer my questions. I manage to make it through yet another class without successfully shifting. Another failure for Master Lioli to hold against me. But I've learned something important that I never knew before. And it's not about shifting.

There is some other secret about why I'm here. And it involves my mother, as well as me. Now I'm even more determined to learn about the Prophecy. I swear, if Aquantans stole my mother from Papi and me, I'll take my revenge. If they had anything to do with her drowning, I'll take everything they've taught me and turn it against them.

In the meantime, all I can do is go to my classes and learn as much as I can. The Aquantan scientists finally fit me with a pair of flexible fins for my feet. Now, between classes I don't need Trill to navigate me through the curved glass hallways. I don't miss her towing me around, but at least she was some kind of a companion. Now, I'm on my own. I swim sidestroke, careful to stay alert for the mobs of rushing students. Sometimes I get a whack with a tail fluke. And I don't know if it's on purpose or just because I'm so awkward in this world.

The next class is my favorite: Marine Arts. I'm strong and fast enough to do some of the upper body moves because I've studied aikido since I was a kid. It was the only way to stop bullies when I had to move to a new school. So I can somersault backward and forward and fight with the best of them.

In the gymnasium, Warrior Master Xylo always begins class with a triple backwards flip, which I can do even without tail flukes. One thing about this world, there's no gravity. It can simply tuck my knees into my chest and spin through the water. Marine Arts is fun, except for the occasional slap I get from my opponent's tail flukes, I could do this all day. Or every tide. I wish Marina could see how good I am at it. She will, if she really does attend my Temple Tests like she promised.

I'm practicing a summersault when I hear a familiar voice that's so seductive I stop mid-spin. "My elder sister doesn't practice Marine Arts much. She's not a Warrior."

"Ah, Pandora!" Master Xylo sings out. He nods approvingly as his pretty protege swims in, followed by her grouchy-looking swordfish Constant, Lak.

I'm going to keep my distance from that fish. But the sight of Pandora is exciting. My body remembers her. Master Xylo gestures for Pandora to float alongside him. Then he turns to all of us in the gymnasium with a dark look. "This is my teaching assistant for today. None of you will beat her at Marine Arts." He pauses and looks around at us all. "But maybe one of you is brave enough to take her on?"

Pandora sashays right over to me. "Here's a volunteer, Master," she practically coos. Then she tosses me a trident. It's a spear with three prongs. I read about it once in a Greek mythology class.

Pandora acts like we've never met before—like our bodies were never pressed closely together as we danced in the secret cave. But that party girl is nowhere to be found. Right now, she's a warrior: cool and confident, as she looks me up and down condescendingly.

I don't want to fight Marina's sister. But her beauty is irresistible. She could ask me to do just about anything and I'd say yes. I'm eager to spar with her sexy body. If it's anything like dancing with her, I'm ready for it. I'd rather wrestle in the sand ring with Pandora than duel, but she's already chosen our weapons.

"En garde," Pandora hums. Of course, she has a stunning voice. A husky and vibrant alto. But I don't listen to her.

I've practiced using swords before in aikido, so I figured this would be pretty easy. But it's really hard to wield a trident underwater—it's all about thrusting and swimming. It's more like spear fishing, knowing the exact moment to strike. And without tail flukes I can't circle Pandora. My only option is to plant my feet on the limestone gymnasium floor and wait for her attack. I can sense that Pandora plans to put on a quite show for everyone before she lunges. I try to relax my knees and wait for her to underestimate me.

She swims circles around me. Literally. I would laugh if I weren't the target. With each slow and threatening circle Pandora gets closer, feigning a few jabs with the trident. But she's not serious. So I don't fall for her bluff. Of course, she's cloaked her thoughts and any strategy, but I tune in to her tail flukes. I've noticed that right before a real attack, Aquantans will twitch their tails reflexively.

It's just the signal I need. As Pandora lunges with her trident, I instinctively evade her attack by shifting to her side. Then I turn and grab her elbow, using the energy of her forward movement to propel her right on past me.

Everyone is stunned, including Master Xylo. Before I can prepare for Pandora's second assault, he roars, "Enough! We are under orders not to hurt this inexperienced human."

He seems on the verge of disobeying orders and taking me on himself. But after a glance from his Constant, an ominous hammerhead shark, Master Xylo shakes his head. "Class dismissed. Go home and practice on your own."

As everybody swims out of the gymnasium, I'm shocked that Pandora stays behind with me. She doesn't seem offended by not winning our joust. Maybe she let me off easy for some reason.

"Nice move, Lukas," Pandora says, floating very close to me.

"Beginner's luck," I respond.

Pandora's face is pale and perfect. Her red lips seem huge—or maybe I'm just very aware of them. As I look at her, I feel a slight vibration in my legs and a spiraling sensation through my body.

With one webbed finger, Pandora reaches out and quickly traces my lips. "You know, I can help you, Lukas."

"Why would you ever help me?" I eye her suspiciously. Pandora is as cunning as she is attractive.

I really wish I could read this girl's acoustic tattoos or even just what she wants to show me. But all I can do is hear the mind-talk she hasn't cloaked and watch her body language. She swims sideways in a stalking sashay like a shark. I can't take my eyes off of her.

"Everybody knows you, Lukas Barrios Rodriguez," she purrs. "You're part of that stupid Prophecy. Like my sister." Pandora frowns as she mentions Marina. There is just the slightest hint of pain in Pandora's blue eyes. Has Marina hurt her little sister somehow? I can imagine Marina, as High Priestess, might be a hard act for Pandora to follow. But Pandora obviously has her own talents and uses them to the fullest. "So what's the big plan for you two?" Pandora demands with an unexpected edge of desperation in her tone. "Tell me!"

"Dunno!" I grin. "I really don't."

Pandora tries another tactic. She hums in her rich, sub-sonic alto. Her scan is like a musical purr and ricochets inside my body. "Please, Lukas, tell me everything you know about the Prophecy."

I shake off her singing. "If I did know, I wouldn't tell you, Pandora. I've heard you don't like humans ... you want to declare war on our world."

"Who told you that?" Pandora momentarily drops her pleasurable sonar. Then she quickly corrects her tone and smiles. "Remember, I'm half-human myself," She says in her compelling voice. "So I want to make sure you succeed in your tests. Show these Aquantans that humans ... I mean we ... are worthy. What is it you need most?"

I'm not buying her "I'm-human-too" act, but I'm curious if she'll really help me. Having a powerful ally like Pandora might get me home sooner. So I tell her the truth. "I need an animal ally ... a Constant like all of you have by your side."

"That's an Aquantan birthright," Pandora frowns. "A lifelong bond. What animal would agree to ...?" She seems to catch herself.

"Listen, in my world my Papi and I save sea turtles! Wouldn't one of them be willing to become my Constant?"

"Dream on!" Pandora tosses her ash-blonde curls and they tinkle like treble chimes. "No turtle would agree to be your Constant. They're Great Elders." She stops and continues in a softer tone. "But perhaps I can be of help to you."

She swims over and floats so near me, my heart races. I know she can hear it. Pandora pulls me inside her electromagnetic field. I feel kind of lulled, like I'm going to fall asleep. Except my body is too excited.

"Listen, Lukas," Pandora continues, her voice warm and liquid. "If I help you find your Constant, will you serve me ... only me?"

"Will you take me back home?" I manage to snap out of her spell long enough to make this demand. But I don't know how much longer I can hold out against Pandora's seductive skills. It feels like the most enjoyable attack.

"Yes, Lukas, I will take you home," Pandora promises. She strokes my arm and her webbed fingers glow a faint blue-green. "Will you swear loyalty to me?"

"I swear!"

My heart is beating in exact synch with Pandora's. I can hear it pulse fast and full. This quickening of hearts is supposed to happen only between potential Aquantan mates. And us mating would be forbidden. Surely Pandora knows this. Why would she ruin her reputation with me? Maybe I'm some sort of trophy.

Without warning, Pandora wraps me in her lean arms. Her mouth against mine is cool but there's a warm flow like lava. It's like drinking hot honey. At first I'm surprised—and then I can't get enough. I can't stop drinking her in. She tastes golden and addictive and I drink as if I'm dying of thirst. With each fiery, fragrant taste my whole body vibrates. Then a surge of pure ecstasy, as Pandora's silver, supple tail flukes wind around my legs.

"My *manna* will make you strong, Lukas," Pandora's voice is as warm and sweet as syrup. "You will impress every citizen of Aquantis ... even your precious High Priestess."

Abruptly, Pandora pushes me away. My head and stomach are still swirling with the warmth of this delicious nectar. It fills me up and yet I still feel a kind of desperate hunger for this *manna*—and for this girl. Maybe this is what Papi feels when he loses himself with liquor and women. Nepenthe, that's what Papi calls his drunken trysts, magic to make him forget his sorrows.

I just call this hot.

"Yes!" I promise Pandora again. "I'll serve you."

I'm hoping she'll let me drink her *manna* again. Just one more intoxicating taste. But she doesn't. She turns and looks both ways in the passageway outside the gymnasium to make sure we haven't been seen.

"You'll want more," Pandora says, nodding with a satisfied smile.

But her face is wan and there are hollows beneath her eyes like bruises. Her expression is anxious, as if her *manna* transfusion has drained her more than she expected. Is this the first time Pandora has ever given anyone her precious *manna*? I've heard about *manna* exchange and how it can heal or even create new life. There's a rumor that Master Lioli gave some of his golden *manna* to help Marina's parents mate and make her. There's also a dark, addictive side to *manna* that some of the other students hinted at. But I don't care. The thought that I might be the first boy that Pandora gives her precious *manna* thrills me. And makes me thirsty once more.

I reach for Pandora again. "More please. Now!"

"Soon," Pandora promises distractedly.

Now, there is real alarm in her eyes and she stumbles a bit on her way out. She seems a little dazed and exhausted. I feel amazing. As Pandora swims away, I touch my lips and taste again a last delicious drop of the honeyed nectar. ˜

PART THREE

CHAPTER 9
Temple Tests

MARINA

I reluctantly refused to wear my official High Priestess headdress of star coral and black pearls for this ceremony. Pandora insisted that we stand together as equals. From this height, at the pinnacle of the stadium, I saw the Golden Gate of Aquantis rising above the city's curved and busy passageways, all adorned with coral and flowing sea grasses. Whenever I saw such Aquantan artistry and splendor, I was grateful to dwell in such a magnificent underwater world.

"Everyone's here to see Lukas," I told Dao, who was floating alongside me.

But it was my sister who answered—eavesdropping, as usual. "Maybe he'll surprise you. Maybe I'll surprise you, too."

How I wished the Blue Beings had never named me High Priestess. It was more a burden than a gift. Ever since the official declaration, my life had been turned upside down. Not only did Pandora resent me even more fiercely, but my friends also kept a new distance, and my parents seemed troubled.

Earlier at low tide, my mother had insisted on braiding my hair for the Temple Tests. Most low tides, my mother would have already been off in her alchemical acoustics lab, and my father would have been busy with other Navigators repairing the unstable WaveHole transit system. But that tide, my parents lingered at home with me in the hearth chamber. Pandora was still sleeping late, as usual, tucked in her slim spun glass alcove on a luxurious bed of sea moss.

"What will they expect of you ... now?" My mother had asked, as she struggled to tame my curls into a sophisticated hairstyle called a

French braid. My mother had learned it from her own Celtic mother in SkyeWorld.

"It will be too much, this high rank of Priestess and the Prophecy. You can count on that," my father concluded, giving me a look of grave concern. His wide brow and bronzed face were so familiar, like looking in a mirror.

Sitting in his favorite carved sandstone chair, his muscular tail flukes were flopped over a soft brain coral hassock. It was his favorite spot, our cozy hearth with shelves filled with pickled mackerel, sea veggies, and herbs picked from our own bungalow's back garden. My father often teased my mother that our hearth looked more like a laboratory than a place to gather and eat. He was the real cook in our family. In the Hawaiian Islands where he'd been born, he came from a large family of devoted fisherman.

Usually I enjoyed his spicy kelp noodles, caviar, and fresh sea scallops. But that tide, I didn't have much of an appetite. There was too much to think about—and worry about. "Do you know the Prophecy?" I asked my parents. "Didn't they have to get your permission to make me High Priestess?"

My mother yanked my braid tighter, but said nothing. My father frowned and floated up from his favorite seat. "We're not exactly aristocrats in this society, dear," he said with an unusual note of bitterness. "They didn't ask us."

"We're just grateful to be here," my mother quickly added.

I knew without looking that she had cast my father a warning glance. There was so much my parents kept secret. Like why they'd decided to stay in Aquantis and never returned to land—when they could have. Before the Skyeworld sickness prohibited any adult Aquantans from traveling there. All I knew was that it had something to do with my father's heart and my mother's scientific research.

My father turned to my mother, his dark eyes narrowed meaningfully. "We might have to protest. We might have to go back up there ourselves."

"But you'll die!" I asserted, thinking of all the other Aquantan adults who could no longer survive the toxicity of SkyeWorld.

As I floated on the stadium steps, my father's words echoing in my head, Pandora sidled up to me. "You should have told them it was our destiny. Our turn. Mom and Dad are too old."

"Stop eavesdropping, Pandora!" I cautioned her.

My little sister, as usual, ignored my request. "You didn't earn the right to be High Priestess," she scoffed. "You didn't even have to fight for it."

I turned away from my sister, who was more irritable than usual. She looked like she had recently lost weight. Pandora didn't need to be thinner. Every boy around appreciated her ample curves. She also looked paler than usual, and her golden hair was thinner, less than glorious today. Maybe my sister was on one of those dumb and dangerous fad diets that all the popular girls fell prey to. Maybe Pandora was pining away for some impossible aristocratic suitor. Or maybe she was still suffering the sting and disappointment of me being chosen for High Priestess. I felt bad for my sister, but what could I do?

A bass gong shimmered golden in the huge stadium where the Sound Temple students would compete and test before they could graduate. I turned to look for Lukas among the passing students. No sign of him yet. I joined in the singing that echoed throughout the glass pillars. I was expected to show off a little to honor Master Lioli.

So far there hadn't been much for a High Priestess to do, except to work harder with Master Lioli on my advanced studies and dress up for more special occasions like this Lower School graduation. Master Lioli was not pleased that I didn't wear my High Priestess headdress. My informality reflected badly on him and his patronage of me.

As the students paraded in, with their Masters below, I nodded courteously to them. Pandora waved grandly as if their bows and nods were meant only for her. It bothered me, but not enough to argue any more while we were in public.

So I just said, "Let's not fight, Pandora." But I couldn't suppress a rising annoyance in my tone. "This is Lukas's ceremony, not ours."

I hadn't seen Lukas since our forbidden dance in the Outer Reef cave. That was several tides ago. A secret I'd kept even from Dao was this: I liked this human boy too much. So I just buried it deep inside and cloaked any thoughts about Lukas. I hoped I had fooled my Constant into thinking I had no special feelings for the boy. If Dao thought I cared for Lukas, there would be no end to his criticism.

I'd also tried not to seem too eager for rumors about Lukas's remarkable progress. Everyone was still very secretive about what exactly his part in the Prophecy was. And no one told me anything. You'd think they'd give a High Priestess more details about her new role. How did they know I could fulfill it?

"Look, there he is," Dao whistled, as he floated alongside me on the steps.

For all of Dao's expressed dislike of Lukas, I could easily hear that his dolphin's heart was beating a little faster. If this was not in appreciation of Lukas's triumphs in his Aquantan studies, at least Dao seemed more open to the boy. After all, Lukas had chosen a career path as a Diplomat-Scholar, just like us.

"The Masters taught him well," Dao nodded. "He has a chance ... if he doesn't do something stupid to show off." My dolphin nodded toward me, "Like someone else I know."

Everyone in Aquantis knew that Lukas had studied hard and was a good student. But he still hadn't managed to Sound Shift, a mandatory requirement for anyone to remain in Aquantis. Maybe Lukas didn't want to be a Shifter or become a Go-Between ambassador, like me. Maybe he just wanted to go home and never return. I wouldn't blame him. I'd miss him, but it would probably be less confusing for me if he left Aquantis and never returned.

"That boy shouldn't be here at all," Pandora snapped. "SkyeWorld should be quarantined." She had the rude habit of tuning into my thoughts even when I tried to cloak them. "I can still hear the noise of Skyeworld in your acoustic tattoos."

"At least I got to explore other dimensions."

"Yeah, right ..." Pandora snorted, "and you did so well on your mission. You accomplished nothing but bringing back a human."

I flushed with anger. Why did I always let my sister get the best of me? Why didn't I know how to fight for myself? I wished I'd taken more Warrior classes, but Diplomat-Spies were discouraged from such rigorous physical training. We excelled at focusing the mind and the senses. For example, Diplomat-Spies were trained in the clandestine skill of scanning acoustic tattoos that were cloaked.

"We did our best—we saved Lukas and the Great Elder *Honu-wahi* from a burning sea, and we figured out what's making Aquantans who travel to Skyeworld so sick."

"Who cares?" Pandora muttered. "Ever since you came back, the Sound Murals are full of static. Who knows what's really going on up there? Next time, they'll have to send Warriors."

"If there is a next time!" I shot back.

Scanning the large crowd, I noticed that Pandora had even more admirers. Her long, braided blonde hair was coifed in an elaborate black coral headdress. She didn't need my mother to do her hair. Pandora was an expert at French braids and many other complicated hairstyles popular in Aquantis. My sister was gorgeous with her cur-vaceous torso and piercing azure eyes. No one knew whose precious Aquantan *manna* had helped our human-born parents create such a dazzling creature.

Was it the haughty Sound Master Lioli, as it had been with my bloodline? Or was it perhaps the mysterious Warrior Master Xylo, who was Pandora's devoted, though somewhat dangerous mentor?

For this momentous event, Master Xylo had dressed Pandora in a tightly woven sea-green gown inlaid with shipwreck sapphires. These gems were rumored to be poisonous if unleashed. Bracelets of moray eels decorated Pandora's muscular arms. Their fearsome scissor-teeth could gnash anyone who came too near. My sister's powerful combina-tion of beauty and aggression had always troubled me.

As the Aquantan dignitaries took their places on the steps along-side us, the crowd sang out its approval in a twelve-octave choir. And when my sister raised her arm to wave, acknowledging their praise, I felt suddenly insignificant. Why had I dressed in such a simple kelp blouse and no adornment? At least I wore my silver sash with all of my scholarly awards. Still, I was no match for Pandora's regal and finely crafted breastplate armor of sharp shells.

A sonorous song rose up in one voice from the crowd. Two oc-topus guards accompanied Lukas into the limestone stadium where he and the other Lower Class students would be tested. I felt a pang of pride and sympathy for Lukas. He was the only student without a Constant to help him in the rigorous ritual tests to qualify for graduation.

Lukas glanced up at the steps as he made his way into the stadium. His training had molded him into a fit and physically confident young man. He seemed much stronger than I remembered. Encircled with knotted kelp bands, Lukas's muscular shoulders were wider from all his swimming. His feet were equipped with artificial webbed flippers made of sea fans.

Around his neck, Lukas wore the Aquantan coral necklace with insignias of all the classes he had successfully completed: Animal Alliances, Mind-Talk 101, Acoustic Hypnosis, Aquantan Ethics, and Marine Arts I. Across his bare chest, he wore the green kelp belt of a beginning marine artist. It was really an impressive array of skills for a human, though Lukas still lacked Sound Shifting, Acoustic Stunning, and Cloaking. Of course, his electromagnetic field held only a few primitive acoustic tattoos. They revealed his conservation work with sea turtles and his singing in a human choir—achievements that Aquantans would admire. If he passed all his difficult tests, he would earn more.

Lukas bowed to the crowds resting in their seats. As his eyes swept the stadium, he spotted me high up on the stadium steps. He bowed with some well-practiced deference.

Impulsively, Lukas grinned at me and then began his first test: a song. Lukas sang out in a clear, high tenor that was surprisingly pure and resonant. Though his voice held no colors, like Aquantan singers, Lukas's tenor was still quite affecting.

Lukas had chosen a Spanish ballad from his Cuban ancestors. The song had both upbeat rhythm and sorrow. It's an interesting combination. Aquantan sad songs were usually monotone and not very complicated. But this song changed with each verse, much like the complex lullabies of humpback whales that were so difficult, even for Sound Masters, to replicate.

Gracias a la vida, que me ha dado tanto.

The Linguistics Masters translated the Spanish lyrics: "Thank you to life, which has given me so much ... "

I was shocked by his supple tenor voice. His singing reminded me of our intimacy in the cave dance. The boy had bragged about many other things, why not his musicality. Maybe Lukas didn't realize when we spent that one night in the Turtle Lab together that it would impress me most to hear him sing. Maybe he thought I only liked Mozart.

Lukas's song stirred the Aquantan crowd. After all, music was our primary art form, and everyone in this underwater civilization knew the value of a fine singing voice. Sometimes it saved your life.

Lukas's singing immediately elevated his standing with the gathered Aquantans. Some in the crowd even picked up the boy's richly woven rhythms and joined in with their own harmonies.

Lukas broke off abruptly and dropped his head. From this distance, I couldn't scan his stomach gases to hear his emotions. But his sagging shoulders and the way he shook his head—it was a posture of grief, and longing. Of course, he was homesick. He was lonely for his world. Anybody could see that he just wanted to go home.

I felt the echo of his sadness in my own body. I desperately wanted to comfort him, but I knew that would not become a High Priestess. Master Lioli had taught me that I must "control my emotions and detach" if I were to be a true leader.

Even though he didn't finish, Lukas's song was a huge hit. The crowd was obviously moved. Bowing, Lukas received the respectful ovation of resonant voices raised in perfect harmony to praise his singing.

Again, searching the stadium steps, Lukas nodded to me. His expression was both relieved and sad. Haunted. Then his gaze shifted to Pandora, and what he did next surprised me. He also bowed to her, less formally, but again with that uncharacteristic courtesy. And Pandora's reaction was also shocking. My little sister waved a hand with its swaying moray eels, as if to bless the boy.

Did Pandora and Lukas know each other? Had they trained together in some of their classes? I thought Pandora despised the boy. Why was she championing him? I could hear my sister's heart; it was not beating with pleasure.

Pandora's heart thudded low and steady, and its light dimmed, just for an instant, but long enough for me to realize that my sister really hated Lukas, almost as much as Pandora despised the human part of herself. Or me.

Why was she being so friendly to Lukas? Did Pandora know something about these tests that might harm him?

I was so alarmed that I took my sister's hand. "Lukas is here because the Blue Beings destined it. You can't hurt him, Pandora!"

"I've heard that if Lukas doesn't pass his tests, he will simply be eliminated." Pandora said with a fervor that was fearsome. "He'll just be another failed experiment."

"Who told you that?" I demanded. "The Blue Beings would never allow his death. He's our guest."

Pandora shook off my hand and turned away from me. Again, she waved and smiled down at Lukas with what might look like benevolence—from a distance. Lukas bowed to acknowledge Pandora's favor.

I fought back my jealousy. As the crowd cheered Lukas on, I tried to scan my sister's acoustic tattoos for information. But they were well cloaked, and I was still learning how to scan hidden tattoos.

"He's a fool," Pandora spat, as she waved at Lukas with false graciousness.

"He's learning!" I countered.

Lukas glanced up at Pandora with his characteristic bravado but there was something else too—desperation. He should be much more alert and focused on the tests to come, if he were not stargazing up at my sister.

"Second test: Marine Arts," Master Xylo announced in his rich baritone.

The crowd clapped appreciatively as Lukas took his place in the sandy arena awaiting his opponent. Surely the Blue Beings would not assign him an advanced student to fight. But when I saw who entered the amphitheater to face-off against Lukas, I gasped. It was Dylan.

"That's not fair!" I burst out. "Everyone knows Dylan has never lost a Marine Arts match. Why would they arrange such an unequal contest?"

"May you win all your matches, Lukas Barrios Rodriguez," Pandora sang out in her seductive alto.

She laid a jeweled hand over her own heart. Her smile for Lukas was false. But there was a strange intensity, even urgency, in her voice. Perhaps only I could hear it. Was there something going on between them?

Lukas gazed up at my little sister with a nervous and rather lopsided smile. He took up a defensive position and squared his shoulders. And then he turned to bravely face his opponent, who was also my best friend and suitor. My destiny. ~

CHAPTER 10
Animal Alliances

My mind raced as Dylan took up his position opposite Lukas in the arena, its sandy floor swept to perfection by meticulous bacteria-eating microbes, tubeworms, and crabs.

Lukas bowed to the crowd. But the applause was all for Dylan, whose family was of the highest rank.

"If I'd known Dylan was going to fight Lukas," I told Dao on our private frequency, "I would've asked him to let Lukas win."

"That would be unfair, Marina," Dao scolded. "And not befitting a High Priestess."

I frowned and focused on Dylan, willing him to glance up at me. But he didn't or wouldn't. For the past several tides, I'd been too busy with High Priestess duties to have a real romance with Dylan, which I knew bothered him. I worried that he would take his frustrations with me out on Lukas.

My gills fluttered in alarm, and I tried to wave at Dylan. But he remained focused on Lukas, his jaw tight. Right there alongside Dylan was his Constant, a young Octopus guardian named Zwo. But Lukas was alone.

Already Dylan and Lukas were circling each other, formally bowing, preparing for the fight. Zwo stayed a little distance behind Dylan, deferring but ever vigilant.

Without thinking about the consequences, I bolted to the edge of the stadium steps. "Stop!" I sang out.

Dylan, then Lukas, looked up at me in confusion.

I didn't know what else to say. I'd shocked even myself by singing out my protest. My first public act as High Priestess—and it was definitely the wrong thing to do. No aristocratic High Priestess would make such a faux pas. For a moment, everyone was silent, but then a reprimanding murmur rippled through the crowd. I accepted the criticism with a slight nod of my head. I regretted my outburst, but at the same time I wanted to do something more to stop this battle.

The announcer, with his baritone authority, spoke only one word: "Commence!"

Lukas grinned at me and made a weird gesture with both of his thumbs sticking up from his fists. It seemed vulgar and made him look silly, but his strange signal suggested that Lukas believed he actually had a chance to win against these overwhelming odds.

"Humans are such idiots!" Pandora's voice was soft, but I heard my sister clearly. "They always overestimate their own powers."

"And you underestimate them, Pandora!"

It all happened so quickly. With a slight, patronizing smile, Dylan allowed Lukas to make the first move, a quite beautifully executed technique we call "Blue Dragon Rising from the Ocean." Lukas rooted himself in the sand and performed an elaborate and calculated series of fist strikes. But the water slowed him down, making it easy for Dylan to maneuver out of the way.

Then Dylan thrashed his tail, spinning in a watery tornado toward the boy. Lukas squatted down. Like springs, he used his legs to propel himself straight toward Dylan, striking him squarely on the jaw. In a nanosecond, Dylan's Constant reached out with his tentacles to grab Lukas.

"No, Zwo, let him be!" Dylan shouted.

Reluctantly, the octopus fell back into a wary position nearby.

Wincing in pain, Dylan held a well-manicured hand to his jaw. We all knew that any blow to any Aquantan's jaw was always very serious. The hollow bone of the jaw is where we transmit and receive sound. This bold strike disoriented Dylan's sonar long enough for Lukas to execute another technique that few Aquantans had ever witnessed before since it required two legs.

106

Lukas leapt onto Dylan's back and wrapped both of his legs around Dylan's tail flukes, essentially scissoring his tail into stillness. Then Lukas grabbed Dylan's elbow and painfully twisted it up and around his back. With his tail paralyzed by Lukas's surprisingly strong legs and his arm bent backwards, Dylan was shockingly trapped. Any more struggling might dislocate Dylan's arm.

The Aquantan crowd was dumbfounded. I was ambivalent—proud of Lukas's skills, but also worried about Dylan. My loyal suitor seemed not only humiliated, but also physically hurt. More murmurs rose from the stadium. I detected in the crowd's mind-talk some darker colors and humming that betrayed dismay and resentment.

Perhaps Lukas had studied enough telepathy to also hear the crowd's disapproval. After a slight bow to the stadium rows, he leaned his head against Dylan's fine-boned aristocratic face and said out loud, "Now, I can see what my opponent sees. I can feel his fears and his sorrows." Lukas seemed to be listening to Dylan's bruised jaw, and a moment of empathy flashed across the boy's face.

"I may not share, but I can experience, my opponent's point of view." Lukas continued his formal mantra, his voice rising. "I know why my opponent has attacked—it is not personal. It is only a required test of strength. I may have won this round. But there are other tests, and I may need my opponent's help to pass them. Therefore, I release him in peace."

It was obviously a speech that one of his masters—which one, I wondered?— had taught Lukas. But the fact that the boy remembered it in the heat of a fight was astonishing.

"At least he didn't gloat," Dao commented.

"Yes, for a change," I said.

I noticed that my sister said nothing. Her lips were pressed tightly together, and her fists were clenched at her side.

Lukas's words seemed to mollify the crowd. They clapped courteously and a few dignitaries even nodded at him. Red-faced and still holding his swollen jaw, Dylan gave Lukas a stiff, formal bow and swam out of the arena quickly. But before Dylan disappeared, he glanced up at the temple steps and at last met my gaze. He bowed and shook his head slightly. Was it a warning? Or was he furious at being bested by a human?

"Did you make Dylan throw the match?" Pandora demanded, sidling up next to me.

"Of course not!" I snapped.

"You care for this boy too much." Pandora haughtily tossed her curls. "He's beneath you."

"And what about you acting like Lukas's champion?" I asked. "You hate humans!"

"Who I love and who I hate is none of your concern!" Pandora hissed. Then she turned and waved benevolently to the crowd. Several songs rose up in Pandora's honor.

I couldn't help but feel hurt by Pandora's rudeness. I knew it was just her manner and was irritated that I always let it get to me.

The announcer's voice echoed around the gleaming amphitheater, "Marine Arts Match One goes to ... Lukas Barrios Rodriguez."

Again the polite, but diffident applause and something new—a low, humming from some in the crowd who were obviously cheering the boy on to the next test: Animal Alliances.

I'd aced this test in my second term of study, but I'd had the advantage of Dao's guidance. His unfailing courtesy once even charmed a great white shark into helping us.

But Lukas was human—a species most sea creatures avoided, either out of fear or the memory of a painful experience. What animal would actually volunteer to accompany Lukas for his whole life? Especially if he returned to SkyeWorld, where wild animals were second-class citizens, rarely equals.

"Choose your animal alliance wisely, Lukas Barrios Rodriguez." The amphitheater rang with the announcer's voice. "Because you must also be chosen."

Glancing over at my Constant, I wondered if I would have deserved Dao, could have drawn him to me for life, if we'd not simply been born together? Would Dao, with all of his skills, have agreed of his own will to always accompany me? What kind of life would Dao have had without me?

With another glance up at Pandora that troubled me, Lukas made his choice.

"Hammerhead shark!" He sang in his clear tenor.

Shock, so loud I could hear it, hummed along Pandora's body as she rocked back and forth, her tail fluttering in agitation. "Fool! What are you doing?" she hissed.

Pandora's mind-talk was sharp as razor clams. Its fury made me wince. But that was all I heard before Pandora completely cloaked her thoughts. She had gripped a spitting moray eel bracelet in her hands as if she had been about to release it. But why would Pandora's eels ever leave her? Was the moray eel meant for Lukas? Had Pandora promised Lukas one of her own accomplices for his animal ally? Why was she giving this boy so much? What else had she promised him? And more importantly, what was Lukas's part of the bargain?

Maybe Pandora's scheme was to accompany Lukas back to Skye-World. The thought of him returning without me—or with only Pandora by his side—made my tail twitch in disappointment. And rage. I wanted to thwack my little sister right there on the stadium steps. Forget decorum. Whatever her secret plans, they must be stopped. I vowed to myself to find out what was going on, even if it meant I had to spy on my sister and Lukas.

There was a hush in the amphitheater as the crowd realized the arrogance of Lukas's request. It was so like a human to call upon such terrible power without considering the consequences.

"Very bad choice," Dao murmured. "So immature."

And dangerous. I didn't have to say it. Everyone here recognized Lukas's mistake as we all nervously awaited a hammerhead.

Animals in Aquantis usually answered our invitations to the Sound Temples out of a sense of diplomacy. There had always been an uneasy yet long-standing truce with the shark clan. Sharks possessed a skill that we sorely lack—a keen sense of smell. It was primary in their navigational abilities. For this, they were highly valued and respected.

Some rare Aquantans were even born with sharks as their Constants. These few usually worked as Warriors or Explorers. Sometimes I was surprised that my sister had not been born with a shark as her Constant, like her Warrior Master Xylo.

With a sidelong swoosh, swoosh of his lethal tail, a hammerhead shark swam out of a nearby reef and straight toward Lukas. The creature was so fast he startled the boy.

"Uhhhhhh, maybe not ..." Panic seized Lukas's face, and he held up his hands, backing away. But Lukas had no place to go. It was obvious that every instinct in his body was alert, terrified.

Even from a distance, I could scan the tumult of his stomach gases, his heart clanged so hard it was visible in his chest. I worried he might actually have a heart attack. I glanced over at my little sister, who pretended to have lost all interest in the boy. Was Pandora turning away from Lukas because she assumed he would die and didn't want to be associated with him?

Lukas was face to face with the hammerhead shark. Everyone in the stadium could hear the boy's gulp of seawater, the flap of the artificial gills. Everyone heard the almost imperceptible click of the shark's teeth, already smelling the human skin, perhaps anticipating the taste of his warm blood.

"I ... I offer ... my alliance ..." Lukas's mind-talk was mostly a stutter as the shark began swimming in slow, calculating circles around him.

"And what do you have to offer me?" the shark demanded. "You humans who hack off my fins for soup. Who torture me without mercy or thought? And why? Just because you fear me."

Lukas's mouth flapped open and closed. But there were no more words or mind-talk. He was paralyzed with terror as the shark opened his huge mouth, revealing rows of jagged teeth. But instead of chomping down on him, the shark snapped his mouth shut and butted the boy hard with his hammerhead.

Arms flailing, Lukas fell back, his feet scraping the ocean floor and sending up little storms of sand.

"Any alliance means trust." The shark seemed to be giving Lukas a moment's reprieve. "Why should I trust you?"

I tried to telepath to Lukas that he should tell the hammerhead about his work in the Turtle Lab, about his campaigns to save sea mammals. But Lukas was lost in his fear, his face a frozen mask of wide eyes and a grimace. "Please, don't ..." Lukas held up his hands to beg the shark for his life.

The crowd was so quiet there was only the pulse of the sea and the nearby sway of the kelp forest. As the shark's obsidian eyes narrowed, and his tail swished menacingly, I wondered why the Blue

Beings didn't interfere. They wouldn't let this boy, their guest, die, would they? But maybe Pandora was right—Lukas would be eliminated. Perhaps this was his destiny, his part in the Prophecy. And mine?

The hammerhead shark turned around. For a moment, I thought he might dismiss this human with the contempt of no contact. But then I realized that the shark was swimming away only to gather speed for a final strike.

"Dao!" I pleaded with my Constant. "Stop him!"

Dao's eyes held mine. He shook his sleek head. "I cannot. It is not my place."

"Then I will!"

With a thrust of my tail flukes, I sped down the stadium steps toward Lukas. I didn't have a plan. Only a memory.

Once Dao had saved me from a shark attack by repeatedly ramming the creature in the soft underbelly until at last, mortally wounded, the shark swam away. But I was nowhere near as strong as Dao, nor were my arms as powerful as my dolphin's beak. And since I was not a Warrior, I had no weapons. All I had was my sonar, my Signature Song, and my wits.

But wait! Didn't Lukas also have a Signature Song that Master Lioli had been trying to teach him ever since he'd arrived in Aquantis? If there were ever a time for Lukas to Sound Shift, it was now. It was the only way he could save his life.

"Lukas, sing!" I yelled. As fast as I was, I knew I couldn't reach him in time to stop the shark's attack. "Shift!"

Hearing me, Lukas began to spin around very fast. He sang out his Signature Song, his voice trembling: "Ahhhhhhhhwhooooooahhhh ..." His tenor broke on the lowest notes, but his upper range was strong.

Lukas clamped his legs tight. He grimaced in pain. Very slowly one leg, then another glowed a silver aura and began to fuse into sleek tail flukes. Scales tinkled in rhythm to his song.

Just as the shark's flat, blunt head rammed his chest, Lukas's tail spun him around. The shark's strike only glanced his body, but its force was enough to double Lukas over in agony. He clutched his broken ribs, his gills gasping.

111

When I reached him, I realized the shark was circling around for another attack. This time his huge mouth was wide open, hungry. Of course, Dao was by my side, ready to ram the shark in my defense—even though we were breaking all the rules. The Blue Beings might be very angry—perhaps even angry enough to let us all be killed by this hammerhead.

"Next time you ask for a Constant, boy," the shark sneered, "have the humility to beseech someone who owes you gratitude."

The hammerhead sped toward us, but now his head was down, his mouth gaping wide. "This is revenge for my kind that you humans have tortured and slaughtered without mercy."

The Aquantan crowd was crying out loud now, "Nooooo . . !"

Lukas swam fast alongside Dao and me, trying to flee the attack. But his tail flukes were not quite fully developed. He was barely strong enough to keep up with us as we swam in circles around the stadium, trying to outrace the shark. But we were still too slow and Dao couldn't carry both Lukas and me in his aerodynamic slipstream.

At last exhausted, pinned against the stadium's curved glass walls, we all turned to face the fury of the hammerhead. At least we would die with some dignity.

Lowering his head, the shark propelled himself toward us at top speed. But just as he reached us, just as his teeth scraped Lukas's hands, which were raised in defense in front of his face—the shark veered off abruptly.

With the ancient dignity that marked his clan, the hammerhead swam back to float before us. The shark snapped shut his great, gaping mouth. Then, he nodded slowly. As he bowed his massive head, the hammerhead was looking beyond us all.

We spun around and recognized the Elder turtle, *Honu-wahi*, floating right behind us. No one could hear what mind-talk passed between the ancient turtle and the terrifying shark. It was so subsonic that even the most talented Sound Masters might not decipher their exchange.

The hammerhead turned his head away from Lukas, somehow making clear by the anger still smoldering in his black eyes that it was not the boy who commanded such restraint. It was *Honu-wahi*.

When the old turtle expanded her winglike flippers to embrace Lukas and me, and even Dao, she addressed everyone in the stadium with her mind-talk.

"This boy tried to save me from a burning sea. It was I who pulled this human back into the water with me so he could study our ways." *Honu-wahi* turned her leathered face to me. "And this girl also saved my life. She transported us all here in her *lanugo*. Marina is worthy to carry us all into the Prophecy."

Then *Honu-wahi* swam to face the Aquantan crowd and bowed respectfully. "It is I who will make the lifelong alliance. I now agree to be this boy's Constant."

There was a murmuring among Aquantans. It was too much of an honor. How could the boy understand that no centuries-old turtle had ever made such an offer? Especially to a human. It was also too much to forgive. The whole city had witnessed in the Sound Murals the images of toxic waves spilling fire and oil in SkyeWorld. The charred and floating bodies of sea turtles trapped within roaring flames. Burning alive.

Softly, so that only Lukas, Dao, and I could hear, *Honu-wahi* confided in a less formal, more humorous tone, "I may be a somewhat inconstant Constant, my boy, because I have much else to do besides swim by your side. But I will always be nearby, if you need me."

"On call," Lukas said, grinning widely. His face was still ghostly pale, and his whole body trembled. "That's what we say in my world."

"Yes." *Honu-wahi* nodded, her face wrinkling in what seemed like a smile. "You have only to call and I will come ... wherever I am, whatever worlds I travel."

The singing from the glass stands began as a respectful trill and then rose up, weaving intricate harmonies of sea green and sapphire blue as the crowd sang. In those stylized and synchronized melodies was the tone of deference, if not complete understanding.

Suddenly, I felt Lukas reach out to take my hand in his. He clenched my fingers much too tightly, and his skin still vibrated with fear. Lukas's hand was warm and by now familiar. I felt a strange fluttering sensation rising in my belly.

I tried to make light of it. "Nice flukes," I told Lukas, nodding to his tail with its bright, silver scales.

"They'll do, I guess," Lukas replied, his tone sounding uncharacterically humble.

"What took you so long ... Shifter?" I teased him.

As we stood hand in hand, I couldn't help but glance up at my sister. Even from this distance, I recognized Pandora's barely contained fury. It twitched at the edges of her smile. But what the crowd saw was the gracious and regal sister of their High Priestess gazing down at everyone.

Pandora placed two fingers on her lips and then held out her hand, first to the crowds. And then to Lukas.

Instantly, a bolt surged through Lukas's body, and all his muscles seized. I also felt the agonizing pain of an electric shock flowing through Lukas's hand to mine. And then the boy collapsed, his tail curling protectively around him—his heart light extinguished. ˜

CHAPTER 11

Manna

*T*he shock of the shark attack had stopped Lukas's heart. That's what the Master Healers told us. Or maybe his collapse had been caused by the effort of Sound Shifting under such duress. It was probably simply too much for a young human's electrical system.

Dao and I waited just outside the Healing Temple, side by side in an uneasy silence with Pandora and her Constant, Lak.

"It's your fault," Pandora insisted. She had obviously been crying. "Lukas was trying too hard to impress you."

I was struck by Pandora's seemingly real distress over Lukas's seizure. "The tests were just too much for him, " I said, watching my sister carefully.

At this, Pandora burst into tears, furiously rubbing her jeweled fists into her eyes to stop the flow.

My sister's reaction surprised me. "What's the matter, Pandora?"

"I offered that boy one of my morays for a Constant," Pandora sobbed. "All Lukas had to do was accept my offer, and he would have been completely mine. I mean ... under my protection."

"Yours?" I burst out. "Lukas doesn't belong to any of us. He's not some kind of pet, Pandora. He's a guest from another world, and we're supposed to treat him with respect."

"Oh, shut up, High Priestess! You don't know anything!"

"Then, why don't you tell me?" I asked softly, reaching out to touch her arm.

Pandora spun around, slapped her tail, and sped away in disgust. But not before her swordfish Constant sliced a fine cut along Dao's sleek face.

I turned to follow her but stopped when Dao advised, "Let her go," his tone weary, and a little wary.

"Does it hurt?" I tenderly touched the small wound from Lak's sword on my dolphin's face.

"No more than usual," Dao said. If he'd had shoulders, he might have shrugged.

I was grateful that *Honu-wahi* was still by Lukas's side as the healers struggled to save his life. They used the most sophisticated tuning forks, herbal medicines from kelp forests, seaweed antibodies, and acoustic acupuncture. I couldn't help but remember the first night I met Lukas on the beach and mistakenly believed he was stealing turtle eggs. Everything now was reversed: It was Lukas who lay unconscious and a turtle who was working with other healers to save him.

Anxiously, Dao and I swam around the glass waiting room. We were not soothed by the soft music echoing through the translucent walls or the small aquarium where tiny clownfish flickered in and out of a bright coral reef. The miniature Sound Murals that usually carried news of Aquantis and other worlds were silent, with only black and white zigzags across the screens.

Obviously, my parents and other scientists had not found a way to fix the unstable WaveHole or our Sound Murals. How long had it been since Aquantis could scan sound pictures from SkyeWorld—or even receive visiting dignitaries from other dimensions? We were essentially cut off. There was a sense of siege in our usually calm city.

Aquantan scientists were still trying to stabilize other transit tunnels in the WaveHole to prepare for the council trial called by the Blue Beings. Aquantans had to decide whether we would finally quarantine and seal off SkyeWorld to protect ourselves from its pollution. Invitations for the trial had been broadcast before the Sound Murals fell silent. Had other worlds received the messages? Would they risk traveling through an unstable WaveHole to attend?

What if my impulsive behavior had convinced everyone, not just highborn Aquantans, that I was not fit to be a Priestess? Perhaps my obvious alliance with a SkyeWorlder like Lukas was perceived as failed diplomacy and bad judgment. I wouldn't mind if they stripped me of my High Priestess position. It was already quite a responsibility; and perhaps Pandora might be more of a sister to me if I lost my title. Besides, what use was power and prestige if you lost people you loved?

"Who claims this human?" Master Healer Hu asked, swimming swiftly into the waiting room. There was an expression of both concern and anger on his chiseled face. His silver mustache and authoritative black eyes, his purple robes of the richest moss, all signified his high rank. "Is any of his family here?"

"I am his ... he's with me," I stuttered.

I feared the worst, and my fears were confirmed when Master Hu took my arm and commanded me to tune my acoustic range to a specific channel, a secret frequency that could only be accessible through physical contact. Even Dao could not hear the Master Healer's mind-talk.

Master Hu demanded, "Are you his guardian here in Aquantis?"

I hesitated a moment. Was Lukas really my responsibility? Why weren't the Blue Beings giving the orders? "I guess so," I said, nodding. "His family is still in SkyeWorld. So I'm the closest to him here. Me and *Honu-wahi*."

"The Elder turtle is with him," Master Hu said. His dark eyes were fixed on me, and there was a tone of accusation in them. "But this boy has received someone's *manna*. . . is it yours?"

"*Manna?*" I was shocked. Who would do such a thing?

"We cannot save this human's life until we identify whose *manna* is affecting his heart and bloodlines. He will need a total transfusion immediately." Master Hu's grasp tightened as he held my eyes meaningfully. "The *manna* must be from the original donor. Or he will die."

Master Hu scanned me intently, as if waiting for me to confess that it was my vital *manna*.

"I swear it is not mine," I assured Master Hu.

"You know very well, Priestess, that if this boy dies, whoever gave him the *manna* will also suffer," Master Hu added.

"But doesn't it depend upon the spirit in which the *manna* was given?"

I felt rising desperation—and something else. A fleeting darkness inside me that was troubling: Could the mysterious *manna* swirling in Lukas's body be a binding gift from my sister? If so, that would explain Lukas's fascination with Pandora during his Temple Tests. The way he hungrily looked to her, instead of me, for reassurance. But what was Pandora's motivation? Why would she ever share her most precious *manna* with a human?

"If the *manna* was freely offered as a gift to this boy without obligation," Master Hu reminded me, "Lukas will be bound to the donor only by devotion. And lifelong gratitude." The Master scowled. "But if the *manna* was used to manipulate and control, the boy will be forever addicted. His death will also diminish and darken the donor's life."

Master Hu went on to explain what every Aquantan knows: Once taken into his body, the *manna* is like a marker, invisible to most except the giver. If Pandora deceitfully gave Lukas her *manna*, she could always track him; Lukas would never be able to cloak his thoughts from Pandora. And he would always thirst for her nectar. If Lukas was possessed by my sister's *manna*, he belonged to her now more than anybody else—even himself. There was no known antidote to what could become the sweetest of poisons, or the hunger for it.

"I think I may know the donor," I told Master Hu. Feeling a sick knot in my stomach, I knew what I had to do.

"We have very little time left before his whole system fails." Master Hu did not let go of my arm. "One more thing. Did this boy have any direct contact with the oil spill?"

"Yes, Master." I nodded, my fears rising. "He fell ... I mean, he was pulled overboard into burning oil, but I protected him with my *lanugo*."

"You didn't protect him quickly enough ... or else he had earlier exposure to the toxic chemicals we found in his bloodstream from the crude oil." Master Hu's oval black eyes fixed me fiercely. "Like many of the dolphins and turtles in that spill, this boy's respiratory system is compromised, perhaps forever." Master Hu gave me a last, penetrating look. "It was the *manna*—not just your *lanugo*—that saved his life. Now, we need more *manna* if he is to survive."

Stunned, I wondered: Had Pandora really meant to save Lukas's life? Would that make a difference if she were ever brought to judgment or retribution? There were strict consequences in Aquantis law for giving *manna* under false pretenses. Banishment was one of them.

"You also know the dangers of any further transfusion to the donor, I assume?"

I nodded, my heart pulsing. "I know."

Without waiting for another admonishment from the Healing Master, I sped off as fast as my tail flukes could propel me. Dao swam alongside, keeping up with my agitated speed. "What did the healer say that was so important you had to use a private frequency?"

"I can't tell you, until I'm sure."

I hated to keep secrets from Dao. But then I remembered that Dao and the Blue Beings had certainly done so by hiding much of the Prophecy from me. How long had my Constant known that I would be chosen for High Priestess? From our birth? Is that why Dao had always been so protective of me?

Dao's eyes betrayed that he was as much hurt as worried by my withholding information. But he did not press. Instead, he swam with one protective fin encircling my waist. "May I at least ask where we're going?"

"To find my sister," I said. "Fast!"

We sped along the spacious, curved glass hallways of the temples, scanning the students' quarters for any sign of Pandora. Rich harmonies resounded from the Sound Healing classes; we saw young Aquantans practicing Marine Arts in the great gymnasium; we heard the prismatic colors of stonemason apprentices as they used highfrequency sound to carve and sculpt limestone into pillars and bricks for building.

The Warrior training quarters were at the far end of the city, separated by a garrison and training arena. Octopus guards halted us as we tried to enter the student barracks.

"Password?" a cool, pale octopus demanded, his tentacles already clenching my wrists.

"I don't need a password." I said, summoning all my High Priestess dignity. "I must see my sister, Pandora."

The octopus guard eyed me with a square yellow eye. He squinted and snapped, "No entrance."

"But I'm—"

"Not even for you, High Priestess," the guard snarled.

"Is my sister here?" I demanded. "It's a matter of life and death."

The octopus guard hesitated and then said, "Warrior Pandora is with Master Xylo in the barracks. I have orders that they are not to be disturbed."

"Please ..." I began, but Dao pulled me away.

"Always go where there's an open door, Marina." Dao tucked me under his fin to speed away. "Don't you remember the first lesson of Diplomacy?"

"But if Pandora doesn't—"

"If your sister has closed her heart to you—and perhaps to Lukas—then you must abide by it," Dao said. "Don't try to gain entrance to Pandora. It is futile. She is a closed door to you."

"You don't understand, Dao." I argued. I finally told him everything that I'd kept secret and felt momentarily relieved to share the burden with someone I trusted. I concluded, "Master Hu told me that without another *manna* transfusion, Lukas will die."

Dao gave me a troubled look. "Your sister is playing in the dark arts," he warned.

I back paddled with my tail flukes. "Maybe I can give Lukas some of my *manna* as an antidote to ..."

"Never!" Dao's voice was so sharp it hurt my ears. Then he turned to the octopus guards. He let out a shrill whistle that focused their attention only on him. "Tell Master Xylo that the boy needs another transfusion of Pandora's *manna* or he'll die. And Pandora is also in grave danger."

Dao paused significantly as the octopi flushed a ghostly white in surprise and alarm. Their reaction revealed that Pandora was acting without Master Xylo's knowledge. My sister was much more reckless than I'd thought. Her actions both angered and worried me.

Floating closer to the guards, Dao added in a very low tone, "And Pandora knows what happens to the donor if this boy dies."

Both octopi nodded and rushed into the Warrior quarters, leaving the door unguarded. Then Dao seized me almost painfully and propelled us toward the central district of the city.

"That's not the way to the Healing Temples," I protested.

"We're not going there now," Dao informed me. "We're going to the Temple of Justice."

"But what about Lukas?" I tried to keep my voice steady. Was he dying? I needed to be with him.

"You're commanded as High Priestess to attend the trial," Dao said and doubled our speed.

In times like these, I wondered just whose side Dao was on, the Blue Beings or mine? As we swam fast to the center of the city and the courthouse, I noticed something seemed different. Glancing around at the underwater fountains, the proud sandstone pillars of every temple, I realized that Aquantis looked somehow dimmer. Had we lost some of our radiance?

At the entrance to the grand courtroom, a richly robed Master Lioli nodded curtly to us. "You're late ... as usual."

I knew better than to argue with him. Master Lioli swept us into the impressive chambers of the white-domed courthouse. In the back of the courtroom, Master Lioli positioned us just out of sight behind salt pillars adorned with coral reefs.

"Let yourselves be seen," he ordered, "but not heard."

Then our Sound Master swam to the front of the room. Every head followed him. Master Lioli was such a feared and majestic creature. His elegant tail was artfully inlaid with musical scales of mica, and his lean upper torso flashed acoustic tattoos that were so bright and quick they were difficult to scan. Most striking of all were Master Lioli's full, sensual lips and his spinning eyes. Like mine, except blue.

It always made me proud to think that Master Lioli's *manna* had helped create me, even though he behaved more like an exacting task-master than a doting uncle.

For this tide's trial, our Sound Master had adorned his mossy silver robes with a starfish and a golden sand dollar pendant. When he moved or spoke, bioluminescence sparked around his head. His obsidian curls were braided with expensive black and white seed pearls. A glorious creature. For the first time, I wondered about Master Lioli's *manna* and how binding its force might be. Was it the Master's *manna* that predestined me to become a High Priestess? Had I profoundly disappointed my mentor by favoring a human boy like Lukas? And worse, would Master Lioli's *manna* prevent me from ever loving anyone of my own choice? Maybe Lukas was wrong about changing one's destiny. Maybe that only happened in other worlds.

"The witnesses are all present," Master Lioli sang out in his deepest baritone. "Let the trial begin."

Octopus guards swept in, their many tentacles securely gripping three huge Sound Murals. Had they at last restored the murals? Scanning the audience, I recognized only Aquantans in attendance, which meant that the WaveHole remained closed for repair. No passage for any other world's ambassadors or dignitaries. And if the WaveHole were forever shut down, contaminated, how would I fulfill my Diplomat-Spy dreams?

As Master Lioli sang out the secret codes to open the Sound Murals, I eagerly leaned forward. It seemed forever since I'd heard any sound pictures from SkyeWorld. Was it possible to long for a place I'd visited only twice? How I wished Lukas was attending the trial, so he could glimpse his homeland. Surely that would help restore his health.

"Our Sound Mural transmissions are still being interrupted by pollution and static from SkyeWorld," Master Lioli announced. His voice rose slightly. "But we have stored recordings from which the Blue Beings might decide their final verdict in this trial."

Where were the Blue Beings? Did they really know the future? Sometimes I couldn't help but mutinously question their wisdom. For example, why didn't they interfere more in the affairs of other worlds? When I finally earned my powers as High Priestess, I knew I would do more to make a difference—in every dimension and certainly in our own Aquantan class hierarchy. I thought maybe I would even defy my Diplomat-Spy training and try to alter the destiny of other worlds.

"These are the exhibits for the prosecution," Master Lioli intoned in his most reverberating voice. It echoed up into the gleaming heart lights of the gathered Aquantan spectators floating high above the courtroom in the balconies. Three Sound Murals flashed to life, each with vivid, moving pictures.

"Narration will not be necessary," continued Master Lioli. "Scan for yourself."

Everyone used their echolocation skills to study each picture. I quickly scanned the first Sound Mural: Fishermen on a Japanese coast surrounded a pod of migrating dolphins at sea. Banging metal poles, they disoriented the dolphins, separating mothers from calves. Terrified, the dolphin families circled tightly together, unwilling to abandon one another. They were herded into a narrow cove. Wielding knives, the fisherman stabbed the dolphins, whose sleek skin is twenty times more sensitive than humans. Wounded and screaming, the dolphins were dragged to a harbor warehouse for slaughter.

I couldn't bear to witness anymore and turned away from the Sound Murals. A hum rose up from the crowd: sepia and dark, red tones of outrage and despair. Not the usual bright and balanced harmonies of Aquantan gatherings. The usual singing and glowing colors were off-pitch and dimmed. Floating near me, Dao slipped his head under my hand. My dolphin hadn't sought protection from me like that since we had been little.

"It's all right, Dao, we will never go back to that savage Skye-World," I told him, realizing even as I spoke that I might be lying. "I promise." Now I was behaving more like Pandora—making promises I couldn't or wouldn't keep.

"Who can atone for such a ruined world?" a voice in the crowd sang out.

"SkyeWorlders deserve their self-destruction! But we don't have to suffer anymore from their taint."

"Yes," Master Lioli agreed, his eyes darkening. "Humans are too primitive to harmonize with our oceans. How can we ever hope to establish diplomatic relations with such creatures?"

"We've tried and failed for centuries," a shout went up.

"Quarantine the humans!" others sang. "Now and ... forever."

Master Lioli held up a hand, but the outrage did not subside.

"Stop them ... now!"

"Close the WaveHole to them so we can survive!"

They were all right, of course. Even I had to acknowledge that SkyeWorld was a terrifyingly violent place. And yet for a moment, the memory of Mozart played in my mind—the music serene and somehow sacred. Then my body remembered the warmth of sunlight, my legs rooted in soft, sugar-white sand, and the wind breezing through palm trees like a whispered song. How could such a vicious world also feel like home?

"Human brutality speaks for itself," Master Lioli sang in a haunting alto. It shimmered like silver. Then he bowed to the courtroom. "The prosecution rests."

Another voice suddenly rang out. My heart light flared, my gills fluttered, my legs vibrated with the memory of earth and his touch.

It was Lukas. ~

PART FOUR

CHAPTER 12
The Trial

LUKAS

"**Y**ou're alive!" Marina shouts, reaching out to hug me. But then she realizes we're standing in the back of a court-room with everybody watching.

For a moment, that smile of hers makes me forget the dull pain from the incision in my chest. The Healing Masters implanted an extra Aqua-Lung after mine collapsed. "Let's get this over with," is all I can manage to say to her.

I don't mean to sound gruff. My mind-talk just comes out that way because I'm working so hard to keep most of my thoughts about Marina hidden, like how happy I am to see her, and how strange it feels to care about Marina, yet at the same time desire her sister. No, not desire. It's more like I need Pandora. It feels like I can't live without her.

"*Manna* can be medicine." That's what Master Hu told me as he was supervising Pandora's transfusion. "If you give it freely and with good intention, it will heal."

During Pandora's transfusion of *manna*, she leaned over me, those full lips fit over mine to keep any of her sweet, hot nectar from escaping. Pandora eyes were bright with regret and rage. Then I knew.

She doesn't like me. She knows she made a big mistake. And now she also somehow needs me just like I need her.

I still don't know whether I was saved or enslaved by Pandora's *manna*. Maybe both. The bond is unbreakable, that's what the Masters say. We'll see about that. When I'm stronger, and now that I've got my tail flukes, maybe I can fight her—for my life, my freedom.

"May we hear from the defense?" Master Lioli calls me to the front of the courtroom.

127

I still don't know why Aquantans blame me for everything my world has done to pollute their precious WaveHole and break their Sound Murals. It's not my fault. All this stuff was going on long before I was born. I guess I'm just the scapegoat.

"Let me help you, Lukas." Marina tries to take my arm.

"No I'm okay." I'm still a little weak from the surgery, but I shake her off. Gently. I don't want to be rude, but I need to do this by myself. And besides, I don't know how to face Marina. Does she know I drank her sister's *manna*? Does she suspect my huge debt to Pandora? If she did, would Marina still want to have anything to do with me?

As I swim through the crowd with my tail flukes unfurled, I try to ignore their anger. What's the punishment for being human? For being born in the wrong world? I can't believe they'll kill me, not after the Healing Masters worked so hard to save my life. No, they've got something else planned. But what? Maybe now they'll tell me about the Prophecy.

I bow and take my place before a giant coral bench. Several stern-looking dignitaries and aristocratic judges float behind it, staring at me. *Honu-wahi* is speaking earnestly on my behalf. I'd like to tell them what I think of their justice system. It's just as rigged and unfair as in my world—where if you're poor or an immigrant or don't have a fancy attorney, you just lose. End of story.

"We request two verdicts," *Honu-wahi* says. "One: To return this boy to his father and his home—such as it is."

I turn sharply to look at the old turtle. What does she mean, "such as it is?" What's changed since I've been gone? Is Papi all right? I'll bet the Masters don't even know, since their Sound Murals are still full of static.

Honu-wahi continues in her formal, subsonic tones, "Second: To keep the WaveHole open for continued diplomacy with SkyeWorld in the hope that—"

"No, no, no!"

Everybody is shouting. It used to be that only the Far Right Aquantans wanted to quarantine my world and seal off the Wave-Hole forever. But now it's everybody, even those who cheered for me in my Temple Tests, and those who welcomed me when I first started taking classes. Now, they all look at me with scorn, just like Master Lioli. Why? What's happened in my world that I don't know about?

I just want to get out of here and go home to Papi. I'm afraid of what he'll be like after losing me. But all the Masters assure me that I haven't been gone that long in SkyeWorld time. Still, it's enough time for my father to lose it—after losing me.

"Let me speak!" *Honu-wahi* commands her audience.

Her status as leader of the Elder Council silences the uproar. It's as if everyone just holds one breath together. Not a sound now, except the old turtle's low voice.

"Humans are a confused species," she says. She glances at me, her eyes crinkled with age. "They bewilder us."

Then she sings out a subsonic code, and the Sound Murals hum to life. It's not a window into SkyeWorld in real time; it's recorded history. But when I see the images, my eyes blur. There's Papi working in his Turtle Lab. He's washing the turtle's oil-slicked flippers tenderly, the way he used to bathe me when I was really little. And he's singing a lullaby, a song he says my mother taught him.

Some of the audience members pick up the song, like they know it, too. And for just a moment, there is a rich harmony echoing through the courtroom. I've never heard such beautiful singing. It's so complicated that it's hard to hear all the parts. "Overtones," that's what Master Lioli calls Aquantan singing.

When the singing ebbs, *Honu-wahi* continues, "Humans believe they are alone in the universe. They search for other life—and then try to conquer or kill it." There is a murmur of agreement. "Yes, they are violent and destructive to themselves, as well as others." She pauses and looks at me with a very slow smile. "But they are also capable of profound acts of kindness ... and care."

Honu-wahi reaches out a flipper to pull me closer. "As you all know, this boy tried to save my life. There are many humans like him in SkyeWorld. Lukas Barrios Rodriguez is real evidence that there is hope that humans can actually ... evolve."

The old turtle nods significantly at my new tail flukes. I have to admit they're pretty cool. Silver and strong with scales that make music when water flows through them. The faster I swim, the more they echo—like xylophone keys.

The old turtle nudges me with a leathery flipper. "Speak now for yourself, Lukas."

What can I say? What do they want to hear? Yes, I owe them my life. But they also stole some of my life. And if I go home and find that Papi is a mess, I'll be really pissed off at this so-called advanced civilization. But I can't say a thing now except the formula. It's what the Master Healers whispered to me right before they dragged me to this trial. It's the promise I must make so they'll let me go home.

"If you allow me to return to my world and my father," I begin, trying to make my spoken voice as much a song as Aquantans do. "I promise to teach others what I've learned here in Aquantis. I promise to—"

"You can't work miracles," someone shouts. "Or stop their pollution."

Others join in. I can hear the anger and fear in their voices.

"You can't hold back their rising seas."

"We are sworn not to interfere with human destiny," others echo. "Besides, they won't let us teach them anymore."

Behind me, the Sound Murals suddenly shriek, like a clarinet squeaking. Everyone in the courtroom covers their sensitive ears and watches static zigzagging across the screens. Then I hear a long, low drone before a picture comes into view. For just a moment, I see a tsunami wave, huge and fast, racing toward a shore. Where? Is Papi there? Then the screens go flat and silent.

In a panic, I yell: "Let me go home! I've got to find my father and stop—"

"What can one boy do when a whole world is drowning?" Master Lioli demands, his tone cynical.

"He will not be alone," *Honu-wahi* says staunchly. She tightens her embrace as if to protect me.

"No, he will not be alone!"

Voices blaze in shades of gold and purple. A rainbow of interwoven harmonies ricochets around the courtroom like lightning. Shocked and confused, I glance around trying to find the source of such astonishing sounds. "What's going on?" I ask *Honu-wahi*, who lays a foreflipper across my shoulders.

"The Blue Beings!" the crowd murmurs in awe.

I've heard of these revered High Masters, but thought they might be make-believe. Master Lioli bows low and then cocks his head to better hear their instructions. Several others—as well as the jury and all the judges—join Master Lioli to try to interpret the Blue Being's declarations. They are all singing at once in an ultrasonic range and language far above even most Aquantan's hearing; it's difficult to understand them.

"This boy has ... a destiny ..." Master Lioli reluctantly translates the harmonies ricocheting around the courtroom. "It is time to send him back to his world and his father."

My heart thuds and my eyes blur. I'm tempted to do a backflip to celebrate. I get to go home! I get to be with Papi. I may never go swimming or out on the boat again. Maybe I'll stay onshore so nobody can ever drag me down here unless I want to visit. I'll try to solve some of the problems in my world, but the Aquantan critics are right. What can just one boy do?

Master Lioli shakes his head, as if he's overheard me. He obviously disagrees with the Blue Beings' decision. Though their music continues, Master Lioli refuses to translate anymore. He folds his arms across his chest and falls silent.

From behind us, I hear another voice: Unfamiliar, but just as authoritative as the Sound Master.

"Our WaveHole is still unstable, but it can be navigated with skillful scouts."

Everyone turns to see Warrior Master Xylo speed into the courtroom in his spectacular silver body armor.

"I offer my Warriors to accompany this boy to SkyeWorld."

Master Xylo appears commanding as he swims to the front of the courtroom. His jet-black hair is arranged in a topknot studded with razor clams and turquoise. With bulging arms, he holds his trident. His acoustic tattoos shimmer with stories of battles won while defending Aquantis against invaders from other worlds. I can hear the tattoos clearly now like in 3-D movies, a side effect of

Pandora's *manna*. For a moment I'm dazzled by these vivid video-like tattoos echoing from Maxter Xylo's skin: Scene after scene of violent battles.

In his wake, Pandora and Lak file in and stand at attention. An entire regiment of octopus guardians follows them. Why? Maybe the Blue Beings intend to at last declare war on my world. Well, I won't lead an army against my own people. Forget that!

Pandora is dressed for battle. Her fierce glow and hum stuns the crowd. She wears the same body armor as her Warrior Master, but Pandora's headdress is a golden helmet of sea stars and tightly woven shells. Lak, with his menacing sword, is the only weapon she needs. That and her *manna*.

I stare in astonishment. Why would Pandora volunteer for such a dangerous mission? And with me? I seriously doubt she cares about me or is interested in helping me. I try to use my remedial sonar to scan Pandora's tattoos. But she's cloaked. I can see, though, that she looks drained and weary. So it really cost her to give me another transfusion. Good. That's nothing compared to what it's going to cost me to get over my addiction to her. Even now, my belly cramps and my mouth twitches with thirst for more of her *manna*.

My tail vibrates, and I'm afraid I might shift back into legs right here in front of everyone. That's how much my body wants her. When Pandora swims past me, she doesn't even give me a look. She tosses her curls and follows her Warrior Master.

"My students are highly trained for this mission," Master Xylo boasts. His rugged face is crisscrossed with jagged scars etched like medals of honor.

"As are mine!" Sound Master Lioli interrupts, his voice soaring into ultrasonic tones. "I offer my best Diplomat-Spies for this mission, as well. They can pass unnoticed among humans. Warriors cannot."

At Master Lioli's signal, a stoic Dylan and his Constant, Zwo, swim into the courtroom. Dylan eyes me coolly—I'm sure he hasn't forgiven me for that blow to his jaw. It still looks swollen.

"We also volunteer!" declares Marina, practically dragging Dao toward me. Her dolphin looks terrified and very upset.

"No! Marina has already risked her life in SkyeWorld," Master Lioli pronounces, as if this were the end of it. "As High Priestess she must stay in Aquantis. Let the others have their chance to—"

"Maybe we don't want her as High Priestess anymore!" Members of the crowd sing out angrily.

"She's made the wrong choices!"

"She favors her human nature over being an Aquantan!"

"It is decided!" The incandescent voices shower us again. It's like marine snow. There is no need now for a translator. This time, the Blue Beings speak clearly as one. Maybe they've tuned their voices down to our level. "We will again open the WaveHole. Go back to SkyeWorld, young ones. There you will find other Aquantans awaiting you. It is Prophecy. They have been waiting for you a very long time—especially you, Lukas Barrios Rodriguez."

Me? What are they talking about? Who cares about the Prophecy? All I care about is finding Papi again and taking Marina with me back to my world. I also care about that—a little too much. I wish Marina and I could just leave Pandora behind. Would that cure me of my need for her?

Marina takes my hand in hers. Her webbed fingers are silken and strong. Pandora glares over at us both. And Lak and Dao are giving each other the evil eye, as always. All these long-standing feuds and enmities are hard to track.

The crowd murmurs in dismay as the Blue Beings continue, "Travel to SkyeWorld well and wisely, Young Ones. Here are your Orders: Pandora and Dylan will undertake a mission to the South to seek counsel and help from an Aquantan Master who is still surviving in SkyeWorld. Lukas and Marina, you will travel together back to Florida to find Lukas's father. You will all meet up again soon. As it is destined."

My heart surges. I'm ecstatic to go home to Papi and I bow my head with gratitude.

There is a flash of dark overtones echoing in the glass arches of the courtroom as the Blue Beings conclude, "If you are to teach others to work in harmony, you must first learn it among yourselves. Remember, many worlds depend upon your success."

Masters Xylo and Lioli scowl across the courtroom. Swiftly, a triumphant, yet depleted Pandora slips right between Marina and me to break our hold.

"Now, it's my Prophecy, too!" she gloats. Hissing moray eels encircle Pandora's arms, and I can see she is shivering. Instantly, my throat constricts with thirst. I hate how much I need her.

"But we're on separate missions," Marina reminds her little sister with a condescending tone that even I can recognize. Times like this, I'm glad I never had a sibling. That intense rivalry seems as complicated and long lasting here as it is in my world.

Marina's response enrages Pandora. "See how well you do without me or my *manna*, Lukas," is all she says as she tosses her head, her curls tinkling.

Then she's gone, and my belly cramps as my withdrawal symptoms begin. ~

CHAPTER 13
The Wrong World

Head over tail flukes, Marina, Dao, and I catapult through the final whirlpool of the WaveHole after a long and harrowing journey. In a great gush, the spiraling waterspout coughs us up onto an empty beach. I recognize this sand—it's cool and sugar-white like my home beach on Siesta Key. But there's a lot of mud mixed in with the sand and there are fallen trees everywhere. Has there been a hurricane?

I feel the late afternoon sun before I see it. And my whole body breathes in the earth's familiar warmth. Overhead a pelican soars. Lying on my back on the sand, I sputter with relief and stare up at the endless blue sky.

"Home!" I shout out loud, laughing.

"SkyeWorld," Marina echoes, with a smile. I can tell she's happy to be back here, too.

All I want is to be human again and in my own world. Maybe here I'll finally be able to get through my *manna* withdrawal. Master Hu told me that one of the reasons the Blue Beings sent me home was because it's my best chance for beating this addiction to Pandora's *manna*.

And Pandora was right. I'm not doing so well without her. My throat burns; my belly cramps, and my muscles ache with a kind of wasting fever. Part of me is glad Pandora is on another mission. But another part can't forget the imprint of her beautiful body. The way her breasts pressed against my chest when we danced in that undersea cave as she swayed her hips beneath my hands to the rhythm of that salsa music. And her *manna* transfusion, the golden nectar pulsing through my body like radiant energy. I owe Pandora my life; do I also owe her my love? Or can I choose Marina, if she wants to be with me?

"Shift, Lukas!" Marina says impatiently, glancing around to make sure we're still alone on the beach.

I notice that Marina is already standing on her legs, tugging her Nirvana t-shirt over her head and wearing shorts she'd packed in her travel satchel. She's a good spy. Ready to fit in. I'm wearing my Turtle Lab t-shirt and my cut-offs are still in my bag. I've to got to shift out of these tail flukes before I can put them on.

Humming, Marina scans the beach with her echolocation. Suddenly, her face clouds over. "Hmmmmmm," she telepaths. "Something's not right here, Lukas. You'll have to lead the way ... while we're here."

"So I'm in charge?" I try to tease her out of her nervousness.

Marina nods somewhat indulgently. "Yes, Lukas. For now."

"Does that mean I'm High Priest?" I joke. "Is that the Prophecy?"

Marina doesn't laugh at my humor. She's scanning again anxiously, as if to make sure there's nobody else around. And nearby in the surf, Dao is leaping up to try to get a better view of this destroyed beach. I wish that my own Constant, *Honu-wahi*, were traveling here with me, too. But I know the Great Elder can't always be by my side.

"Hurry, Lukas," Dao orders me, as if he's in charge.

I want to remind the know-it-all dolphin that he has no skills on land, not like I do. But Marina is looking so anxious I don't want to argue with her Constant. Why is she so worried? Is it really because there's some danger lurking on this strange beach? Or, is she unnerved by my *manna* addiction to her sister? Does Marina know how much my body still desires Pandora?

Whenever Pandora was near, I felt her strength flowing through me. The bond between us let me borrow Pandora's abilities and power. Now that I'm with Marina, all I can feel is our simple affection for one another. Does my addiction even matter to Marina? I'm sure by now she's scanned me and recognized my desperation. But she says nothing. The Blue Beings have forbidden Marina to give me a drop of her own *manna*. Even if I'm dying.

136

A minute more I lie on the soft sand. My tail flukes flop over a beach rock, and I can feel a balmy breeze welcoming me home. It's a relief to breathe air again with its delicate fragrance of wild gardenias, and to be back on solid, dry land. Now, to find Papi.

I sing out my Sound Signature to shift. A bolt of pain shoots up my backbone, and then my tail flukes shudder. Silver scales scatter and trill in the sand. A crack like an earthquake in my lower body and my tail splits into legs. Ouch! It always hurts, this shifting. You'd think the Healing Masters could have come up with some way to make it less painful. Then again maybe it's supposed to hurt. Just like getting free of someone's *manna* is supposed to be a real ordeal. Another Aquantan test.

I stand up slowly, my legs aching like I've run a marathon. My feet sink into the sand. I don't care what they say about my "primitive" world, I'd still rather be here than Aquantis. There will be some things I miss—like swimming fast underwater and my powerful flukes. And *manna*.

"Do we still have use to use telepathy?" I ask Marina.

Of course, she's cloaking most of her thoughts from me. I'm pretty remedial in mind-talk. And though Marina can hear my telepathy, she can't hear my deepest thoughts. Thank God. Otherwise, she'd know when I break all the Aquantan rules against interspecies mating by fantasizing—about her and me. And Pandora.

"Yes, we'll need our mind-talk, especially in this world," Marina answers. "Someone might overhear our plans. But we'll also have to talk out loud so we fit in." She pauses and then shakes her head. "I'm sure you won't mind doing most of the talking for us, Lukas. Humans seem to have some trouble with Aquantan accents."

"No problem," I say with more confidence than I feel. "Follow me!"

I glance up and down the beach. Nobody. That's so strange. There's still a little sun left. Where are all the beachgoers? We may have overshot our destination and landed on one of the zillions of uninhabited islands off Florida. This sand is gritty and full of gravel. Who knows if the WaveHole actually brought us back to my home? It doesn't look familiar at all.

"Can't quite get my bearings," I confess to Marina as we stride down the beach, with Dao following us in the surf. From this stretch of sand, I can't see any condos or other buildings. "Where is everybody?"

"I don't think we're all alone here," Marina telepaths. Again, she's scanning with her echolocation. "We're being followed."

"Don't be so paranoid, Marina. This place is deserted. C'mon."

This beach is muddy and it's full of debris—shingles, rusted bi- cycles, mountains of bricks, and panel siding piled up everywhere. It looks like this beach was recently flooded.

I scan the shoreline. So many of the palm trees are dead and fallen over, with bark peeling back. Our science teacher once asked me to do a research paper on the plant-hopping bug that chews on Florida palm leaves and then vomits on them. It was gross. But now it looks like that tiny pest has eaten its way through our palm trees like a plague. How could that bug do this much damage in the short time since I've been gone? Suddenly, I remember the loud images of that terrible tsunami in the Sound Murals. Is that what happened here on my home beach? Is my father still alive?

"Let's get into town!" I say and stride off down the battered beach.

"Keep guard, Dao," Marina cautions her Constant as she catches up with me. Dao is whistling at us wildly from the shallow waves. He never wants to let Marina out of his sight.

"Don't go too far away from me or the beach," Dao advises. "There's something very wrong with this world. I sense you're in grave danger."

"I'll take care of her," I promise Dao.

But he and I both know this may not be possible. Dao fixes me with his unblinking, brown eyes. His expression is fierce, resentful. I'm sure Marina's Constant wishes that she had never met me.

"We'll be back at high tide," Marina promises Dao. How can she know that? I'm not sure when we'll be back, but I don't tell Marina that. She turns to follow me and then abruptly grabs my arm, "Quiet," she cautions. "Did you hear that? I can hear breathing."

I pause for a moment to listen. "No, I don't hear anything." I respond, not telling her how good it feels when she holds on to me. Natural. Soothing.

We follow a rough path through the underbrush. Bushes and fallen trees on either side of us are so dense I wish I had a machete. Birds chatter overhead and I hear a menacing growl from a nearby tangle of wild vines. Florida panther? Impossible. Those big cats were declared officially extinct several years ago. Maybe a pack of wild dogs? I glance up through the thick canopy of green and see a huge black snake curled around a branch.

"Wild animals ... here?" I say, my heart racing. "Must be what you're hearing, Marina. But where are all the people?"

"I don't know. Do you think people are ... extinct?" Marina asks.

I take a deep breath. "Marina," I confess, pausing mid-trail. "This isn't the Siesta Key I know."

"Then where are we in your world?" Marina asks.

I'm sure she can hear my pounding heartbeat. "Dunno," I admit, glancing around. I don't want to show Marina I'm spooked. But this beach is so overgrown. Humans don't allow this much wildlife near their civilization. Dao's right, there's something terribly wrong. My heart sinks a little—it's not going to be as easy to find Papi as I thought.

"The WaveHole was unstable," Marina says thoughtfully like she's just solving a problem. Like this isn't a complete catastrophe. "Maybe our destination coordinates got thrown off." She betrays more emotion when she adds, "I wonder if my little sister and Dylan are lost, too."

"We're not lost," I try to reassure Marina. "I just haven't figured out where we are ... yet."

Watching Marina acoustically scan the noisy jungle and empty beach, her eyes calculating, I realize something about Marina: All her life, Marina's trained to travel and explore new worlds. To be an ambassador. But all my life, I've just tried to fit in and find a safe home. That's what exiles do. We're so different I wonder if Marina and I could really ever be together.

She takes my arm and whispers, "You think we're back in the same time as when we left here, Lukas? Remember, the WaveHole allows us to travel between the past and future too."

At last I concede, "Something terrible has happened here, Marina. It looks like a disaster area. There should be people around—at least rescue workers."

"I think there is somebody here." Marina cocks her head, listening again. "Not just wild animals ... humans. I can hear the difference."

"Well, they might be more afraid of us than we are of them," I say. At least I hope that's true and that some savages aren't tracking us. Or survivors.

Spooked, I squeeze Marina's hand, more to reassure myself than her. It feels cool, the blue webbing between her fingers soft and almost transparent. Webbed fingers don't change when we shift. But the webbing is so translucent that few humans notice. Marina seems to like my touch. She actually blushes. I can't help but remember that stolen kiss we shared in the cave. I wonder if Marina will ever let me kiss her again. Maybe that will help me get over my craving for her sister. If I had a choice, I'd rather be with Marina. But my body may have other plans.

"Well," Marina says hopefully. "Maybe the Blue Beings sent us here to help whoever is hiding from us."

"Or tracking us," I remind her.

How can we help anyone? We'll be lucky if we survive ourselves. "Looks like this coast just got hit with a huge hurricane," I explain. "Don't know how far inland the flooding reaches. We won't know the damage—or anything more—until we explore. Let's keep going before we lose the light," I say, trying to sound bold.

I doubt there is any electricity working in this flooded shoreline. Soon we will have to find a place to make camp. At least I need sleep. Without another word, I just keep striding through the underbrush. The overgrown path is narrow and winding. Overhead strange birds cry. I glance up just in time to see a bright red parrot dive-bomb us. Marina ducks.

"Maybe you should hide here while I try to see if there's a town left," I suggest and release her hand.

Suddenly, I double over with cramps in my belly. Damn Pandora! But I can't help noticing that as long as I hold Marina's hand, my withdrawal symptoms aren't as bad. Does this mean that physical contact with Marina is healing? Even if she doesn't give me any of her own *manna*?

I fight off an impulse to wrap my arms tightly around Marina to see if my shivering and nausea stops. But I know better than to push myself on her.

"I know ... *manna* withdrawal ... you'll get through it," Marina says sympathetically. "I hear it's pretty awful."

So she does know about my addiction. At least, she doesn't seem to hold it against me. I don't tell Marina that it feels like my insides are grinding to a halt and that my heart is going to thud out of my chest. It feels like running a marathon in a desert without any water, like my Aqua-Lung is slowly filling with sand and grit.

"I'll go on ahead," Marina says, with determination. "Maybe whoever's following us won't be afraid of a girl."

When I look up at Marina, she is so full of vigor and purpose. Next to her, I feel weak and useless. It's humiliating. I'm the one supposed to be taking care of her in this world.

"No, Marina," I say. "We're in this together. And this is my world." I try to grin, but it's an effort. "Besides, you said I could lead, right?"

"Like slow dancing." Marina smiles suddenly. Her warm emerald eyes are glowing. "Remember?"

I do. A clear image of Marina slowly wrapping her tail around my legs as we twirl weightlessly, our bodies swaying to the melodic chants and singing at the cave party. Does she know this is a memory that is always with me? For the first time, I realize I'm actually alone here in this world with Marina, a girl I really like. No supervision. No Masters. No Blue Beings telling us what we can and cannot do. Even though I feel awful, I also feel a hint of excitement. Anything is possible. It really is a new world. It may be ruined—but it's still mine. Maybe ours.

"I'm fine—I'll lead the way," I insist. But it's so obvious that Marina has me completely in her power.

As we trudge along the beach together, Marina takes my hand again. I can feel the electric pulse of her skin and hear the echo of her heartbeat. Her touch is reassuring. After awhile, I feel myself growing tired. I hate to admit it but the *manna* withdrawal is zapping my stamina.

"Let's rest here a little," I suggest, stopping in a small clearing.

Marina nods in agreement, her green eyes understanding. She can see how fatigued I am.

As the pink-tinged sun sets, it occurs to me that we should probably find some shelter before it gets dark. Ahead of us, beneath a stand of palm trees, I spy a little storage shed made of metal that must have washed up from somebody's back yard. It's no five-star hotel but it will do.

"We could spend the night in here," I say, pulling open the shed's door. It's broken and sagging on its aluminum hinges, but at least it's got half a roof left.

"Sure," Marina agrees. "After we eat, I'll keep watch while you sleep, Lukas."

"You still think we're being followed?"

"Yes," Marina says, cocking her head to listen. "They're human, that's all I know. And they've been tracking us for a long time."

Glancing around the empty beach, the little stand of trees shading us, I still can't see or hear anything. But I trust her acute senses. "You think they're dangerous?"

"I don't know humans well enough to tell," Marina says with a frown. "Maybe they're plotting something against us. Or, maybe they're as scared as we are."

"I'm not scared," I lie.

"Me, neither," Marina says, but I don't really believe her.

For the first time, I sense that Marina is really as spooked as I am about this devastated beach. She's far from home and probably wishes she were back in Aquantis with her own kind, her family. Without me. I know I'm a burden to Marina, when all I want to be is someone she admires. Someone she might even choose for a mate. Not this wreck. I'm as much a disaster area as this beach.

We enter the storage shed and settle ourselves amidst a scattering of junk—paint cans, rusted tools, and old tires. We can sit on the tires and use the rotted workbench for a table. There are no windows in the aluminum siding, so we leave the door slightly open to better see outside.

"Hungry?" I open my backpack and lay out several seaweed cakes and fish bars from our food stash.

Marina nods and gratefully accepts the food. I know I need to eat to build my strength, but my stomach recoils at the sight of yet another Aquantan meal of fish and seaweed cakes. By this time, I had expected Marina and I would be dining on peeled shrimp, fries, coleslaw, and my favorite pie, strawberry-rhubarb from Sid's Fish Shack. But who knows where we are or what we'll encounter tomorrow?

"We're in the wrong world, Marina," I admit at last. "You know that now, right?"

"Yes, Lukas," Marina says quietly. Her tone is almost tender and her eyes hold mine. "I've known that for awhile. I think we've landed somewhere in the near future."

"The future?" Alarm rises in me. "How far into the future?"

"Don't know, Lukas," Marina replies. "Tomorrow, we'll figure it out."

"Yes, tomorrow," I say.

I'm in a state of shock and complete exhaustion. All I want to do is lie down and forget all about this mess of a world we've landed in. There's a dusty old rug leaning against the wall in the corner of the storage shed. I pull it down and create a make-shift bed for both of us. Then I lay back, trying not to think about how uncomfortable and filthy it is. My eyes flutter, and I wonder if I'm already dreaming.

Marina sits down next to me, and her fingers intertwine with mine. It's so much better with her touching me. I feel more like myself and less invaded by Pandora's energy still swirling inside my body. Marina can keep watch all night, but I'm still human enough to need the rest, the darkness, and the oblivion. It's like another drug, this gravitational pull into sleep.

Even though I feel fatigued, my body is still excited by lying next to Marina. For the first time, we're not underwater. In the tropical air, I can smell Marina's scent—her skin is sun-warmed and smells like the wild ginger and jasmine we've been trekking through. Her light fragrance makes me hungry for her. The only time Marina has been this close to me was when we were cave dancing. I can feel the blue pulse of her electromagnetic field like a tingling all along my legs and circling up into my groin and belly. My body shivers now, and my heartbeat quickens.

Marina's braids are loosened, auburn curls straying from their usual woven confines. Her skin is dark and smooth. Those spinning sea-green eyes look like bright jewels set in a face that is as refined as it is thoughtful. Marina is lean and feline, and she perches on the rotten rug with all the grace and vigilance of a jaguar.

I want to take Marina into my arms and pull her down on top of me. What would it be like to kiss her again? Certainly, nothing like the fiery hot and manipulative feel of Pandora's kiss, when she gave me her *manna*. I realize how much I long for the simple warmth and loyalty of Marina's affection. But how could she care for me when my body helplessly craves her sister?

"Lukas," Marina says quietly. "Are you still awake?"

"Yes." My eyes flutter open. I've been hovering somewhere between sleep and wakefulness. My whole body is throbbing—not because of *manna* withdrawal but because I desire Marina. Does she know how much I want her? Not like she's an addiction. But something else. Something better.

"Get some sleep," Marina says. Her tone is musical, and I know she's acoustically lulling me into my dreams.

"It feels ... good," I manage to say before Marina's humming spell works on me. "With you near me ... together."

"Yes, Lukas," she echoes. "Together."

I struggle to keep my eyes open to watch Marina as she sits next to me. Her head turns from side to side while her sonar scans outside the door and far into the bushes. Marina is completely alert to every noise—the snap of a branch, the wind stirring through the diseased palm trees, the high-pitched whistles from the surf where Dao is also still watching and calling out to her.

Even though it's dangerous, even though I'd much rather stay awake with Marina and feel the cool touch of her hand in mine, the last things I see are stars glinting overhead—the familiar constellations I've studied all my life—and then nothing. ~

CHAPTER 14
The Gang

"Lukas, wake up!"

It's Marina's mind-talk startling me from sleep. Her tone betrays alarm.

Groggily, I sit up, my head aching. "What's the matter?"

"They're here." Marina's voice is very soft, almost inaudible.

"Who?" I scan the trees and early morning beach. No one.

"The people who've been following us," Marina says. "We're surrounded!"

She's so frightened that I can hear the mental pictures swirling through her mind: Medical labs where scientists perform tests on her as she struggles to break free of the straps binding her to a steel table.

From the surf, I can hear Dao screaming to us, "Danger! Come back!"

Only then do I hear the shushing of fallen leaves and the snap of twigs. Kids emerge from the trees looking like aborigines, their faces covered in dirt for camouflage. It's some kind of gang. Six of them. I'd say about our age with two very scraggly but menacing dogs. These kids look pretty rough with their tattered shorts and T-shirts, their grimy faces. Some of them have tattoos all over their arms and legs. And piercings. They seem poised to leap on us. Fierce and feral. Their dogs sniff the air and snarl. One looks like a pit bull mix with a huge jaw ready to crush you.

I spring up from the ground, even though my legs are rubber. "Hey there," I call, trying to sound casual. I step in front of Marina protectively to stand at the open door of the shed. "What's up?"

For a moment, the gang just gawks at us. I wonder if they even speak English. Maybe I've given us away by speaking. Marina told me the first rule of being a Diplomat-Spy is to avoid communicating until you're spoken to—only then can you figure out the language, the culture, the etiquette —and maybe the exit.

The gang stares in suspicious silence. Something's not right with them. They look like they've been on their own for a long time. Then I notice that they all have small machetes and knives. And there's no doubt they know how to use them. The leader of this gang looks like a mulatto. His tanned skin is coffee-colored like Marina's. But he's got high cheekbones and piercing hazel eyes. He's some kind of mixed blood. Maybe Seminole and African-American. Lots of those mixed kids here in Florida. They're tough; they've had to be to survive all the redneck prejudice. This guy is sleek and toned like a marathon runner.

He's about sixteen. The other kids look a little younger, and they're all different ethnicities: Asian, Black, Hispanic (Maybe Cuban?), and White. I'm surprised to see a few girls in the gang, too. They look like wild cats with their matted hair and lean, angular bodies. Who needs makeup when you've got such a crazy glow in your eyes? Are they on drugs? Then I notice that quite a few of them are wearing really big glasses. All they do is stare at us really hard. They must all have pretty bad eyesight.

I try again, looking straight at the leader with his filthy baseball cap. "So what happened here? Hurricane?"

"Ya think?" The boy mocks me and jerks his head toward the shoreline, acknowledging the devastation all around us.

"Duuuuuuuuuh," his gang snickers.

"Where're you from?" I ask, ignoring their jeers and keeping my eyes on the leader. I don't have to glance back at Marina. I know she's ready to defend herself, if necessary. She's got a small knife in her backpack. And she's much stronger than I am right now.

"Where're you from?" he shoots back.

"Uh," I hesitate and then remember our cover story. "Cuba, we escaped. Please don't report us."

"Report you?" The leader bursts out laughing. But his tone is harsh. Obviously, he knows we're lying.

146

He has a very slight accent, not Spanish. More like Cajun or a South Florida drawl. I recognize the rhythm. It's the way I would've talked if Papi hadn't raised me in a neighborhood of Cuban exiles.

The gang surrounds us in a close circle. They seem a little less menacing now. Maybe they're hiding out from authorities. I'm not as scared of them as Marina, but they do outnumber us. I could probably handle most of them. When I took my black belt test in aikido, I could throw four attackers at once. I relax my body, preparing to defend us.

Behind me, I can feel Marina scanning them carefully as they close in on our shed. "You all look really hungry," she ventures. She's using her most musical voice to soothe them.

Marina steps out of the shed into the little clearing. She reaches into her backpack and pulls out a stash of protein-rich seaweed bars sweetened with azave from Aquantan gardens. "Here ... we have enough to share."

"They're like uh ... Japanese power bars," I add, moving quickly to stand beside Marina.

The gang ignores us now and falls upon our food stash like starving animals. They don't thank Marina; they just rip into the seaweed treats, baring their teeth. Still watching us. Even though they are obviously hungry, they share their food with their dogs, who seem a little less frightening when they're chowing down on our stash.

The leader doesn't accept Marina's offerings. He stands very still, his hazel eyes riveted on her. I don't like the intensity of his scrutiny. He seems mesmerized by Marina. If we were in some normal setting, not this overgrown jungle, I'd think the guy was attracted to her. The way he follows her every move alerts me to the fact that he might sense she's alien. Someone he could capture—or worse.

"Back off, buddy." I say, glaring at him. It has little effect. He keeps his eyes intently focused on Marina.

"Why'd you come here?" he demands. "Is Cuba underwater, too? Or are you pirates?"

"If we were pirates, d'ya think we'd give you anything?" I ask testily.

I notice his hand is on the machete handle looped through his dirty belt. My body tenses, and I inch toward the guy. But Marina's frown holds me back.

Marina says softly, "We're here looking for Lukas's father."

I can't believe she's told this stranger the truth. But it seems to somewhat satisfy him.

"Everybody's looking for somebody," he spits out. There's a hint of pain in his voice. "Except us."

What does he mean? Is this gang homeless, without any family at all? I remember some kids in my high school were living in their cars because their parents lost their jobs and their homes. Is that what happened to these kids?

"Well," Marina says in her most calming tones. "We found you."

"No," the boy says. "We found you."

"We mean you no harm," Marina says.

Her voice is lulling as she uses her low-frequency hum to disarm their nervous systems. At its highest frequency, her sonar could stun them. But for that, Marina would need her tail flukes. No need for stunning now. Marina's melodic voice is having its effect. As are the seaweed bars. Both dogs wag their tails and saunter over to Marina. The pit bull mutt actually leans against her, his eyes half-lidded and calm. The other dog, a husky mix, plops on the ground with a relaxed sigh. She also leans against Marina and raises her snout in the air to let out a happy yodel-howl.

"What are your dogs' names?" Marina asks.

"Alexander," a tall Black girl answers.

"Alexander the Great," a boy with a blonde buzz cut adds, grinning.

"And LuLu," chimes in another guy. He's got the biggest glasses of all. They've slid halfway down his nose.

"Sounds like a nice old retired couple," I say nonchalantly. But I'm still on edge, especially with the leader.

"They're good watchdogs," the guy informs me sharply. But his words seem a little silly now as both dogs settle against Marina with all the contentment of having identified their pack's alpha female leader.

The whole gang sits down on the ground, chewing. They look up at us, their eyes fixed and drowsy. Behind those enormous glasses, they all seem suddenly very weary. How long has it been since they've slept or eaten their fill?

"What d'ya really want here?" the leader demands. But his eyes, at last, shift to the food Marina is offering. He snatches it.

"We need your help," Marina says simply, but she's still transmitting that low pleasurable humming. It's subsonic, so the guy can't really hear it. But his body does. His breathing deepens, and his shoulders slump a little. Sure signs of fatigue—and surrender. His unsettling eyes are still suspicious.

"What's your name?" Marina asks.

"Jake," the boy spits out.

His dark face is all angles and shadows and his changeable eyes are ovals. Jake's pretty good-looking for a guy. I wonder if Marina thinks so, too. He never takes those wary eyes off of her.

"Jake, will you lead us?" Marina says. "We're lost here."

I can't believe she's asking this other guy to take charge. Why does she trust him? Marina really must have lost faith in me. Can't say I blame her. I'm a mess. Still shivering, even though it's blazing hot, and my heart beats too rapidly. Hungrily. Unfortunately, it's nothing sweetened seaweed can satisfy.

I watch Marina as she smiles at Jake, and it occurs to me that she might really like humans. Maybe I'm not really that special after all. She might be attracted to a strong leader like Jake—not some weak addict like me. What if Marina finds love in this world and chooses a boy like Jake? A bolt of jealousy rises up in me like bile. Damn Pandora and her stupid *manna*! If I'm ever going to keep Marina connected to me, I've got to get over my thirst for her sister. It's what I want now more than anything—except finding Papi, of course.

"What's with him?" Jake jerks his head toward me. "Strung out?"

"He got sick ..." Marina lies. "He'll get better soon."

"Feds looking for you? Lots of you pirates out there on the uninhabited islands running drugs."

"We're not pirates." Marina says, her eyes wide. Even Aquantans understand thieves. Every world has them. "We're diplomats."

"Yeah, right," Jake snorts, his voice mocking. "From Cuba."

"Marina," I telepath, trying to distract her from Jake. "Let's get outta here. Lose these kids."

"Not yet," Marina says firmly. "I think they can help us."

Frowning, I turn to Jake. "Why'd you follow us?"

"Got any money?" Jake asks Marina, ignoring me.

Marina reaches into her backpack for a Spanish doubloon. She's often told me the story of how well that golden currency worked on a waitress at Sid's Fish Shack. But now she's way out of her depth. Diplomats may bargain with gold, but Marina doesn't realize we're among savages. No official etiquette here. It's survival of the fittest in this world. These kids might attack us if they know we have a fortune in shipwreck gold and silver. I telepath to Marina, "Stop! Let me talk to him."

"Yeah, Jake," I take over the conversation. "We got a little money. But we need to get to ... to town. We can pay you for being our scouts." I'm hoping he'll mention which town is nearby.

"So ... you'll hire us?" Jake asks. "How much?"

"Hundred dollars if you take us into town."

"Deal," he says.

I can see Jake's chest actually let out a small sigh. It must be hard to lead this gang. All of the kids, their hunger sated, now gather around us again in an expectant and tight circle. But this time they're not so wild. More curious than threatening. And the dogs now take their cues from Marina more than anybody else. Jake notices their desertion with a scowl.

I sit down on the ground, right in front of Jake. To allow him to stand over me gives him the supposed authority he so craves. My seeming subservience appears to satisfy Jake. He shrugs and asks. "How'd you get lost here?"

"Our boat capsized," I explain, making up the story as I go along. "We got chased by pirates. We don't want the feds to catch us, either."

Jake nods soberly. It's obvious now his gang is running and hiding from someone, too. But who? "Yeah," Jake says. "The feds deported a lot of environmental refugees like you all after Hurricane Malachi hit Florida last year."

Marina telepaths to me, "So the WaveHole coordinates are correct. We're back in your home, Lukas!"

What a relief! But what time are we in? How many years have passed since I was abducted and taken to Aquantis? And more importantly, where's Papi now?

"Hurricane Malachi ...?" I fish for more details.

Jake looks at me suspiciously and then slowly nods. "Direct hit of the whole East Coast. Floods all the way into Sarasota."

A little shock wave shudders through my body. Sarasota was the only home I've ever known. I can't believe it's devastated. Trying to hide my dismay, I turn to Jake and reach for his arm, "You got a watch? We lost ours ... at sea."

"Stay back!" Jake suddenly shouts and steps back from us. His hand again hovers over his machete.

But then I see that he also has a battered cell phone attached to his belt. It looks complicated and really futuristic—not like any smart phone I've ever seen. If I can get my hands on that phone, I can try to call Papi. If he's home. If he has a home. If he's even still in Florida.

I calculate the risks of tackling Jake and stealing his phone versus trying to get more information out of him. His crouch and dilated eyes tell me that he's ready to fight if I make any advance.

"No." Marina's mind-talk stops me from leaping on Jake. "We need to know what they know. Be a spy, Lukas—no attacks unless it's in self-defense. These kids are really in trouble. Can't you see that?"

Marina's right. I've been so focused on what I want that I haven't really noticed much about what this gang needs. I remember the Spanish conquistadors we studied in World History. When those invaders landed on these shores so many centuries ago, all they did was steal and enslave. I can show these kids better diplomacy. Our Aquantan Ethics teacher taught us an important rule about visiting other worlds: "Ask what you can give, not what you can take."

Even though I'm human and have my species' bloody history running through every cell in my body, I'm still also here representing Aquantis and the Blue Beings. Even if I don't agree with all their rules and laws, I do agree with their ethics. It was my second favorite class in the Sound Temples. So I take a deep breath from my aching Aqua-Lung. For the first time, I scan these kids with my rudimentary sonar to assess their health and well being. I'm sure Marina scanned them the minute they appeared out of the bushes, and has already gotten the whole picture.

"Hey, Jake," I tell him in my most soothing tones. "I didn't say you're a thief." It's like singing a lullaby, this acoustic scanning. All the while I'm using my new ultrasound skills to see the history of the boy's body: He's suffered two broken arms and a broken leg when he was a child; his bones lack calcium from malnourishment, he's got rotten teeth—and he's very underweight. But Jake is still very strong.

"I just need to see your watch because ... well, we've just lost track of time out there floating in the ocean for days."

Grudgingly, Jake shows Marina and me his arm. Strapped to his thin wrist is a silver contraption that is so strange I can hardly read it. There are a lot of little gears and bleeping lights, then a digital read out that flashes—3.10.2030.

"What?" I shout, jumping up. "Impossible!" I'm so shocked that we've time traveled ten years I don't even bother to hide my dismay.

"Oh," Marina telepaths, as if she knew this all along. She's not overwhelmed like I am, just curious. How quickly she adapts to change and new information. I envy her that. "Well, I guess the WaveHole did throw us slightly off target."

"Slightly?" I straighten, gasping. "You think ten years is nothing?" My whole body is shuddering with fear, withdrawal, and shock.

Jake eyes me coolly, assessing my anxiety. But I don't care what he thinks.

I'm so furious I can hardly contain myself. How will we ever find my father? We've lost a decade! I'm still sixteen. A minor. No power at all here.

I'd be 26 if I'd stayed in my own world. What skills do I have to survive in this future? How can I adapt when I don't recognize any-thing? If Papi's no longer here, how will I take care of myself—and Marina? No wonder she's turning to Jake for help. He's a better bet for her survival than I am. Disoriented, I again consider jumping on Jake and grabbing his cell phone. But it may also be as sophisticated as his watch. Will I even know how to use it?

Marina's mind-talk restrains me. "It's even more important now to watch, listen, and learn," she advises on our private channel. "We can figure this out, Lukas ... together."

"I thought I was in charge," I say lamely. I hate that she always seems right, even in my own world. But I guess it's really not my world. Not anymore.

"So ... what happened to you all?" Marina motions for me to join her on the ground.

But Jake sits down right next to Marina. It's obvious he's instinctively drawn to her. Just like the dogs. It never occurred to me that I'd have a rival for Marina's affections. I've been so focused on finding my father and bringing Marina back here with me that I never once thought I might lose her to somebody else. But I'm damaged goods now. Why wouldn't she be more interested in a guy who can survive and navigate this place? It's Jake's world now.

Benevolently, Marina smiles at everyone. She acts as if we're in some library story time. No action. Just listening. I'm still so unhinged by the fact that we're in the wrong time that I don't know what else to do but follow her lead. I sit down on the other side of her.

"How long have you all been on your own here?" Marina asks.

"We lost everything," one of the little kids says hoarsely.

"I'm so sorry," Marina reaches out to the kid.

Marina is so obviously a natural leader, someone who people can trust. Even the gang senses it. She's handing out more of our food to them and to the salivating dogs, LuLu and Alexander the Great. I don't even bother telling her to save it for us. She won't. Generosity is Marina's biggest flaw.

"Right before Hurricane Malachi hit, there was a freak snowstorm, and then twisters," a scrawny Black girl named Sissy says.

"Yeah." One of the other girls shrugs her narrow shoulders, "Global weirding."

"And then that killer hurricane ... she flooded us real bad," Sissy continues. "We were living in a used car junkyard up on the hill. So when the big waves hit ... we watched it all ..."

Now the other kids join in, words coming so fast I can barely understand them all.

"Couldn't stop the flooding, waves just slammed into all the buildings."

"Floated everything away ... cars, houses, sometimes people still inside."

"Screaming!"

"Some up on their roofs."

"No one came to rescue them. . ."

"Or us."

"We waited," Jake interjects, taking over the story. "But no one could get to us for a long time. Helicopters didn't see us. Roads washed out. We ate stuff from abandoned houses and waited. There were lots of canned goods floating around then. Now, not so much."

"And money," Sissy pipes up helpfully. Jake shoots her a cautionary look.

"But then we realized ..." Sissy continues. "If they found us, we'd all be split up and just taken to refugee camps."

"To live with strangers," Jake mutters. "Or they'd put us in environmental refugee labor camps and make us work."

"We wanted to stay together," Sissy adds, sniffling. Her legs are covered in scars and scabs. I wonder what she's been through.

"Besides," another boy in the group scowls. "Nobody misses homeless kids."

"But how do you survive?" Marina asks. Her voice is so kind it breaks my heart. And opens theirs.

"We do okay in the flood lands," Jake says. "Nobody comes here now, not on purpose. Not even pirates loot the place much anymore. Only the trash bots come to clean up all the debris."

"Bots?" Marina asks.

Jake stares back at us curiously. "You two really aren't from around here, are you? Doesn't Cuba have any robots?"

"Not many," I say. I remember reading that in the near future robots were practically going to take over the world. Maybe they have by now.

"Well, even with the bots, nobody can live on the coast anymore," Jake continues. "It's all ..."

"Washed up!" some of the other kids scream, giggling almost hysterically.

"And what about Siesta Key?" I ask, trying to keep my voice steady.

"A refugee camp. Thousands of people there and out on the floating cities," Jake says. "Security is tight with all the pirates in the Atlantic. We're better off staying here in the flood lands on our own."

"What about ... " I can barely bring myself to ask, " ... what about Sarasota?" It's where Papi and I lived in our little apartment over a Cuban bakery. Near the beach and the Turtle Lab.

"Half of Sarasota made it, the other half's a ghost town," says Jake. "There were so many bad hurricanes the last couple of years. Then, just as everybody rebuilt, the monster storm Malachi made that direct hit."

My Aqua-Lungs feel like they might collapse, and my breathing is quick and shallow. Sweat pours down my face and armpits. I can't stop the torrent of terrible thoughts:

What if everything in our little apartment is flooded and covered in mud? What if I'm also homeless like this gang? What if Papi is dead? What if I'm an orphan? ~

CHAPTER 15
Flood Lands

"Careful, Marina, there's nails and metal and lots of sharp stuff," Jake advises as he slashes with his machete to bushwhack through the overgrown path to Siesta Key. "It'll cut right through your shoes."

Jake's calculating eyes light up every time he talks to her. He's taking way too much interest in Marina, while he ignores me completely. Marina readily appreciates Jake's care and concern. It makes me suspicious and also envious. He's so strong and sure of himself. I'm stumbling and lost in this changed world. Why wouldn't Marina follow Jake instead of me? He's obviously a real survivor.

I glance at the other kids' feet, clad in old flip-flops, plastic clogs, and leather sandals. Many have bruised toes and fresh scratches that look a little infected. One of the girls is limping, and her legs are black and blue, covered in gashes and scabs. These homeless kids have it really rough.

"Looks like she got into a swordfight with Lak," Marina telepaths.

"Or worse," I say.

At least Marina hasn't forgotten about me completely. We can still share a private joke. But that's about all we share, now that Jake and his gang have taken over. I feel a pang of regret and anger. Marina and I had so little time alone before getting swept up with these other kids. And who knows if we can even trust them?

Trying to keep up with Jake's pace, Marina is no longer half-dragging me along, so her touch doesn't ease my body's aches and weakness. I struggle to keep up, but find myself falling to the back of the pack. For the first time, I notice that the familiar skyline of high-rise

157

condominiums that used to dot Siesta Beach is gone. Windows are blown out of dilapidated buildings and parking lots are full of cars filled with mud. No lights on. It's eerie to see my hometown so abandoned.

"You okay?" Sissy asks.

"Yeah, yeah," I say, hardly able to catch my breath. "How long has the power been out here?"

"Couple months." Sissy shrugs nonchalantly. "No electricity in the flood lands. Live wires out here would be too dangerous."

"Flood lands are off-limits. Too much looting and squatting. After Hurricane Malachi, they gave people one week to salvage their homes and stores. Then they shut down Siesta Key. So much for paradise. Now, it's just a ghost town," adds Bruce, one of the guys with a blond buzz cut.

As we emerge from the muddy underbrush, I gasp. I can't believe the wreckage. "What's this street?"

"Beach Road," Jake says.

It's unrecognizable. This once quaint and expensive street is just a rutted deer trail now. Beach Road was once valuable waterfront property boasting rich mansions and elegant bungalows. But now all those cottages and estates are boarded up, covered in filth and debris.

Asphalt streets are potholed and tilt at crazy angles. Mud slimes everything. Trash, plywood, mangled bicycles, mountains of bricks and shingles, upside-down trucks, fallen power lines and telephone poles—that's all that's left of Siesta Key. So my science teacher was right: The rising seas and extreme weather caused by climate change have taken their terrible toll. If Jake is right and the rest of the eastern seaboard looks like this, how will we ever survive? How could Papi have survived?

"Why aren't people coming back to clean things up?" I ask Jake. "Rebuild?"

"No use rebuilding when another hurricane will just knock everything down again." Jake shrugs. "Government's got big plans to start over out here on the coast—to make eco-villages on stilts. Fat chance, with all the flooding and storms."

I notice that Marina seems more fascinated now than upset by the devastation around us. Maybe that's because Jake's in control, and Marina doesn't have to worry so much about just surviving. I feel terrible that I can't take better care of her here. But it's not my world anymore. And Marina doesn't belong to me. Never did.

"I've got a friend who can help us," Jake says. He reaches out a hand to help Marina over a fallen tree, but she just leaps over by herself. I'm glad she's not allowing him to treat her like a damsel-in-distress. It almost makes me laugh—Jake has no idea how powerful Marina actually is. If he did, he might not be so cocky.

"How?" Marina asks Jake.

"He can get us out of the flood lands into the part of the city that's still functioning."

"Okay, good," Marina says, without even consulting me.

Jake quickens his pace. Soon he and Marina are so far ahead I can't quite hear their conversation. But I can see that Marina is hanging on Jake's every word, taking everything in—just as her Diplomat-Spy training taught her. I remind myself that Marina is not just here to help me; she's also on an important mission to study SkyeWorld. Of course, she'll return to Aquantis when she's done with her research—and me. For a moment, I imagine returning to Marina's submarine world alongside her. I might consider that if I can't find Papi. But would the Blue Beings let me come back? Would Marina even want me with her?

"So ..." Jake yells as we all tromp through the mudflats and debris, "How long you two been ... together?"

He means as a couple. Jake's fishing for information about Marina and me.

Before I can answer, Marina says very loudly, "Lukas is my ... my little brother."

Little brother! I stop. Fury swirls in my stomach. Marina won't even claim me as a partner, an equal. Is it because she's suddenly smitten with Jake or because she's trying to protect us? Maybe Marina thinks she's making me less threatening to Jake. Whatever her motivation is, it's humiliating.

"What're you doing?" I telepath to Marina. "Why don't you tell him that we're . . ?" I don't know what to say. That's we're a couple? That we belong together? We don't, except in my head.

"Tell him what, Lukas?" Marina's voice is soft.

"That we ... that we're ... together," I say firmly.

"Trust me," Marina urges. "That won't work with Jake. He needs to believe that we're just brother and sister. That way he'll keep helping us."

"Are you flirting with him?" I demand. "Because we don't need Jake. We can handle this by ourselves!"

"No, Lukas," Marina's voice is flat. "We obviously can't. Not until we get you through your withdrawal and find your father. Diplomat-Spies graciously receive help when it is truly offered, and Jake is—"

"He's up to no good, Marina!" I protest so loudly that she shakes her head and stops in her tracks. She turns back to look at me.

"How do you know that?" Marina telepaths. She studies me with an expression as exasperated and imperious as Master Lioli. Times like these I realize why they declared Marina their High Priestess. She'd never admit it, but Marina can be downright high-handed.

I don't back down. "I ... I sense it, Marina," I insist. "You may have your Aquantan powers, but in this world I know a conman when I see one."

"A what?"

"Someone who's using you for his own purposes."

"But aren't we using him, too? Lukas," Marina asks. There is just the slightest bit of self-doubt in her tone, as if she might at last consider deferring to me in my own world.

"What're you two staring at?" Jake asks, interrupting our mind-talk. "You got your own channel or something?"

"Nothing." Marina turns her back on me. "Let's keep going ... please."

Her genial attitude toward the guy infuriates me. And that rage gives me enough energy to pick up my pace and make my way to the front, closer to Jake and Marina.

I'm panting with the effort, but at least I'm not falling so far behind.

"I'm not her little brother," I tell Jake stubbornly.

He turns around and frowns at me. Good. I hope Marina can see Jake's barely contained aggression. I hope it makes her more suspicious of him. "Then who are you?" he demands.

"We're ... cousins," Marina tells him, but stumbles over her words as well as the underbrush.

"You don't look alike and you two don't have the same accent," Jake comments. He's glaring at me now, his arms crossed over his chest. A classic defensive posture. "Why don't you stop lying?"

I could leap on Jake now and take him down. I could grip his neck and cut off the blood supply to his carotid artery, a simple move. Jake would fall unconscious at my feet. And Marina would see me defeat this bossy guy.

"Don't do it, Lukas," Marina's mind-talk cautions me.

Then she lays a gentle hand on Jake's arm and explains, "Lukas and I are ... distant cousins. Raised in different countries. We've only recently met each other—that's why we have to find Lukas's father. It's a ... a reunion for us all."

Jake considers this, his eyes darting from Marina to me. His furrowed brow and narrowed eyes clearly show that he doesn't believe Marina's story. And I don't blame him—it's lame. Jake's gang awaits their leader's decision. There's an electric tension in the air. What will they do if Jake denounces us?

"Listen, I'm sorry we lied. Our family situation is just too complicated to explain." I add, trying to smooth things over. "Any chance I can use your cell to call my father? He'll pay you big money for helping us out."

"I can't believe a word you two say," Jake scowls, considering what to do with us. "But you're too clueless to be feds or pirates."

Another long moment of wariness. There's no loyalty here now. Even the dogs have left Marina's side, sensing that their master doesn't trust us. Danger shrouds us all like humidity.

Jake's eyes dilate. I know that subtle signal. It's what happens right before somebody attacks. I sink my feet into the sand and get ready to fight. Jake moves toward me, but then suddenly his eyes dart up at the sky.

"Drones!" he yells. "Take cover!"

The gang dives back into the underbrush again, scrambling on all fours across the mudflats. Marina and I drop to the ground and crawl after them. Glass and jagged metal slice my hands like shrapnel.

Drones? They're using predator drones on kids now? Why? I thought those radio-controlled airplanes were just used in wars and spy patrol missions. Is America at war in 2030? Are we an occupied country? Who is our enemy?

"Hey, wait for us!" I gasp. I try to keep up with them, but my knees are gashed and trembling; my Aqua-Lungs feel like they're going to collapse.

Suddenly, the gang is running in zigzag patterns across an open stretch of mud. They speed past collapsed mansions and upside-down boats shipwrecked in what used to be front yards.

Marina grabs my waist and drags me along. I'm kind of pathetically happy she's holding onto me and not Jake. Where is the guy anyway? Has he deserted us all?

"In here!" Jake cries. "Quick!"

We all scuttle inside the back door of a decrepit colonial-style villa. Its three stories and sagging balconies are almost completely overgrown with kudzu and climbing ivy. The whole estate is completely covered in mud. The grime is good camouflage.

"What are drones?" Marina telepaths as we flee inside, following the gang.

"They're for war," I shout. "Not disaster relief!"

As though he can hear us, Jake calls back over his shoulder, "Drones patrol the flood lands looking for trespassers, survivors, or looters ..."

"Yeah, like us!" Sissy giggles. Her big glasses have slipped down her nose from running.

I'm just about to ask the kids why they all have such bad eyesight when Jake shuts me up with a stern look. Then everybody scatters throughout the wrecked house like they're on a well-rehearsed drill. The kids duck under huge panes of spider-cracked glass.

"Hide under that!" Jake orders Marina and me to slide beneath a huge glass coffee table.

We crawl through piles of debris to slide underneath it. I cover Marina with one arm and pull her close against me. Her eyes are huge, alert.

"Infrared can't see through glass," Jake explains from under his own windowpane.

I remember Papi telling me that the feds once used infrared devices to find Cuban refugees or people lost at sea. Firefighters also used it to detect people trapped in smoky buildings. But drones using infrared in the flood lands seem like overkill.

I hunker down under the glass with Marina tucked against me. She's strong, but surprisingly slender. Marina's long-waisted, her land legs shapely and smooth in her shorts. Don't need a thermal recognition device to feel her living warmth. Marina's nearness eases my shivering, but she's trembling now, no doubt plagued by her worst fears: capture by authorities. Being imprisoned in medical labs for experiments. My worst fears: not finding Papi and losing Marina.

I crane my neck to look over at Jake. He's lying flat on his back staring up through the windowpane. Absolutely still. Then I notice that his eyes are darting back and forth behind his glasses. Like he's reading. What's he doing?

"Okay, hacked into the patrol system," Jake nods firmly. "They're gone. Flew off this grid ... for now."

Grid? How does Jake know the drones have left our area? Before I can ask him, all the kids gather in what's left of this mansion's kitchen. Inside the huge walk-in cupboard closet, they toss canned goods into a pile on the floor. Each kids fills his backpack with cans. So that's how they eat.

"Hey, good idea!" I say.

At the sight of towers of canned soups, stews, corn, beans, peppers, and even Spaghetti-Os, my stomach growls. It's been a long time since I've had human food. Some of it looks really weird in strange, futuristic packaging. But I'm suddenly ravenous. I'm sick of eating seaweed, no matter how sweet or slimy, uncooked fish, and sea vegetables. I pop the aluminum top of a can of smoked mussels and eat a few of the delicate shellfish. Salt and smoke tingle on my tongue.

"Yuuuum," I say, with my mouth full. I toss Marina a tin of sardines.

Marina catches it but hesitates to open the tin. Jake whips out his Swiss Army Knife. It takes some effort to open the sardines, but when he offers Marina the neat little row of tiny, oiled fish, she smiles and nibbles them tentatively.

"Delicious!" She eats several more. "Almost as good as peeled shrimp." Then she abruptly stops eating and turns to me, "Lukas, we're not supposed to eat anything... here."

"Let me get this straight," Jake says, suddenly on edge again. "You two got shipwrecked and lost at sea for days and you don't want our food, just that seaweed stuff you brought in your backpacks?"

I try to head him off. "Hey man, give us a break. We're just a little freaked out by all of this." I hesitate, and then add, "She has food allergies, okay? She has to be careful about what she eats."

This seems to satisfy Jake. He busies himself with opening cans for the other kids who are sitting on the floor, eating heartily. The others are exploring the tumbledown house.

"Hey, down here!" one of the girls calls out. "You'll never believe what I found in the wine cellar."

We all run through the master study. It's a clutter of fallen bookshelves, overstuffed chairs covered in mud, and a desk crazily tilted. On the walls are huge, blank TV screens as big as picture windows. They take up the whole room. But these screens are still miniature compared to the Sound Murals in Aquantis.

"So much for this ritzy smart house," Jake sniggers. "Not so smart now without electricity, is it?"

The basement stairs are splattered with hardened mud, leaves, and glass. In the cellar the smell of rot and ruin is almost overwhelming. Rows of wooden shelves are filled with grimy wine bottles.

"Here!" Sissy calls from the back of the cellar. "It's a safe."

My heart sinks. If the kids find money, they won't need Marina and me any more. But probably the safe is empty. What kind of rich person would leave money behind? The safe's door is hanging ajar. I'm the tallest, so they allow me to reach inside.

"What is it?" the kids clamor.

When I feel the little metal boxes inside the wall safe, I grin. Maybe we're lucky. No money, just waterlogged papers. Pulling the wet, grimy containers out, I hand them to Jake.

He nods, a sign that he begrudgingly trusts me a little more now. I don't like him being in charge, but Marina's right—we do need his help. Everyone gathers around Jake as he pries open the metal boxes with his knife. I see a glint of gold. Is it gold bouillon bars?

Jake grunts in disgust as he holds up a bar of Swiss chocolate wrapped in gold foil. He sniffs it and throws it down on the muddy floor. "Nothing!"

"Nothing?" I laugh. "Don't you know what this is?" Now, I've got everybody's attention. I take the lead.

I bend down and pick up the thick chocolate bar, my mouth already watering. I'd only had chocolate once in my life—and that was on my twelfth birthday when Papi managed to get a small fortune together to buy two chocolate bars on the black market. Even then, chocolate was a luxury item because of the usual suspects: African droughts and unsustainable farming.

"Looks like shit," Jake says.

His spectacled eyes grow huge when I break off a big piece of the bar and plop it in my mouth. It's obvious none of the kids have eaten chocolate before or they would have jumped on me, devouring it.

The taste is amazing—rich, velvety chocolate drizzled with caramel and some kind of nut. Pecan? Cashew? The dense concoction coats my mouth with a rush of sugared bliss. There is enough chocolate for all of us. Except the dogs. ˜

CHAPTER 16
Eye-Net

"Here, try one of the best inventions of mankind." I offer each gang member a chocolate bar wrapped in gold foil. "But don't share it with the dogs. It'll kill them."

The gang's reaction is comical. At first, they sniff and nibble the chocolate suspiciously—then their eyes widen with pleasure as they gobble bigger and bigger bites. Jake finishes his chocolate bar in seconds.

"No wonder they keep this in their safe," he says. Jake's lips are smeared with chocolate, and there's even a dark, creamy smudge on his nose. It's nice to see him not acting like such a know-it-all for once. Maybe there are things about this world I can teach him and his gang.

Alexander the Great and LuLu jump up on Jake begging for the treat. Their combined weight almost knocks him down.

"Here," Marina offers. "The dogs can have some of our fish."

Before she can fetch the salmon from her backpack, Alexander the Great and LuLu are sitting before her in rapt attention, tails wagging. They devour the fish she tosses them.

"Hey, can we sell this chocolate?" Jake asks me reluctantly. Giving up this newfound marvel looks like the last thing he wants to do.

"Are you kidding?" I ask. "Chocolate is as good as gold. And this is a huge stash." I count up all the bars. There's at least a hundred. Why didn't the rich people take it with them? Maybe the same reason they didn't save their wine. Too rushed. And they could always buy more.

167

"Will you ...?" Jake begins, and then hesitates. It's unlike him to be so timid. He fixes me with a frown and asks, "Will you sell it in town for us?"

"Sure," I say. "But why me? You can take your share and sell it yourself, can't you?"

"Someone in town might recognize us," Jake explains. "And turn us in to ORR."

"What's that?" I ask.

"Office of Refugee Resettlement," Jake says. His voice is low. It's the first time I've seen him look even vaguely scared. As a minor, of course, he'd get turned in, too. "Once ORR gets their hands on us, we'll be their slaves. And my gang would never see each other again."

"I understand," I tell Jake.

And I do. I know how it feels to be wary of the authorities. They claim to have the best intentions like Castro's re-education or communal camps. But it always ends up being just one more way to track and control you. Papi taught me that. It's why he left Cuba.

I glance over at Marina, and she nods. But first I have to bargain with Jake. "If I do this for you, will you let me use your cell phone to call my father?" I ask.

Jake snorts. "It's dead."

"That's right, there's no electricity. You can't charge it."

"It's solar-powered," Jake answers, giving me a suspicious look. He glances at Marina and admits, "But no money to pay for the cell anymore. Besides, we don't ever want to bleep on their GPS. They're always searching for people off the grid—like us."

"Maybe we can contact Lukas's dad for him," Sissy suggests. "He's on our side."

Again Jake hesitates, eyeing me. What does he see? A boy who is taller and maybe smarter, but at a foreigner's disadvantage? He takes in my pallor and the shivering that has returned, now that Marina no longer has hold of me. Obviously, Jake believes I'm an addict and not to be trusted. But I'm also a refugee, like him.

"Okay," Jake says, nodding. "But I'll do it."

The gang agrees and returns to gobbling their chocolate bars. Quickly, Jake hands four little metal boxes of chocolate to me. He stows several other boxes for himself in his tattered backpack. "Just in case you don't come through with any money," he mutters.

"Sure, okay," I say. "Now, your part of the deal. How're you going to contact my father?"

Jake stares at me real hard, and then his hazel eyes shift again behind those big glasses. "What's his name?" he asks.

"Manuel Barrios Rodriguez."

The sound of my father's full name makes my eyes blur. Ten years gone. He will be an old man now. Almost fifty. Papi was never in the greatest health. Is he even still alive?

Again, Jake's pupils dart back and forth like he's reading. Only then do I realize that he's scanning something that seems to be inside his oversized glasses.

"Nothing on Eye-Net," Jake announces.

"Your glasses!" I burst out. "You've got the Internet inside them?"

Jake looks at me strangely. "I know it took Cuba decades to get cell phones, but don't you have Eye-Net yet?"

"Uh, no ..."

I glance over at Marina who is equally bewildered. Then I look at all the kids with their super-sized glasses and realize that the glass in their frames must double as tiny computer screens. I remember in 2020 they predicted small microchips would be implanted in our clothes, our skin, even our brains, so we could always be online. And anybody could track or spy on us. I wonder what other changes ten years of technology has brought my world. Is everybody wired?

"Wireless still works out here in the flood lands?" I ask.

"Yeah," Jake replies curtly. "We can hack in on emergency satellite channels."

I give him Papi's email—the one I chose for him, but he didn't use. My father was never very tech-savvy, so this is a long shot. But maybe in the past ten years he's finally figured out how to get online.

Jake speaks his message out loud—"Your son is here"—and the voice text turns into an email. He must have some sort of acoustic chip implanted in his ear. "Nope." Jake shakes his head. "That email bounces back. No good anymore." His eyes dart back and forth behind his glasses. "And there's nobody by that name in the Sarasota directory."

No surprise there. We never answered census takers and tried to stay "off the grid," as Papi called it, as much as we could. Kind of like this gang of kids. We always used the Turtle Lab's address for everything from Papi's driver's license to his mail and credit cards.

"Try looking up Turtle Lab," I tell Jake. "It's on ... or was on Conway Road."

Again, Jake's eyes shift back and forth, and I can now see a faint glow in his glasses. I wonder if Eye-Net is solar-powered, too.

Jake frowns. "Closed for the weekend. Got another contact?"

Why didn't I accept Lyla's email or cell phone number one of the million times she offered it to me? I know it was my way of shutting her out. If I didn't acknowledge her as Papi's girlfriend, then she didn't exist. I wish I hadn't been so resistant because now I need her.

"No," I say hopelessly.

Who else can I call? It dawns on me then that all of my friends from high school are ten years older, probably long gone. Suddenly, I realize how alone and cut off I am from my old life. Just like these homeless kids. If I can't find Papi, will anybody help me survive? Maybe I can find my old girlfriend, Jenny, if she hasn't married and moved away. Or, my science teacher, Mr. Meeker, if he's still at Grove High and my school isn't underwater.

Sensing my despair, Marina comes over and places her hand on my shoulder. I take a deep breath to steady myself. "We've got to get into town," I tell her.

"No, not 'til tomorrow," Jake counters. Whether I like it or not, he's still in charge. Leader of our little pack. "Weather report shows another hurricane headed our way. Full and mandatory evacuation for Sarasota all the way down to the Keys." He shrugs. "Hurricane season year-round now."

"Should we go into the town shelters this time?" Sissy asks tentatively. She's obviously afraid. All of the other kids cluster behind her. One girl even holds onto her skinny arm.

"No, it's not worth the risk of getting caught." Jake says firmly. "We can ride out another storm ..." His eyes dart back and forth as he checks Eye-Net. "Let's go!"

The gang knows the hurricane drill. Grabbing the chocolate and stuffing their backpacks with canned goods, wine, and bottled water, they run out of the cellar—the dark, cool depths where rich people hide their treasures. The part of me that is weakened by withdrawal, that even chocolate can't ease just wants to lie down here and rest.

But a quick, expectant look from Marina checks that instinct. She practically leaps up the stairs with me behind her, a little breathless. Again the kids are zigzagging through the muddy wreckage as though they're members of Special Forces, well trained in flood land surveillance and survival. Is this our future? Kids scavenging and running from military drones, like we're living in an occupied third-world country? It's hard to believe that our conquering enemy is climate change—horrible hurricanes and rising seas. Enemies my world could have stopped but chose not to.

As if it's instinct by now, Marina grabs my hand as we follow the gang. I'm grateful that she's staying with me and not sticking so close to Jake anymore. Maybe she got what she needed from him. Or maybe she thinks I'm such a wreck she can't, in good faith, desert me.

The wind is whipping up what's left of the palm trees, and overhead the sky is dark, threatening. There's an ominous yellow and charcoal streak across the sun. Hard to tell what time of day it is. I guess it only matters that it's hurricane time.

Jake leads us out across open fields. "Drones can't fly in bad weather," he explains when I balk at crossing the exposed mudflats. "And they call off the trash bots during big storms. C'mon!"

Soon we're back at the beach near a vacant estate of pink stucco and white columns. It's so huge and pretentious it's almost funny. How many people once lived here—one or two? Now there are eight of us. Even that's too few for such a grand, empty house. It could easily sleep dozens. Why do some people get to take up so much space? Where are all the rich people now? Probably taking up more than their fair share, just farther inland. The land and sea may have changed, but the people haven't. No wonder Aquantans despise us. I remember Master Lioli declaring, "Humans don't seem to understand they also have to evolve. Nothing stays the same."

"Upstairs," Jake orders us all. "Hurry!"

We run up a grand staircase covered in tiny shards of glass from a chandelier that must have fallen from the domed ceiling. If I weren't in withdrawal, I could ace these stairs. But I have to hold onto the banister. I'm the last to climb up the three stories to the very top of the mansion.

Lungs burning, gasping for air, I enter the attic room with its blown-out picture windows and its expansive view of Siesta Beach, or what's left of it. Wind is already howling through the attic, and rain slashes inside from the north. I look up and see that half of the roof is missing and right in the middle of this attic is a yacht that must have been lifted by a storm surge and then crashed through the top of the house, lodging in the attic.

"It's perfect!" Marina tells Jake with a grin. She's obviously back to believing in him, instead of me. "If the waters get too high, we can float right out of here." She doesn't mention, of course, that she and I can easily shift and swim safely through rising waters.

Jake nods proudly. "This is where we sleep and sit out the storms. You two can stay with us ... tonight."

The gang climbs up a rope ladder into the boat. Jake graciously offers Marina a hand to help her up and over the railing. Even though she doesn't need his help, she accepts it, perhaps sensing it would please Jake. As he hefts me up on to the boat, Jake says in a whisper, "My big brother was a junkie, man. I know what you're going through. You can beat this!"

"Yeah," I say, trying not to sound too winded. Who wants this guy's cheerleading? I doubt it's Jake's true motivation to help me. He only wants Marina.

The yacht's cabin is like a glassed-in solarium. Useless, if you were going fishing. But working in a Siesta Key fancy marina taught me that most yacht captains don't know how to sail. They mostly stay in dry dock, hosting parties on their pretty, impractical boats. But in this case the glass cabin is useful: It will hide us from the drones' infrared and float us back out to sea in floods.

Under the cushions are shelves with a few canned goods, wine bottles, and water. The kids empty their backpacks and stow their salvaged food carefully. Who knows how long this supply has to last them? Until they find another stocked house to loot? I carefully pack up my precious chocolate stash to sell in Sarasota.

The wind is screaming now, and the kids hunker down around Marina and me. Jake drapes a few quilts over Sissy and several of the other girls. Quite the gentleman. Then he pulls out a ratty blanket, which he offers to Marina.

"I'm not really cold ... yet," he shrugs. It's obvious that's not true, which I consider pointing out until Jake extends his gallantry to me, as well, when he tosses me a windbreaker. "You two get warm first."

Marina offers me the blanket. "I'm fine," she says.

I know she's used to much deeper cold than even a Florida hurricane. So I take her blanket and Jake's tattered canvas jacket and pull it on. "Thanks, Jake."

I feel a grudging gratitude to this guy who has taken us into his fold. But I'm also aware that he's got ulterior motives. And his fascination with Marina is troubling. What's more disturbing is that Marina seems equally curious about Jake. Her eyes follow him as Jake takes his position in the front of the glass cabin. Like the pirate captain of this beached boat.

As Marina studies Jake, her face in the shadows is dark, wide, and high-boned. Her curly auburn hair is braided and woven in Aquantan style. But it's beautiful without any adornment of seed pearls or sapphires. How pretty Marina looks in her simple T-shirt and shorts, so human. So unlike Pandora with her pale radiance, her aristocratic airs, her jewels, and glinting black pearl armor.

Though I prefer Marina, I can't help but still crave her sister. Sometimes in my night sweats, I dream about Pandora. Even wide-awake, every time I close my eyes, I see Pandora's piercing gaze, her lips brushing mine, her golden curls floating out from her beautiful face. Then she kisses me, and I drink in the exquisite rush of her *manna*—like fire and honey.

In the glass cabin, Jake busies himself with ropes and supplies. He pretends not to notice Marina's attention. But it's obvious he's used to basking in female admiration. He's practically got a harem already. And the boys follow Jake without question. I doubt any of them would follow me anywhere. Unless I had money. Or more chocolate.

"Will you sing to us?" Sissy asks Marina. "You've got such a pretty voice."

With an expression of surprise and then delight, Marina nods. Her laugh is musical as she begins to sing. And then her soft humming mesmerizes them all. Even Jake's watchful eyes blink back sleep.

My own breathing steadies, the burning ache in my Aqua-Lungs eases a little. As I lie on a boat cushion next to Marina, I can't help but notice how sculpted her tawny legs are—lean but also strong. The memory of her tail flukes curling around my body makes me feel suddenly very warm, aroused. I feel a pulsing along my lower body. A subtle heat. I hope Marina can't hear my helpless desire for her.

Now that Marina's shifted to her legs, I realize we could have sex. I'm not a virgin. A quick release on the beach with Sally Lowen when I was a freshman took care of that. Would Marina even want to do it with me—when she could be with someone as powerful and fast as Jake? Someone not weak and addicted to her sister? Jake is equally human and forbidden, but he's a better bet now than I am. We probably need Jake more than he needs us.

Still I can't help but want to get Marina alone again. Is it wrong to be this selfish? Our chances of survival here are not as good without Jake and his gang, but that doesn't matter as much to me as keeping Marina's favor and attention.

So as soon as Jake and the gang are all asleep, I tell Marina, "Quick! Let's sneak outta here."

"Why, Lukas?" she asks. "What's wrong with Jake and his gang? They're giving us shelter and will help us into town tomorrow."

She turns those changeable, bright eyes on me, so trusting. I know I'm not really doing the right thing. But I can't help it. I say in a harsh tone. "Jake's not the good guy he's pretending to be. I know it."

"How do you know?" Marina frowns.

"I think Jake's gonna turn us into the authorities as soon as we get to town. Sell us ... sell you ..."

Now, I've got Marina really worried and the dark part of my heart is thrilled. I can see her struggling with her own terror at being captured for medical experiments. I hate that I'm causing Marina this alarm, but it's the only way to get her to doubt Jake. And choose me.

And who knows? Maybe Jake really is plotting against us. We don't really know anything about him or his motives.

"I wish ..." Marina begins, her mind-talk trembling.

"Wish what?"

"That Dao was here to help me decide. He's always my best counsel."

"Well, Dao can't hear you now!" I insist. "You have to listen to me. It's still my world, and I know it better than you or Dao." Inside my own heart, I can feel my light diminish. Can Marina fathom my deceit?

"But do you know this future world better than Jake?" Marina looks straight at me, her eyes shining in the dark.

"Yes," I lie. "Trust me."

But she doesn't. Marina looks away and seems to disappear inside herself for a long time. At last she says, "I'll think about it, Lukas. Get some rest."

Is it a reprimand? Or just a reminder that she can stand guard sleepless while the rest of us humans must zone out for eight hours. Marina has all night to consider my plan. Will she put her faith in me? Do I deserve her trust?

A faint shadow of disappointment crosses Marina's face as she gazes down at me, lying so near her. I close my eyes. I don't want to remember Marina's expression: regret and confusion. Even though I'm right next to her, Marina looks as if she feels suddenly alone. Abandoned.

"I will never desert you, Marina," I tell her. "Or betray you. I can protect you." But I know that I've already betrayed her by my demands, and Jake can probably take much better care of her than I can.

Marina says nothing. Not out loud. Not on our own private frequency. She's humming softly as if to comfort herself now.

My heart is beating fast and my breathing quickens. Does Marina sense how much I want her? I can smell her—salt and sea and the warmth of the sun still echoing in her skin. If she feels my yearning for her, does this make her trust or doubt me? ~

PART FIVE

CHAPTER 17
Hurricane

MARINA

*E*ven when Lukas slept, he looked worried. His forehead was creased and his lips tense. Outside our little glass-boat cabin, the hurricane winds roared so loudly it hurt my ears. The whole house rocked and shuddered.

For the second time, this human boy slept next to me. Even though I was trained as a Diplomat-Spy, it felt wrong to pry into Lukas's thoughts while he was sleeping, so I had to be content with simply watching him. That rumpled hair and moody, handsome face, the way his eyebrows knit and his black eyelashes curled, impossibly long. I couldn't take my eyes off Lukas.

Was he right about Jake and his gang? Would they sell us to survive in this dangerous world? Ever since I met Lukas, I'd instinctively trusted him. But now I wasn't so sure he had our best interests at heart. His light was not as bright—strangely shadowed. Was that just his addiction to Pandora or was Lukas hiding something from me? His animosity toward Jake didn't make much sense. Jake had done nothing but help us—so far. But humans were never to be completely trusted. That's what Master Lioli drilled into us during Diplomat-Spy training.

"Why not?" I'd asked the Master one class.

"Because humans can't even trust themselves," Master Lioli had answered with a meaningful glance at me.

Being half-human, I'd taken it as one of his usual criticisms. Master Lioli had never quite gotten over the fact that I didn't belong to

177

him alone. That he had only contributed his *manna* to my creation—
that I was still half-human. He didn't completely control my fate or
me. I did. That's probably what made me less Aquantan than any High
Priestess should ever be. It also made me unpredictable. Would my
own half-human heart break trust with Aquantis and decide for itself
who was my mate? Choose someone like Lukas? Or maybe a stronger
boy, like Jake?

Even though Lukas was still suffering the symptoms of withdrawal, even though he was addicted to my sister and not me, I couldn't
help but feel something more than friendship for Lukas. Was it love?
Diplomat-Spies were trained in emotional espionage, not love. And if
we fell in love in a world other than our own, it always seemed to end
badly.

Maybe I couldn't control whom I loved. Jake's attention was flat-
tering, even intriguing. Did he think I was pretty? Or was he plotting
to betray me? Lukas didn't trust Jake. Should I?

I lightly touched Lukas's forehead to feel for fever. He was much
too warm and his skin clammy. But he shivered in his sleep. What
could I do?

Almost by instinct, I lay down next to Lukas and wrapped my arms
around him. He shifted in his sleep and fit his body more closely into
mine, so his back was against my breasts. His heart beat more steadily,
more surely. It was the first time I'd ever embraced anybody like this,
and suddenly a memory from my childhood returned.

I'd seen my father nap with my mother the same way I was lying
with Lukas. "Spoons," he'd called it fondly. "Cuddling." As human-
born, half-Aquantans, my parents no longer needed to sleep. But
sometimes they still napped together just like that.

"You'll understand when you're older," my father had said, winking at me.

Lying this close to Lukas made me realize that perhaps sleep was not
such a waste of time. Perhaps my parents knew what they were doing in
their long naps. As I held Lukas, I felt a new sensation—warmth tingling
and glowing along my skin like sunlight, even though it was night. Then
my land legs trembled as if I might unexpectedly shift. I realized that ever
since that cave party, my body had been longing to curl again around

Lukas the way it did when we danced together. It was the reason I was sometimes irritated with him or worried so much about his withdrawal symptoms. My body somehow needed his body.

It felt so natural lying with my arms and legs interlaced with Lukas's. All my senses were heightened as if I'd drunk *manna*. It must be desire. Why had I never felt this way toward Dylan? Was this how Lukas felt about my sister? Or me? A thrill. Craving. I wondered if what I felt thrumming through my body was similar to the power of Pandora's transfusion. Was this how Lukas felt when he drank her golden nectar? No wonder I was forbidden from giving him my *manna*. I already felt intoxicated, just lying next to this boy.

But I also felt a jolt of fear. Lukas might abandon me. That would be pain, perhaps even withdrawal. Was love an addiction? Did Lukas love Pandora—or just need her? Was there a difference?

With a sleepy sigh, Lukas's tense muscles relaxed and his breathing steadied, slowed down. Without trying, we inhaled and exhaled together, the way dolphins breathe in synch all their lives. The way I breathe together with Dao. How I missed my Constant now! Dao would know how to advise me. Soon Lukas and I were both enveloped in an energy field of vibrating blue lights. Warm and pleasurable. Like we were floating on the same wave.

Somehow, Lukas felt like home. My heart's light was so bright it lit up the glass cabin, bathing the sleeping humans. It was so beautiful, it was a shame they couldn't see my light. As the darkness eased into sunlight, I reluctantly slipped away from Lukas's body and sat up on the boat cushions a small distance away. Immediately, Lukas began tossing and turning, his legs thrashing. He murmured and then shouted something unintelligible. Who was he calling for in his dreams? His father? My sister? Me?

Would he ever really heal from his addiction to Pandora and her *manna*? My sister had managed to steal the first boy I'd ever really liked. Even though Pandora wasn't there, her blight fell over us. How I missed the Lukas I'd rescued from the burning boat, the Lukas who always tried to impress me in the Sound Temples, the boy who had held me to his heart and danced slowly with me, spinning together in the cave.

Restless, Lukas's legs twitched, like he was running away. Was this agitation just his addiction swirling through his veins like a golden chain cruelly wielded by Pandora? Where was my sister now? Perhaps the WaveHole sent her into the future too. And what about Dylan? Would Pandora try to steal him from me as well? As I watched Lukas and Jake and his little gang sleep in the glass boat cabin, suddenly, I felt very alone. Alien. How I longed for my Constant, who had always been so near me.

"Dao?" I telepathed. I turned toward the sea as the rain slashed through the roof and pattered against the glass cabin. "You out there?"

We weren't that far away from the surf, but I doubted Dao was anywhere near shore where the waves were wild and unpredictable. He would be far out at sea to better survive the hurricane. I resolved that as soon as everybody woke up, I'd shift and find Dao.

How could Lukas, Jake, and his gang sleep through such screeching winds and debris flying everywhere? They had to be beyond exhaustion. Or maybe the kids were accustomed to such dangerous weather.

"I'm hungry," Sissy whispered to me as she awoke and stretched on the opposite boat cushion bed. "Any more chocolate?"

Sissy was so scrawny and her expression so expectant, I couldn't resist reaching into Lukas's backpack and tossing her a slim chocolate bar from our stash.

"No!" Jake was immediately up and snatching the chocolate from her hands. "We have to sell that, Sissy. If you're hungry, have some ..." He reached under the bed in the storage shelf. " ... Tuna fish."

"I'm sick of tuna," Sissy pouted. She looked suddenly very young as she turned to me hopefully. "I'd rather have more of Marina's Japanese power bars. At least they're sweet."

I handed Sissy another seaweed bar and smiled as she nibbled it. She ate carefully, as if trying to make her treat last. Tiny wrinkles fanned out under her bloodshot eyes.

"How old are you, Sissy?" I asked.

"Old enough," Jake answered for her.

He seemed to have awoken with a renewed sense of distrust toward me. Or maybe it was an effect of the disturbing winds. Like a noisy intruder battering us, causing both irritation and alarm. We didn't have such terrible winds under the sea. My Aquantan hearing was so acute that the roar made it difficult to concentrate. I kept holding my hands over my ears when the blasts got too painful.

"Here," Jake said, offering me a strange headset from his backpack. "Noise-cancelling headphones. There's still a little battery life left."

The silver and black headphones cupped my ears like soft hands, and suddenly the storm's fury was magically muted. It was like acoustic cloaking, except done by instrument rather than Aquantan sonar.

"Thank you so much," I said. It was a kind gesture, so I didn't ask where he found such obviously expensive equipment.

Jake shrugged. "Looks like you need 'em more than we do."

His mistrust of me seemed to be ebbing. I wondered if acts of kindness softened humans. Helped them let down their many defenses. They didn't have *lanugo* cloaks. Human defenses seemed centered deep inside their hearts, interfering with their ability to create their own light and forcing them to rely on their technology.

Wedged in the ruined attic, our boat creaked and rattled, tilting sideways, just as if it were riding gigantic waves. What moved us was not water, but wind.

"I'm fifteen." Sissy answered my earlier question, while frowning at Jake. "And you're not my boss."

Jake ignored her small rebellion. Turning to me, he said in a loud voice I could hear even with my headphones, "You seem like a smart girl. How'd you end up with this junkie?

The way he dismissed Lukas pained me. I didn't have to ask what a "junkie" was in this world. Obviously, Jake recognized addiction when he saw it. "He's trying to get through withdrawal," I explained. "Lukas is doing the best he can."

"Yeah, yeah," Jake snorted. "That's what they all say. I had a brother like him. Tried to take care of me after our parents died, but he was a junkie, too."

"What happened to your brother?" I asked, scanning Jake's heart. There was little light there. But he was resilient.

Jake hesitated, as if debating whether to confide anything more in me. At last he scowled and added, "He got really messed up one night on Oxyzon. Then he broke into my bedroom and stole all my baseball cards. He was trying to hawk them on the street—that's when somebody shot him."

I wasn't quite sure what Jake was talking about. What was Oxyzon? And why would it make someone steal baseball cards? But I understood how Jake ended up homeless. Glancing around at the other sleeping children, I wondered who had died or abandoned all of them? In Aquantis, it was considered one's ethical duty and an honor to adopt any children whose parents or family perished. Even Outer Reef orphans were adopted. We raised our children communally. The idea of children being thrown away like that was shocking.

"I'm so sorry, Jake," I said and sent him some low-frequency sonar to soothe him. For just a moment, his heart echoed with a little borrowed light.

"Thanks," Jake replied, with sincerity, "And I'm sorry that you gotta lug this guy around. How long has he been off the junk?"

If by "junk," Jake meant *manna*, it was hard to calculate. Aquantans told time in tides; our cycles were so different than in SkyeWorld. Master Hu had told me there was no way to tell how long Lukas would struggle with his *manna* withdrawal. It depended on the laws of this world, not Aquantis. Without proper initiation and official ceremony, Pandora's *manna* transfusion was unprecedented. Its effects were actually unknown. How could my sister have been so reckless?

"Uh ... not long," I said.

"Well, there used to be a good rehab center in Sarasota," Jake ventured. "I could take you there."

"But I thought you wanted Lukas and me to sell the chocolate in town for you, so you wouldn't get caught?"

"Yeah, like he's in a position to help anybody—but himself." Jake sighed and nodded at Lukas who was now drenched in sweat, his legs twitching.

I feared that Lukas would accidently Sound Shift in his sleep and give us away. Sometimes, beginning shifters weren't able to control their flukes. Extreme fear or anger—even arousal—might cause one's body to suddenly shift. It's what happened to me on the beach the first night I met Lukas.

"Lukas." I reached down and shook him gently. "Wake up!"

No response, except for a grimace and a snore as Lukas pushed me away. His unconscious rejection hurt me. I tried to hide my pain, but Jake recognized my expression.

"Hey, as soon as the storm dies down," Jake offered, "you and I can go into town and sell that chocolate ourselves."

"No, Jake," I was firm. "Lukas has to find his father ... my ... uncle."

"You two aren't really family, are you?" Jake asked. It was his turn to be hurt. "Why are you lying to me, Marina?"

My whole body flushed with panic. How could I have forgotten such an important rule of being a Diplomat-Spy? Never tell the exact truth. Stick to the cover story. I stumbled over my words trying to explain. "Like Lukas said, it's a long story. Our family is ..." What had he called it? "We're ... really complicated."

Jake hunched his shoulders and frowned. He knew I was hiding something. But what could I do? Tell him the WaveHole overshot our destination by ten years? Reveal to him that I was not a refugee, but an alien? Would Jake turn us into the authorities, maybe even sell me to a medical laboratory, like Lukas warned? How I wished I could truly trust this boy and his gang.

And what about Lukas? He was human. I trusted him for the most part, even though he was sickened by my sister's *manna*. I still believed in him. And I hoped Lukas felt the same about me. I guess I would find out soon. When Lukas found his father, he would be done with me. He wouldn't need me anymore. Lukas would be with his own kind. Jake was right. Lukas and I were not really family. We barely knew each other.

Besides, I was under direct orders to leave Lukas there and return to Aquantis, as soon as we found his father. After all, I was turning seventeen soon and would lose my protective *lanugo* cloak. Then Skye-World would be as toxic to me as any Aquantan adult. We had only this brief time left together, Lukas and me. Best to complete my mission before I got any more involved with this human boy.

"Well," Jake murmured. "None of us is really family, either. It's okay." He hesitated and then blurted, "C'mon, Marina, the winds are dying down a little—let's brave the storm. We can take a trip to town, just you and me, before Lukas even wakes up. If he ever decides to wake up. Sometimes my brother slept for days when he was really doped up. He called it, 'low tide.'"

"Sounds right," I nodded. But I had to wonder why Jake was so anxious to get into town now, without Lukas. Maybe Lukas was right and Jake really wasn't to be trusted. Or maybe Jake was trying to give Lukas a rest. Lukas was functioning like his body and spirit were at their lowest ebb. How long before the tide would turn for him? "What was your brother's name?" I asked Jake.

The boy hesitated and then answered grudgingly, "Angus. He always hated that name."

"And your parents?"

"Never knew 'em," Jake shrugged. "Maybe they were junkies, too."

At last Lukas stirred and coughed. Lifting himself up groggily on one elbow, Lukas stared blearily as if he didn't recognize me. As if he was still lost in his nightmare. Or a seductive dream about Pandora. Maybe when he seemed to fit himself so close against me, Lukas was really just fantasizing about my sister. The thought hurt my feelings so I tried to shake it away.

"We're heading to town," Jake told Lukas firmly. "With or without you, man."

Lukas shook his head and rubbed his eyes. He sat up on the boat cushion, cocked his head to listen to the raging storm, and then his eyes finally focused on me. Immediately, his expression shifted from a look of agitation to what I hoped was tenderness. "Okay," he managed to say, though I could see he was still very unsettled. "With me!"

"What if we get caught?" Sissy asked the question that was on all of our minds.

"You're not going, Sissy," Jake snapped. "You're in charge of the others while I'm gone."

"No way!" Sissy protested. But her disappointed eyes acquiesced.

The rest of the gang began to rouse, rummaging through the stash of canned goods looking for breakfast. Others clambered down from the boat cabin to an under-deck bathroom they inexplicably called "the head."

"How long do they predict the storm will last?" Lukas asked Jake.

Jake scanned his Eye-Net glasses quickly. "Not supposed to make landfall here until tomorrow," he said. "We gotta make our move today."

"You don't have to come with us, Jake ... " Lukas began, and then stopped. Obviously Lukas would rather we leave Jake behind. But we all knew I might truly need Jake's help if Lukas faltered on our way to Sarasota.

In answer, Jake yanked open a big storage box and started hurling clothes at us that were slick and musty.

"Raincoats," Lukas told me. "You're going to need them out there."

I pulled on a grimy yellow raincoat. It was much too big for me, but I could see how practical it would be against the savage rain. I had some trouble fitting my small backpack filled with chocolate bars over the bulky raincoat. But Lukas helped me.

"We look like sailors," he said, managing a grin. Though he was shaky, Lukas was determined. His backpack was heavy with more chocolate and extra gear. He reached out to help me down the rickety ladder of the beached boat.

"Come back soon!" Sissy called after us. She seemed suddenly forlorn. But then she gathered her courage and stood taller. "We'll be okay," she declared.

"Bring us some more food," one of the other girls pleaded.

"They don't really care about me." Jake said, grinning good-naturedly and shrugging. He jumped down from the boat nimbly, not even bothering with the ladder. "Just food." ~

CHAPTER 18
Salvagers

$\mathcal{J}$ ake seemed excited about the prospect of going into town. Was he tired of being the leader of his little ragtag gang? Maybe Jake felt a sense of freedom to be traveling without any responsibility—except for Lukas and me.

When I scanned Jake, I could tell he was feeling less defensive. His heart was not so closed. He moved purposefully through the underbrush and debris even though his huge backpack and orange rain gear weighed him down. Why did Lukas think Jake was so untrustworthy? In his own world, Lukas seemed much more guarded than in Aquantis.

It occurred to me that perhaps everything Lukas had been through was finally taking a toll. After all, he'd lost his mother when he was just a baby. And then he'd gone from living a nomadic and somewhat impoverished life with his father to being stranded in a future world without family or friends. And what did I really knew about this boy whose destiny seemed so interwoven with mine? How could Lukas and I be part of the same Prophecy?

"How long since you been into town?" Lukas asked Jake suspiciously.

I wished the boys would try to get along better. We needed to work in harmony, with nobody singing the lead. Ensemble. That's what we called our cooperative skills in Aquantis.

"Not since Hurricane Malachi," Jake admitted.

Jake seemed to be telling the truth. Why lie? As we trudged, Lukas was breathing hard with the effort of slogging through the tumultuous rain. Leaning forward against the wind, Lukas pulled his rain slicker hood over his face. I couldn't see his expression. But a quick scan told me Lukas had nothing in his stomach.

I hadn't suggested that Lukas eat to fortify himself for the trip; I didn't want him to think I was watching him too closely. I knew he was ashamed of his addiction, though it wasn't his fault. If he chose to try and ignore it, so would I.

But Jake also seemed to be keeping watch over Lukas. He would slow his pace if he heard Lukas gasp for air. For several miles, we trudged slowly, bent over against the gusts of fierce wind and rain. So far, there was not much flooding, just rainwater and muddy debris running down rutted streets. The empty neighborhoods were spooky. Wooden shutters rattled, automobiles full of mud sat useless in driveways, and debris flowed down the streets, some of which were impassable.

"Is this really all that's left of Siesta Key?" Lukas asked, shocked. "It will take us hours to hike to Sarasota. Any way we could get there faster?"

Jake was practically yelling now so we could hear him above the storm. "I think I know where they got some fusion or air motorcycles that still work."

"Air bikes?" Lukas perked up. "That's the fuel you use now?"

"Don't got air bikes in Cuba, yet?" Jake shook his head, surprised. "How do you guys get around on that island?"

"Uh..." Lukas stalled for time. "Mostly by boat. And horses."

Jake nodded, "Yeah, Cuba got hit pretty hard, too. I hear it's mostly underwater ... like our eastern coast."

"All of the East Coast?" Lukas asked.

"Yeah, the Keys sank a long time ago, and half of New York City is a flood zone. Nothing left in Boston but the harbor." Jake turned around and gave us a curious look. "Didn't you see any of the Eco-Arks offshore when you were sailing here from Cuba?"

"Oh, yeah," Lukas nodded, as if he knew what Jake was talking about. "Saw a few."

"Good thing you didn't capsize off a Floating City," Jake said. "That's where most of the refugees live now. Once you get sent to one of those Eco-Arks, it's hard to get off—even though I hear they're pretty swank digs. Security is really tight because of all the pirates in these waters."

Suddenly, a blast of wind threw Jake sideways against a fallen tree. Lukas grabbed Jake and righted him. "You okay, buddy?"

Jake seemed shocked by Lukas's unexpected strength. "Yeah ..." he muttered. But Jake regarded Lukas as if for the first time, as if he had been wrong to completely write Lukas off.

That small gesture was enough to encourage Jake to see us as potential allies. "Listen," Jake explained. "Just before a hurricane hits, the government calls off their trash bots and their drones ... that's when the salvagers can come out."

"Salvagers?" I asked.

"You know, the only ones who still help people like us."

"Doesn't the government help disaster victims?" Lukas asked.

"Nope, no money in it. Too many disasters. Salvagers are out saving things and each other. It's a barter system. You'll see. That's where we can sell the chocolate."

"But I need to get into Sarasota to find Papi," Lukas began, and then stopped. "Or at least get a phone. Do salvagers barter cell phones?"

"Anything you want." Jake said, grinning. "They trade."

I telepathed to Lukas, "Maybe we could trade our Spanish doubloons?"

"Maybe," Lukas said. For the first time since we landed in this future disaster area, Lukas's tone was almost hopeful.

Lukas straightened up against the windy deluge, zipped his slicker firmly and reached out to take my hand. It was the first time he'd touched me since yesterday. And though his hand was slick and cold, it felt solid, resolute. Maybe he was getting through his withdrawal.

"You know, Marina," Lukas's mind-talk was hardly a whisper. "It's always better when you're near me." He hesitated, and then added with a shy smile, "like last night."

It was my turn to feel shy, as if he'd suddenly caught me. So he was half-awake when I'd embraced him. Had it thrilled Lukas as much as it had thrilled me? "You mean that ..." I struggled to find the words. "Your symptoms ... are better—when you're near me?"

Lukas held my hand more tightly. Delicately, he traced the webs between my fingers. I felt a fluttering in my legs.

"I mean, everything's better when you're touching me, Marina." Then, embarrassed, Lukas picked up his pace, pulling me along against the storm.

As we slogged through the empty streets of Sarasota Key, I saw just how much had changed since my first visit to SkyeWorld. All the boutiques were boarded up, mudslides caked the storefronts, and debris from past storms piled up along the sidewalks. We had to pick our way carefully through plywood, broken neon signs, and downed telephone or electric poles.

"What a mess!" Lukas exclaimed.

"The bots cleared out most of the valuables already," Jake explained. "But there's still stuff we can score here."

I stopped abruptly at the sight of Sid's Fish Shack. It had collapsed sideways like a flattened box. There was a swordfish trophy that I'd once seen on the wall, sticking straight up from a pile of metal debris. I couldn't help but think about Lak and my sister, and about my own Constant.

Where were they? I had promised to find Dao that morning, but with the hurricane moving in, I knew he'd be far from shore. I could have shifted and swum out to find him, but that would have meant abandoning Lukas in his search for his father. I felt torn between my loyalty to Dao and my duty to Lukas. Was I making the right decision? Maybe this was more than a mission; maybe I was putting Lukas's needs first—even before Dao's and my own. That frightened me.

"What're you waiting for?" Jake asked me. I didn't realize I'd stopped so long to stare at Sid's Fish Shack, or what was left of it. "C'mon!"

"I know it's hard to fathom all this," Lukas telepathed, squeezing my hand. "But you're not alone here."

He pulled me close to him for a moment. Our quick hug was made all the more awkward by our backpacks and bulky rain slickers. But I could hear his heart beating through the grimy layers, and it seemed surprisingly strong. Humans were hard to understand. You'd think the sight of his destroyed homeland would make Lukas weaker.

Instead, he seemed strangely buoyed. Was it by the simple tasks of surviving? Or was it something more?

"Ahoy there, Mateys!" We heard a man's gruff voice before we saw him. "Ah, I've always wanted to say that."

A robust man stepped out of a dilapidated machine strung under a colorful sail. Was it some kind of flying boat? It looked like it was handcrafted out of junk and debris. The only thing recognizable was its shape, like a huge chambered nautilus with a pointed metal dorsal fin sticking out the top. I wondered if it was for navigation.

"Wow!" Lukas telepathed. "It's some kind of homemade airship. Maybe we can get him to fly us to Sarasota."

The man was dressed head-to-toe in leather that somehow shed the rain. He wore golden goggles and knee-high black-laced boots and had some kind of iron tool strapped to his belt. Was he a pirate? When I scanned him, I was shocked to see his hands were not really flesh and blood. Each hand was a well-designed and very lifelike machine made of whirring gears and flashing circuit boards.

"Hey there, Grist," Jake grinned. "Thought you might be out and about in this fine weather."

"Right-o, my boy," Grist laughed heartily. "Thank God for hurricanes." He nodded toward Lukas and me. "Friends of yours?"

"Uh ... yeah, sure," Jake said. He turned to us and made a formal introduction. "This is Grist, one of the best salvagers in Sarasota. And these two are ..." Jake started to say, correcting himself at a frown from Lukas. "Well ... they're refugees."

"So you're on the run, too?" Grist didn't miss a beat. Obviously, we fit right in where so many people were dislocated and avoiding authorities.

Lukas nodded tersely. "You got a cell phone or a charger to trade?"

Grist shook his head. "Nope, kid, all out of luxury items. What d'ya got?"

Jake hesitated a moment, then began, "Not much. We've just got—"

"Chocolate!" Lukas interrupted. There was an edge of desperation in his voice. "We got delicious chocolate."

Grist whistled softly. "Whoa! So you're the one with the luxury items. How much?"

Before Jake could take over the bargaining, Lukas said, "Can this contraption get us to Sarasota?"

"That'll cost you a lot of chocolate, kid."

"We got a lot."

Jake glared at Lukas. "No, we don't! We can't trade him all our chocolate just to hitch a ride to Sarasota. What about food for all the others? We need money for that."

"He's right, Lukas," I had to telepath, even though I saw Lukas's face drop. "We can't just think of ourselves. Jake's gang is depending on us."

"Then how about a few doubloons?" Lukas's mind-talk had a pleading tone. He was sweating now, as the rain slashed against us.

"Get inside, kids," Grist commanded. Even he had noticed Lukas's condition. "We can bargain without being blown away."

The muscular man pulled open a small doorway with a porthole in its center. I'd seen such round windows in passing ships. The airship was very different from the expensive yacht that we had used for shelter during the hurricane. Inside were rough wooden seats like planks along the sides.

"Turbine," Grist explained as Lukas leaned over a circular and spinning instrument in the center of the ship. "Designed it myself. But don't put your hands in there!" Grist held up his gloved hands, and I could see Lukas scanning them.

"You got robotic hands!" Lukas marveled. "My science teacher said it was just a matter of time ..."

"Best thing that ever happened to me," Grist said. "Now, there's no such thing as "hands-off" for this man!"

He clapped his black bionic hands together and suddenly the door slammed shut behind us. Were we his prisoners? Or was it just to stop the ferocious wind from swirling inside?

"Now, let's get down to business." Grist moved into the front of his contraption where a set of windows gave us an 180-degree view. Flying bicycles, signs, and other debris swept past, carried by the wind.

"Soon, it'll hit gale force," Grist said, pursing his lips. "Better catch the wind before they catch us here." He placed his hand on a huge lever and studied the dials on his instrument panel. "Got anything besides chocolate to pay for this flight?"

Lukas glanced at me, and I nodded in agreement. "Spanish doubloons," Lukas said. "For collectors."

"You salvage shipwrecks?" Grist eyed Lukas in surprise. There was a tone of respect in his voice. "Who you work with?"

"Uh, my father," Lukas said. "Ever heard of Turtle Lab?"

"Nope, but I don't trade in turtles, kid. They're endangered. Gotta draw the line somewhere."

"Not killing turtles, it's a rehab center. My Papi works there. It's on Conway Avenue in South Sarasota."

"Never seen it, but I could get you there, I reckon," Grist snorted. "How much gold you got?"

I reached into my backpack and pulled out two large golden doubloons. Just like the waitress in Sid's Fish Shack, this rough man's demeanor changed when he saw my treasure. He even pushed his goggles up onto his forehead. For a moment, I thought he might confiscate all of our possessions.

Grist laughed when he saw me back away, protectively gripping my backpack. "Hey, little lady, I might be a thief, but I'm still a gentleman. We all gotta have something left to trade, right?"

"Right!" Jake piped up.

He seemed as shocked as Grist at the Spanish doubloons. I noticed the two of them exchange a quick look that suddenly made me wary. Were Grist and Jake striking a deal—and did it involve us? Maybe they were both really pirates. Maybe Lukas was right to suspect Jake.

"These doubloons are worth a small fortune," Grist murmured as he held them up to study their golden inscriptions. "As much as I'd like to rip you off, sweetheart, one of them will do just fine. After all, there is such a thing as honor among thieves!" He turned to Lukas, "But I will take a chocolate bar. Can't remember the last time I tasted it ... probably your age."

Grist quickly pocketed the Spanish doubloon, but ripped open the golden foil of the bar and ate it in one mouthful. "Holy Mother, that's good," he declared.

Grist could have stolen all of our Spanish doubloons, but he only asked for one. Maybe I was wrong to distrust him and Jake. Maybe they were really going to help us. Maybe I had nothing to worry about.

"Now, steady yourselves!" Grist yelled.

He reached out and jerked back a huge metal lever. His robotic hands flashed with audible lights that made a whirring, silver sound. The flying contraption shuddered and groaned, but slowly began to lift off the ground. "You ready to ride this storm?" Grist asked with a wild grin.

Jake scrambled up to look out the small windows. "Ready!" He reached over for my hand to steady me, but Lukas had beaten him to it.

Pulling me closer to him, Lukas squeezed my hand, almost painfully. Even I knew what this meant. He was letting Jake know: She's mine, my territory. It's the same in any culture. It was a little irritating, but also exciting that these two boys seemed to be in a not-so-subtle struggle over me. Pandora was usually the one with suitors who fought for her attention. I'd only ever had Dylan. And he felt more like a brother to me than a mate. I wondered if Jake and Lukas would actually declare a Marine Arts duel over me, as two of my sister's suitors had in Aquantis.

With his other hand, Lukas grabbed onto a railing to anchor us. "How's this thing powered?" he shouted. "Oil, gas, solar?"

Jake laughed, but he was scowling now at Lukas. "Dude, that's so twentieth century. . ." he said with a shadow of contempt in his tone. Then Jake nodded to Grist, as if to apologize for our backwardness. "They're from Cuba. Lost in time, ya know."

Grist guffawed at Lukas and spat out one word of explanation. "Wind!"

It took all Grist's considerable strength to work the lever as the airship lurched, buffeted back and forth by the gale outside.

"Hold onto me, Marina!" Lukas shouted.

He seemed suddenly like his old self. Willful and self-assured. And even a little proud. Was it because Lukas was at last going to find his father or because he was holding so triumphantly on to me? Maybe both.

Jake glared at Lukas, his hazel eyes darkening, his jaw set. The boy's obvious envy made me shift uncomfortably. Then the airship made a horrible screeching noise and I thought we might explode. At last, it jerked upward and sailed into the turbulent, blackening sky. ˜

CHAPTER 19
Sarasota

"What in the world is that?" Lukas asked Grist, pointing through the airship's porthole to the rolling turquoise sea below us.

Off the shoreline was a gigantic metallic and blue structure floating securely on the wild waves. It was as big as an island. The round building looked like a giant conch shell with many levels, green forests in the center, and some kind of metal fronds sticking out on all sides. It was beautiful yet ominous.

"Eco-Arks," Grist explained. "Floating cities for all the refugees."

"I thought you two said you saw these when you were floating at sea?" Jake asked, crossing his arms.

"We did—they just look different from up here, I guess." Lukas replied, trying to appear casual. "What are they like?"

"Lots of modern conveniences like solar, electric, smart cottages, rainwater recycling, and public transportation. Eco-Arks power themselves. Forty thousand people in each one. Perfectly energy efficient."

"It's perfect in every way," Grist said slyly. "And in a floating city, you don't have to worry anymore about getting flooded."

"But you don't want to end up there," Jake warned.

"Why not?" I asked.

The floating Eco-Ark was impressive with its splendid architecture and brightly lit silver-blue stories. It looked like something an Aquantan builder might spin out of sand and stone and glass. The spy in me took mental photos to bring back to Aquantis.

"Well, once you're onboard those floating cities, you never get off. Unless you can swim hundreds of miles," Grist said. "Refugees, immigrants, it takes time to process everybody."

"Yeah," Jake snorted. "Sometimes your whole life."

"But there's plenty of food and culture ... the good life," Grist said. "As long as you don't care about your freedom."

"And plenty of weird experiments," Jake added. "If you know what I mean." The fact that Jake glanced at me when he said this sent a little chill through my body. Had Jake already figured out that I was an alien?

"And then, of course," Jake added, "there's always the pirates. They attack Eco-Arks for food and anything valuable they can trade or salvage."

"Are you ...?" I had to ask Grist. "Are you a pirate?"

"Grist is one of the best." Jake grinned and winked at him and then turned to me. "But he's a friend, too, Marina. If you ever get trapped on an Eco-Ark, Grist is the guy to get you off."

I didn't know whether to be reassured or frightened.

"You see," Lukas telepathed to me. "I told you Jake was not to be trusted." Lukas tightened his grip on me. "I'll protect us," he said. "And so will Papi."

Grist banked the airship as a slap of wind sent us flying east, away from the Eco-Ark and toward land.

"Hey, most of the city is flooded," Lukas observed. He was now glued to the porthole. "What's going on down there?" He pointed to vast fields below. They looked like a system of little rivers and terraces.

"Refugee farming," Grist shouted over the lurch and din of his airship's wind turbines. "With all the floods, the legalized refugees now work their rice paddies. It's what they trade."

We zoomed and dipped and tilted sideways, caught inside a crazy undertow of air. I felt light-headed, bending double with an awful queasy feeling. My stomach churned.

"Humans get sea sick, Marina ..." Lukas telepathed, patting my back a little too firmly. "So of course, you'd get airsick," His thumping my back made me hiccup and belch—very embarrassing sounds.

What must Lukas think of my body with its gurgles and loud noises? It wasn't at all attractive. "Sorry," I managed to say, but then covered my mouth to stop the bile surging up my throat. No use. My stomach urgently emptied out on the floor.

Lukas smiled sympathetically and rummaged in his backpack; at last he pulled out some woven kelp cloth. "You'll feel much better now, Marina."

I did. Almost tenderly, Lukas wiped my lips and then bent down to scrub the floor. His mood seemed to have lightened. Was it because we were even? I felt almost as bad as he did with his *manna* withdrawal. Why did that cheer Lukas up?

"Nothing I can do about the turbulence, kids," Grist called out, turning around to grin at us. He exchanged another look with Jake, who shrugged his shoulders.

No one seemed terribly offended by my body's upheaval. It was the least of our problems. Yet, I wondered if Pandora would have done such a rude thing in public. The more I pondered my role as High Priestess, the more I realized it was my sister who was really born to play the regal part. Where was she? And Dylan—had Pandora also seduced him? Would we find them in Sarasota? So far I was not very impressed with the Blue Beings' plan. Maybe they weren't such Masters after all.

The queasy feeling began to dissipate, but then I felt something else almost as uncomfortable: Jake was studying me as if he was seeing me clearly for the first time. Humans don't have sonar, but Jake had an obvious sixth sense, heightened by his need to adapt to and survive such harrowing conditions. I wondered what humans used to scan each other's true motives, to figure out their lies. Something told me I would learn soon enough.

As the airship swayed and dipped, Jake grabbed onto the copper railings and made his way over to perch near me on a storage box. "You're ... you're really not from around here, are you?" Jake asked.

"Uh ..." I began, but one snort from Jake silenced me.

Then he noted drily. "Tell me, in Cuba do they eat fish whole, raw ... and with all the little bones?" Jake asked, keeping his voice low so that Grist wouldn't hear him. "What are you? Some kind of sea monsters?"

It never occurred to me that my stomach contents would reveal my true identity. All the strategies and planning to keep my Aquantan nature secret were useless as soon as the boy saw what I'd eaten. A bolt of panic ran up my spine. What if Jake traded me to the salvagers or turned me in as some kind of prize trophy for scientists? I'm sure I'd bring in enough money to keep his little gang fed for a long time.

Lukas swiftly pulled his hand from my back and placed it, with some pressure, on Jake's small shoulder. "Hey, man, you'd eat fish whole if you were starving, too. And like I told you, Marina has to be really picky about what she eats or she gets sick."

"But you had all those Japanese Power Bars ..." Jake began suspiciously.

"Yeah, we had enough to share with you," Lukas reminded the boy.

Slightly more pressure from Lukas's hand checked Jake's next question. Jake still scrutinized me, slowly looking me up and down. Then his eyes rested on my hands where the faintest veil of blue webbing connected my fingers. There was no way to explain that.

The boy's eyes widened. For a moment, I thought he might blurt out something. But instead, he seemed to store his perception deep inside his own thoughts. It was as if he was hiding his realization from us. Was Jake saving his discovery for some later bargaining deal—when he would betray us? Would he sell us to Grist as bounty?

"Well, whatever." Jake shrugged. "Japanese eat all sorts of weird fish. Ever had sushi?"

Lukas's whole body relaxed. He hadn't noticed Jake's skillful scrutiny. So Lukas let go of Jake's shoulder. "Nope," he said good-naturedly. "You?"

"Are you kidding, man?" Jake smiled slightly, but his eyes were still watchful. "Raw fish?"

"Whoa, stop it, Nellie!" Grist's shout startled us. "Settle down! Drop altitude to 1,000 feet." He was working the lever on his wind turbine and yelling at someone who wasn't there. Or was she?

I glanced around to see if someone else was hiding onboard this rattletrap airship that seemed held together more by Grist's willpower than its many spinning gears and giant clicking gauges. The wind was hissing and blowing us sideways. I couldn't help wondering if we'd actually make it to Sarasota without crashing.

"Who's Nellie?" I asked, but Lukas only shrugged.

As if overhearing my mind-talk, Jake answered, "This must be a 'smart' airship" ... you know, like smart homes or cars."

"Oh, yeah, right. Like smart phones," Lukas nodded, intrigued.

"Descending to 1,000 feet ..." A mechanical woman's voice said as the flat screens on each side of our airship shimmered into life.

"Good girl, Nellie!" Grist yelled, his gloved hands flashing with the same green and red lights that popped out on the flat screens. "Now, can you keep us steady in this wind shear?"

The airship shimmied mid-air, dropped so precipitously my stomach again lurched. But then we caught what felt like an updraft of wind, and the turbulence eased slightly. Below us, the architecture of human buildings seemed to float. It was hard to see the sprawling city through the small porthole.

"Hey, Nellie," Jake yelled. "Give us a visual."

Did this robotic computer program respond to anybody's voice? Not just Grist's? Would she do what I asked her?

"Oh, God," Lukas breathed as the large, flat screens, much like our Aquantan Sound Murals, flashed into vivid life. "Sarasota ... where we ... where my Papi lives." Lukas didn't see Jake cast him another wary glance.

Was there really any use in pretending anymore when Jake knew we were lying? What would he do with us? Would he betray our trust? I wished Dao were there. He'd know what to do.

Below us were neatly plotted streets with tall stone buildings, some of which looked vacant. Others were lit up brightly with solar panels and lush, tropical gardens planted on rooftops. How ingenious of humans to plant their gardens in the air when their streets were so often running with floodwaters.

There were all kinds of transportation, much of it different than in the outdated documentaries of SkyeWorld I'd seen on the Sound Murals. There were small airships zipping above the traffic, bicycles that zoomed along above streets, and many aerial trains running on suspended tracks that wove in and out of the city. The traffic was more airborne than on the ground—maybe that was the way they dealt with so many floods. Many buildings had small circular landing pads on their roofs and were linked together by sky bridges.

"Sarasota looks like a giant, green honeycomb ..."Lukas breathed, fascinated. "A lot can happen in ten years ..."

"Ten years?" Jake quizzed, on the alert again. "You visited here ten years ago?"

"Uh, yeah." Lukas recovered himself quickly, "Tourist visa ... and the old postcards we got in Cuba are from 2020."

"Give it up, man." Jake shook his head. "Your story sucks. Don't bother with any more lies."

There was an edge of irritation in his voice, and I could see that Lukas's forehead was beaded in sweat. Again, Jake was studying us from head to toe. But this time his considerable attention was focused on Lukas. Not me. I felt a wave of relief. At least Lukas could probably still pass for human.

"Don't know if I can land on the ground in this deluge, kids," Grist called out to us. "Might have to drop you on a rooftop landing pod."

The airship tilted and nosedived downward as if we might crash right atop one of the many gleaming buildings.

Grist shouted. "Grab hold!" Then he yelled at Nellie as the airship shuddered and lost more altitude. "Don't just drop us. Take us down gently ... yes, that's right." With a loud whirring sound, the airship hovered over a landing pod and then, with a teeth-jarring wobble, dropped us down. "Good girl, Nellie," Grist said, with obvious relief.

"That was more like a dribble than a landing," Lukas commented, his face ashen. Sweat dotted his forehead.

My stomach had strangely settled, now that we weren't being tossed around in the wind. Funny, how quickly the human body adjusts when the motion suddenly stops. I felt a little dizzy, but otherwise all right. Lukas grabbed hold of the railings, moving hand-over-hand toward the door. But it didn't open for us. Would Grist and Jake really let us leave?

"Are we anywhere near the Turtle Lab?" Lukas asked.

From his raincoat pocket, Jake gingerly took out his big glasses. Scanning Eye-Net, he nodded. "GPS says it's just four blocks south on Highfill Avenue, right?"

Lukas stood up to his full height and took a deep breath. I could see that it took all of his energy to pull himself together. His heart thudded wildly, and he grinned ear to ear, his expression so hopeful. "Yes, that's right," he said and his voice was stronger. "My Papi lives here! " For a moment his eyes blurred with tears. I knew he was happy, so close to finally finding his father.

I was glad for him. But I also felt tears start in my eyes, and they weren't tears of happiness. When Lukas found his father, my mission would be over. His reunion with Papi meant my separation from Lukas. It would be wonderful, of course, to return to Dao and journey the WaveHole home. But the idea of never seeing Lukas again was so unexpectedly painful. Why? We really had no future together. After all, we were from two very different worlds. In my long career as a Diplomat-Spy, would I ever be allowed to visit SkyeWorld again? Would Lukas forget about me? I already knew that I would never forget him.

"Diplomat-Spies don't ever get deeply involved," Master Lioli had taught us in Emotional Espionage 101. "Romances—if you must have them during your missions—are to be brief and uncommitted. It's the only way we can remain neutral. It's the only way we can negotiate with and sometimes spy on those who trust us."

Diplomat-Spies were never assigned to a world very long. My mission there was almost over. It was right that I return. Why then, did I feel a mutinous rebellion rising up in me, just as surely as that bile had surged up from my belly? What if I wanted to stay there—not just for Lukas, but also for myself? It wasn't that I loved this troubled Skye-World so much. Not yet. I just didn't want anyone telling me it was time to go home before I was ready.

"Okay, the doubloon got you two this far," Grist said, nodding to Lukas. "But how about a little more chocolate?" He was licking his lips in anticipation of another chocolate bar.

Obligingly, Lukas dug in his backpack and tossed Grist the precious chocolate, its gold foil glinting in the dim cabin.

"Muchas gracias, kiddos!" Grist said.

With a whoosh, the airship door clanged open. Jake leapt out onto the launchpad before Lukas could even get out the door.

"Hey, you don't need to come any farther with us, Jake," Lukas said, hopping down onto the rain-swept ground.

"Gotta trade that chocolate for food," Jake reminded Lukas. "You promised."

"Oh, yeah," Lukas said. He was obviously distracted.

It bothered me that Lukas seemed so often to forget his promises or even his duty when his own needs were primary. I didn't admire this kind of selfishness. It probably meant that he would promptly forget about me as soon as he found his father. But to Lukas's credit, he turned to help me down from the airship and then nodded to Jake.

"Course we got to get you some food for your gang," Lukas said firmly. " I didn't mean to forget—I'm just so excited to see my Papi. He can also give you some money."

Jake seemed to accept Lukas's explanation. I wondered if he had other plans for trade, as well. Trading me. I would have to keep my eye on Jake, since Lukas seemed oblivious to anything now except finding his father.

It occurred to me that Jake, more than Lukas, might actually make a very good Diplomat-Spy. Observant and farsighted, Jake could delay his own gratification to help others. These were survival and leadership skills that Lukas seemed to have lost. I couldn't help but feel disappointed in Lukas, even though I realized it probably wasn't his fault that he was devolving. It was my sister's fault. *Manna* addiction seemed to reveal one's worst character traits.

"I'd wait for you kids," Grist called out to us from his airship. "But I gotta get back to Siesta Key before this hurricane hits for real."

"Good luck!" Jake waved at Grist. "We'll find our own way back."

How, I wondered? And then I remembered that Lukas's father would help us. Maybe he even had a fusion motorcycle or another kind of truck like the Turtle Lab van I'd taken my first ride in long ago. Maybe I'd finally learn what Lukas's father wanted to tell us that night.

Grist's airship was up and off before we had time to say goodbye. Not that we could linger on the launchpad while such a fierce wind swirled around us. Lukas reached over and pulled my rain hood over my face, then grabbed my hand.

"C'mon, before we get blown off this roof!" he yelled.

Jake, bent double against the wind, found a door that said, "Exit."
"Can't risk the elevators," he shouted. "Too many people."

So we all ran down what seemed like hundreds of stairs. I was still
getting used to using stairways and it took a few moments of stumbling
to get the rhythm in my land legs. By the time we got to the ground
floor, Lukas was gasping for breath, but I was just getting the hang of
stairways. It was a little like dancing.

It took all Jake's strength to push open a huge metal door to a
narrow passageway that seemed deserted. One look at the ground told
me why. Flooding. There was only a solitary, disheveled-looking man
moving down the alley, and he was wading almost waist-deep in dirty,
debris-filled water. On his head he carried a bulging suitcase.

"Probably all his worldly possessions," Jake muttered. He turned
to me. "I notice you two travel awfully light."

I didn't know how exactly to answer him and was relieved when
Lukas, who had at last caught his breath, said curtly, "Of course. Refugees know what's important to carry—and what's not."

This seemed to somewhat satisfy Jake, who shrugged and darted
into a side passage. Triumphantly, he emerged with a battered bicycle
that had some kind of rickety motor attached to it. But how would
that help us in these flooded streets?

"Hop on!" Jake ordered.

The engine sputtered. Lucky I was slender enough that the three
of us could fit on the bicycle. With a whoosh, our air bike lifted off
and into the traffic stalled above flooded streets. On what appeared
to be a main thoroughfare below, a few dilapidated buses and trucks
full of people moved through streets running high with water over the
wheels. Above all this city traffic zipped a few small airships and sleek
aerial scooters. There seemed to be no rules to this chaos of transportation. How did people keep from smashing into each other? On the
flooded streets below people rowed frantically in small boats—canoes
and others with engines. Where was everybody going?

As if Jake read my mind-talk, he explained, "They're trying to get
to hurricane shelters and high ground."

I wondered if somehow Jake had been able to tune in to my frequency. After all, Lukas had shocked me by being able to hear my

mind-talk before we even got to his Aquantan training. If Jake could now hear my telepathy, did he suspect my true nature? If so, we might be in grave danger.

"We'll take this ramp," Jake shouted and we zoomed up onto a bridge that was dry and high. I held onto Jake's waist a little more tightly as I looked around to get more of a sense of this city.

It sprawled and then rose up in tall buildings. There were loud sirens and horns and people yelling. But they didn't seem angry. The voices were high-pitched and surprisingly buoyant. It was like a huge reunion with everybody helping everybody else. I saw a man dive into the floodwater and pluck up a dog who was yelping as he drifted by. There was a woman nursing two babies, one at each breast, as she floated in a boat filled with toddlers. Surely, they weren't all her children. Was she saving them?

"Everybody seems so ..." I didn't know how to explain it, even to myself. "Well, why such high spirits?"

Jake grinned. "Hurricanes and floods bring out the best in us," he remarked. "It's all the times in between when you really gotta watch your back."

This human behavior didn't make a lot of sense to me. Why would disasters bring out the best in them? Was it because humans preferred catastrophe to calm? That was opposite than Aquantan life.

Lukas's grip on my waist suddenly tightened. "There it is!" He shouted with so much joy, I envied him. "The Turtle Lab ... turn here, Jake."

Jake maneuvered our bicycle above turbid waters on a back street near a bay, which was flooding all the empty cottages. But the Turtle Lab was raised up on what looked like poles so the floodwaters washed beneath it without getting inside.

Lukas seemed overcome with happiness. He released his grip on my waist and leapt off the motorcycle, plunging himself waist-high in the grimy water. Without even looking back, Lukas half-swam, half-strode toward the stairs. Bounding up the steps, he used his fist to batter the door.

"Open up!" Lukas cried out. "Where's Papi?"

There was no answer.

Lukas kept calling out and pounding the door. At last, it was opened by a round, blonde woman dressed in blue laboratory scrubs smeared with blood. I vaguely remembered seeing her before in the Turtle Lab.

"Lyla!" Lukas cried out. "Where's Papi?"

For a moment the woman was confused. She seemed deeply exhausted. No recognition. All she saw at first was a teenager begging for food. But slowly her expression changed and her dull eyes widened. "Lukas!" the woman screamed. Then she burst out sobbing.

Before Lukas could protest, she grabbed him and almost lifted him off the ground, holding him fast. The woman kissed Lukas's cheeks, his hands, and the top of his head. Then she clasped him again very tightly. I felt a strange feeling that I didn't at first recognize. Then it struck me: pure loss. Like when we lost Master Loo to SkyeWorld medical experiments.

But this loss was worse. It was his choice. Lukas had so easily leapt away from me—and hadn't looked back. Everything in me collapsed and again, my eyes blurred. I knew my mission was over. This reunion meant that I must leave Lukas and SkyeWorld. That was always the duty of a Diplomat-Spy: Observe, engage, detach. ~

PART SIX

CHAPTER 20
The Floating City

LUKAS

With one hand on her arm, Jake stands next to Marina in the Turtle Lab's examining room. He's too close to her. It makes me want to throttle him. But I can't move, standing practically naked in front of a smart screen. Now, it's not just the turtles who are being scanned by Robo-Doc on silver wheels, it's me.

Robo-Doc's face is female with blonde hair and lifeless blue eyes. She's supposed to appear real and helpful. But she looks more like a life-size mechanical monster to me. I expected something like this in the future. Even when I was living here, there were robotic surgeons and domestic robots that cleaned houses or tended to kids and elders. There were also robots that offered companionship—they looked like pet dogs or seals. Papi and I could never afford robots—and besides we had our work with real animals, which were better, anyway.

"Stand still, Lukas," Lyla says. "Or we won't get a proper diagnosis."

"What's to diagnose?" I hear Jake whisper to Marina. "Once an addict, always a addict."

To her credit, Marina shakes her head in reprimand and looks down. But she doesn't move away from Jake's possessive touch. Maybe she needs to lean on Jake. I certainly haven't been able to be as strong for Marina as I'd hoped.

Even Lyla recognizes I'm sick. It must be a shock to her that I still look sixteen years old when ten years have passed. I should be a full-grown man. Maybe what betrayed my identity was collapsing into Lyla's arms like some kind of girl when she told me that Papi wasn't here anymore— that he had returned to Cuba several years ago on a marine mammal research grant. Lyla has lost contact with my father and he never answered her emails. Maybe he's dead.

What's the point of anything now? I'll never find Papi. Lyla says that it's still very hard to get into Cuba, even with the fragile detente. And Marina has to return to Aquantis soon. She'll never stay here with me to keep searching for my father. It's hopeless. Who cares what happens to me?

"I don't need a doctor," I protest. And I certainly don't need some robot discovering that I have an Aqua-Lung and Aquantan *manna* swirling through my system.

"Maybe they can heal you, Lukas," Marina says in her ever-hopeful voice.

"But what if they find out that I'm not ...?" I protest, quickly shutting up. Jake is listening acutely to everything Marina and I say now. So I shift into mind-talk.

"Gotta get rid of Robo-Doc before she discovers I'm not just human anymore."

"No, you need help, Lukas. It's worth the risk," Marina argues. "Don't you want to be well again?"

Next to finding Papi, that's what I want most in this world. "Yeah, okay," I say. But I don't think I've ever felt so helpless.

Pandora's *manna* has ruined my life. The Aquantans are always talking about living ethically and facing moral dilemmas with courage and skill. How ethical was it to send me back to a world that has no idea how to cure *manna* addiction?

Why couldn't the Healing Masters fix me first? Then Marina wouldn't have to see me like this. She wouldn't have to take refuge in a guy like Jake. Now, more than ever, I'm convinced that Jake's going to betray us. Glancing at him holding onto Marina, I scowl. He's obviously a traitor. Why can't Marina see that?

"Ouch!" I yell in surprise as Robo-Doc draws blood from my arm.

"Anomaly," her mechanical voice muses, her eyes clicking as if in surprise. "More tests required."

Sweat begins to run down my body so that I'm standing in a shower of my own perspiration. My legs feel weak, like they might buckle under me. And dizziness swirls inside my head. I can hardly remember what it's like to feel normal, strong.

"Turn to the side," Robo-Doc commands. Even though her electronic voice is designed to soothe patients, this prying machine is anything but calming. "Now, the other side. Thank you, sir."

"Oh, I'm a 'sir,' now," I try to laugh, looking over at Marina. But my voice is hoarse, and she doesn't smile.

Sweating and shivering, I must look terrible. Red splotches dot my arms and legs like poison ivy blisters. The worst part is not being able to breathe right; it's like my lungs are filling with sand. It's so humiliating. And scary, like suffocating.

I don't need Marina feeling sorry for me like I'm some kind of pathetic invalid. Even though it's the last thing I want, I telepath to her, "Why don't you and Jake get out of here for awhile? Try to sell the chocolate bars or something."

"Did you forget the hurricane outside?" Marina's mind-talk is strained. Maybe she wonders about my memory now.

"Oh, yeah," I telepath. "Well, it's blowing over. At least go talk to the turtles. See if you can figure out what to do next." Then I suggest what I know will make Marina leave me. "Maybe the turtles will know where Dao is."

Find a simple task. It's what my Papi always taught me to do when things spin out of control, when I'm stressed beyond my ability to cope. Make a plan. Finish a task. It just might take Marina's mind off our predicament. And keep her from seeing me like this any longer.

"Jake," Marina turns to him. He's still resting his hand on her arm. Like she belongs to him more than me. "Let's give Lukas some privacy."

"Sure," Jake whispers to Marina. I can hear him because of my Aquantan acoustics training. "Come on—I know a guy who has Zitrope, the miracle drug they use to help addicts like Lukas. It will cost a lot, but it'll help him get off...whatever he's on," Jake says with a dark tone in his voice. Judgmental and superior.

Marina gives me a long, worried look. Then the two of them stroll out of the examining room, not exactly arm-in-arm, but they're together now in a way that Marina used to always ally herself with me. Survival of the fittest. That's my world. And Marina is just adapting to it. As I hear the air motorcycle whoosh away from the lab I wonder:

Will Marina come back for me? Or is the Zitrope run only a ruse for Jake to get Marina all to himself?

I stand there alone now, except for Lyla, in front of the smart screen, my arms stretched out as Robo-Doc whirrs and bleeps gathering information about my body: A hand-held MRI the size of a cell phone clicks and flashes 3-D lights along my spine and around my head. Then an unexpected cotton swab swirls inside my mouth.

There is a long pause while bleeps and clicks ricochet inside Robo-Doc. "Human genome complete." Then the flat repetition, "Anomaly. Anomaly..."

But this time there are hundreds of bright strobe lights and clicks of a camera shutter as photos are shot like fireworks.

At last Robo-Doc concludes firmly, "Second opinion required."

"No!" Lyla rushes in between me and Robo-Doc. "Not that!" She clutches me by the shoulders. "Get dressed, Lukas, and get out of here quick!"

But it's too late. There's an urgent knocking at the Turtle Lab door, and three burly men in black uniforms stride in. They push Lyla aside and rush to Robo-Doc, who is spitting out a series of holograms. One of the men grabs the printouts, and his eyebrows knit in surprise.

"This is your genome?" he glares at me. "Are you Lukas Barrios Rodriguez?"

I'm half-dressed now and calculating how fast I can bolt for the door of the lab. I'd have a better chance of surviving the hurricane winds than fighting off these guys. They look more like soldiers than medics.

"Leave him alone!" Lyla cries out and stands in front of me. Like she can protect me from these thugs. "How did you get here so fast? Robo-Doc barely had time to call you before ..."

And then I know. It was Jake. Somehow he must have contacted these soldier-medics. He got Marina out of here just in time so the authorities would only find me, not her. If he betrayed me, what dangers are in store for Marina? I feel horrible. I failed to protect her.

"You can't take Lukas!" Lyla shouts. "He's under my care."

"Lady, you only got a medical license for animals," one of the men snaps.

Another medic-soldier laughs harshly. "Or maybe he does need a vet."

I'm screwed. I can't outrun them, and in my condition there's no way I could take down one, much less four, grown men. If we were on the beach, I might be able to escape—shift and swim far away, maybe find Dao. Right about now, I'd be thrilled to see that know-it-all dolphin.

One of the men wraps a silver blanket around me roughly and hoists me up in the air like I'm a baby. "Ready, Captain."

"Where are you taking him?" Lyla screams, begging the man. "You can't arrest him. He's done nothing wrong."

"His genome is not just human," the captain says. "He's been spliced with animal DNA. We need to run more tests in the lab."

Robo-Doc must have discovered my Aqua-Lung and *manna*. Who knows what else the Aquantan healers implanted in me that this machine exposed? I begin laughing almost hysterically. All this time I've been worrying about Marina being captured for medical research, when I should have been the one fearing imprisonment.

Lyla runs over and grabs my face in her hands. If she could telepath she would have. But all she can say is: "We'll find you, Lukas. I promise."

As the soldier carries me away, I call back to her, "Tell Marina ...!" I stop.

Tell her what? She's with Jake now. She shouldn't try to rescue me because that would put her at great risk. Maybe it's better for her this way. Maybe she's better off without me.

I try to reach for the man's carotid artery to knock him out. But he holds me at arm's length as I struggle against him. My body starts trembling. With all my strength I try to leap out of the soldier's grasp. But it's no use. Then, against my will, my legs begin to shudder. No, not now! Why now?

I didn't sing my Signature Song; I had no plan to shift. But driven by terror, my body has a will of its own. It adapts to give me the most strength—my tail flukes.

"What the ... ?" the soldier shouts and drops me as my legs fuse and my flukes flail, thrashing him. "We got a fuckin' fish here, Captain!"

I lie on the ground, my tail flukes strong but useless here on land. Anyone who comes near gets lashed. The men surround me, their faces glazed in amazement.

"Get a net," the captain orders, obviously a fisherman when he's off-duty.

Suddenly, a wide net falls over me. Its sharp plastic cinches my arms tightly to my side. Then I'm dangling mid-air between two guys like some trophy fish.

They carry me outside the Turtle Lab with Lyla running after them, screaming. They pay her no mind and toss me in the back of an air truck that has some official insignia on it I don't recognize. One of the guys hops in the truck bed to secure me with more rope and tighten the net. As we speed off in the hurricane winds and the high waters, the guys joke roughly.

"Look what we caught!" one of them snorts.

"They'll never believe this fish tale."

"Hey, let's not take him back to the lab," the captain says after awhile, like he's reconsidering my fate. "He's just a kid. You know what they do to zenotransplant hybrids there."

"But the labs pay big money!" one of the other guys protests.

"I got a kid," the captain says hoarsely. "Or I used to ... before Malachi hit."

There's a tense silence. Like the men are still arguing, but without words. My head is thudding wildly as I await their decision.

At last the captain says, "I know what we'll do. Sell him to the Eco-Ark. They've got a brand new research facility and an aquarium. It's where they bring stranded sea creatures to study. They'll check this hybrid out and figure out how he got those tail flukes." The captain laughs drily and lights a cigarette. "A tail like that might come in handy in the next tsunami. Wouldn't you want one?"

"Okay, okay," the soldiers grudgingly agree.

"They might make him perform tricks—but at least the boy will live."

The captain glances at me in the rearview mirror, his eyes not quite hidden behind shaded glasses. He's not a thug; he's just trying to get by. He's lost a son. And I've lost a father. That makes him a loner, like me.

It's night and the Eco-Ark aquarium and research center is empty except for a watchman who dozes in front of a 3-D hologram TV. His snores echo throughout the aquarium. With the lapping of my tank's chlorinated water and the weird night shadows, it's kind of spooky here. Some of the researchers, like Courtney, are kind to me. Others think I'm a freak of nature and are one step away from dissecting me.

The watchman hardly ever patrols the aquarium. The first night here I tried to leap out of the tank and shift into my legs. But the tank is covered in a thick ceiling of Plexiglas with a hatch that opens when they feed me or when the vet wants to poke and prod at me. It's locked from the outside. My first few days I sang out my Signature Song non-stop and tried desperately to shift. If they saw a real boy with two legs floating in this tank, they'd rescue me. But nothing works. My tail flukes seem permanent now. I don't know why. It's like the reverse of when I first arrived in Aquantis and couldn't for the life of me shift into my tail flukes.

It feels like I've been in this tank forever, swimming around with a whale shark, a captive dolphin, Loki, and a zillion clownfish. During viewing hours, people gawk at the boy with the beautiful, but bizarre tail flukes.

"Is he a dolphin boy?" kids ask. They put their hands on the aquarium glass, hoping I'll swim over to them. But I never do anymore. Not since the first frustrating day.

During my first few forced performances, I screamed out at the crowd, "I'm human! I'm like you. My name is Lukas Barrios Rodriguez and I live here in Siesta Key. Please get me out of here!"

The trainers put an end to my attempts at communication by shutting off the sound system every time I talked. So my shouting just looks like a big guppy gulping saltwater. Even though I repeatedly explained to the keepers that I was born human and had been dragged down to Aquantis against my will, they thought I was crazy and told me to shut up. Courtney still lets me talk to her—but only when nobody else is around. She's quiet, but very skilled. She reminds me of my old girlfriend and lab partner, Jenny. Like me, Courtney has a stylized dolphin tattoo, but on her forearm.

I've told Courtney everything. Who knows if she believes me? But she always listens. Courtney is the only one who treats me with any respect. Maybe she thinks I'm some escapee from a medical lab experiment in human-animal hybrids.

The trainers still let me sing. They think it's amusing. I'm hoping that someone will hear me and admit that I'm still human, still one of them. But so far they don't. They just listen to me sing "Gracias a la Vida," and then they marvel at how well I've been trained. Like I'm some sort of smart parrot or talking gorilla in a circus act. Papi would be horrified at the way they treat me and the other animals.

I've given up on humans. Maybe Master Lioli was right to think of us as a primitive species. I try to hide out behind the gentle whale shark or behind the huge coral reef display. There's a small sign saying, "90% of our oceans' coral reefs have been destroyed."

"You think he's a mutant?" the kids ask, mesmerized.

Their parents don't know how to answer. They point at the sign outside my tank: "Sea Creature of the Deep. Genus Unknown," and a few paragraphs about how I was discovered during a research expedition in an ocean trench in the Atlantic. They point in amazement, believing that I was never human. That I was always this freakish mer-man.

Without a clock, with no window to the outside world, it's hard to tell time. I count the days by my daily performance schedule. I figure I've been imprisoned here for about a month, and no one seems to know where I am. Lyla hasn't found me. And who knows where Jake has taken Marina or even if they're looking for me. Maybe he betrayed Marina too and sold her to a different floating city. Or, he might have convinced Marina to explore SkyeWorld with him. To forget about me.

I'm half crazy with swimming round and round in this concrete pool. My sonar bounces off the walls and comes right back to me in maddening echoes. They feed me fish like I'm some sort of trained seal. The most horrible thing of all is that every day they make me perform tricks for the crowd: I leap up in synch with Loki, spin in midair, and splash down into the tank. And they'll only feed me if I sing for them. Talk about singing for your supper.

Some days I wish I weren't a hybrid but a dolphin like Loki. Then I could stop breathing consciously and just die. As voluntary breathers, dolphins choose to take each breath. If they get depressed in aquariums, they just stop breathing and sink to the bottom of the cement tank. But I'm still human enough to have a reptilian brain that breathes, even if I knock myself unconscious.

There are really bad days, like today, when I float listlessly at the top of the tank, not even bothering to eat the fish thrown in at feeding time.

"You've got to find a reason to keep living ... keep breathing." Loki often tries to comfort me.

But I'm inconsolable.

"What do you believe in, Lukas?" Loki's telepathy is tender.

"Not much ... anymore," I say.

"If you're going to stay alive, it really helps to have some purpose," Loki tells me, his brown eyes holding mine.

Loki has a cool way of swimming with his tail wagging sideways. The kids love it. Loki looks a lot like Dao. But Loki was born in captivity and sold to this floating Eco-Ark off Sarasota when he was a year old. He will never see his family pod again. And he's never swum in the open sea, only round and round in circles in this cement tank. You'd think he'd be nuts by now.

"What's your purpose?" I ask. "You've lost your family, you're imprisoned here for your whole life, and none of these humans know how smart you are. It's hopeless. What keeps you going?"

"I think of myself as a kind of teacher or diplomat who's been imprisoned—just for being a different species," Loki explains thoughtfully. "Think of how many people and animals around this world are in prison, just because of what they believe or who they are."

I've never thought much about that. But in this tank there isn't much else to do but think. One interesting development: My withdrawal symptoms seem to be ebbing. My mind is clearer, and my body is gaining strength every day. Maybe it's all the vitamins Courtney's giving me, little pellets of B3 and high antiviral doses of vitamin C hidden inside my fish. Could it be that with Courtney's vitamin therapy

I'm getting free of my addiction at last? At least, one good thing has come out of this wretched experience, I guess.

"Teacher, huh? What can you teach humans? They don't seem interested in learning much from us." I tell Loki.

"That they're not alone here," Loki says simply. "And they're not the only smart ones on this planet. In fact, the dolphin brain is more evolved than the human brain."

"Good luck with convincing people of that!" I laugh. "For them, we're just entertainment."

Loki swims alongside me in silence for a while. He knows all about my history: losing my father, my training in Aquantis. Loki has actually heard of that underwater civilization. He thought it was a myth.

"What would you do if you could get out of here?" I ask him.

"Well, I'd like to swim in the ocean," Loki says with a wistful tone in his mind-talk. How can he still dream of freedom? "I'd like to travel the WaveHole I've heard so much about from other dolphins that used to live here in this tank with me before they were sold. And now you tell me it's real. It's so exciting! Would you take me back to Aquantis with you, Lukas?"

"Oh, sure," I laugh. "Let's go tonight!"

Before Loki can respond with his good-natured whistle, I hear a loud noise, like something hitting the floor and a shout. Then a voice I never expected to hear again, especially not here.

"Yes, let's go, Lukas ... now!"

I look out into the darkened exhibit room, and there she is. Pandora is radiant in her sharp silver mesh breastplate armor and trident held above her head. I can't help but notice her strong and lovely land legs. Beside Pandora is Dylan, looking wary.

Desperately, I swim to the glass and place my palms on the cold wall, my heart thundering. "Pandora!" I shout.

"Did you think I couldn't find you again, Lukas, if I wanted to?"

Pandora's voice is the same rich purr that vibrates through my body with the remembered pleasure of her *manna*.

"But how?"

"I can always track my *manna* in you." Pandora smiles with satisfaction. But then she admits, "Although your signal was getting weaker."

I don't reply that Pandora looks a little weaker, too. Her face is strangely gaunt, her eyes hollowed and bruised. Her legendary curves are more angular, as if she's been starving. Have Pandora and Dylan fallen ill or not been able to find food? I glance at Dylan; he looks as strong and buff as always. It's just Pandora who seems diminished.

Even though I'm worried about Pandora, a desperate craving for her rises up in my body. I fight it, but feel a surge of raw desire that's so strong my tail flukes begin to shudder and shed silver scales. Can Pandora help me shift into my legs? Could another transfusion of her powerful *manna*—just one more honeyed kiss—set me free? ~

CHAPTER 21
Leap

With her golden trident, Pandora smashes open the lock on the hatch above my tank. "Leap, Lukas!" she commands. Dylan is leaning over, his muscular arms stretched out for me. His expression is cool, dutiful.

With all my strength, I thwack my tail flukes twice and propel myself upward. Dylan catches me in both arms and hoists me onto the cover of the pool. I gasp with the effort, my whole body shaking.

"Now, shift back to your land legs!" Pandora orders. "And let's get out of here before the watchman comes to."

"I can't shift!" I yell. "Think I'd still be captive here if I could use my legs?"

Pandora scowls, and for just a moment seems bewildered. Then she gathers herself and commands Dylan. "Carry Lukas."

I catch just a flash of Dylan's fury—after all, I'm not his favorite person. I'm a rival for Marina's favor, and I beat him in the Marine Arts match. He'll never live that down. But Dylan is obviously still under orders from the Blue Beings to protect me and obey Pandora.

"Where's Marina?" Dylan demands. He grabs me by the shoulders and shakes me.

I'm still trying to catch my breath after the mighty effort to leap out of the aquarium pool. "Dunno," I manage to say.

"What d'ya mean, you don't know?" Dylan shouts. "You were supposed to stay with Marina. Why did you leave her?"

"I didn't leave her!" I yell right back at him. "She dumped me. Ran off with some guy named Jake she met here." Yeah, it's a lie, but she did leave me, after all. And where has Marina been all this time?

"She ... left ... you?" Dylan is shocked and stares at me hard. "Why would Marina do that?" he asks. But his eyes are pensive.

I can see Dylan trying to figure it out: Marina, his beloved, choosing to run away with someone she'd just met. And a human. Slowly, a realization spreads over Dylan's handsome face. Marina did this before. She abandoned Dylan for another human she'd just met. Me.

"Women aren't as fickle as you think, boys." Pandora says, uncharacteristically sticking up for her sister. Or maybe just making a point about her superior gender. "If Marina left you, she had a very good reason."

As I lay on top of the tank looking up at Pandora and Dylan, I'm too ashamed to tell them the truth: Marina went with Jake because he promised her a cure for my addiction. I hope that Pandora and Dylan can't tell how much I still crave her *manna*. Just being near Pandora again makes my belly twist and heat rise up my spine. Just a drop of her *manna*—that's all I need now. I hate myself for asking, but I do.

"Pandora," I begin, my voice trembling. "If you gave me more *manna*, just a little, I could shift into my legs. Dylan wouldn't have to carry me. We'd all have a better chance of escaping if I could run."

It strikes me how crazy backward this all is: I'm the human with tail flukes, helpless on land, while these two highly-trained Aquantans are stuck using their land legs.

Pandora pauses to consider my plea. She looks ashen, like the blood has been drained from her. Or the *manna*. Did it lessen Pandora's own life force to give her *manna* to me? Or was Master Hu right when he told me that Pandora also needed to be near me, from time to time, to truly thrive? Did Pandora really come back for me or for herself? Maybe she lost some of her luster because she's also strung out—on me? The idea makes me shiver. And crave her even more.

"Pandora," Dylan advises in that aristocratic know-it-all mind-talk of his. "you can't give Lukas any more of your *manna*. The Blue Beings strictly forbid it, especially in SkyeWorld."

"Why not?" Pandora asks.

She tosses her golden curls, and I notice they make no music. Her hair doesn't shine like it used to, and it's wrapped in a haphazard braid. This once glorious beauty now reminds me of those anorexic high school girls who diet themselves to death.

Dylan presses his cause. "Because, Pandora, you and Lukas need the Healing Masters to oversee any more *manna* transfusions. It's not safe for either of you to do it by yourselves," he adds darkly. "There are side affects, Pandora ... you're already suffering from—"

"You're not the leader of this mission, Dylan," Pandora snaps defiantly. "I am."

She looks at me a long time, her eyes calculating. My whole body craves her, and I can hardly keep myself from begging. But I'm also concerned that another *manna* transfusion might really harm Pandora. Now is the time for me to remember my Aquantan ethics training: "Do not ask for others to give what you need—if it costs them too much."

Studying me with her red-rimmed eyes, Pandora seems to also be struggling with her decision. I remember my first impression of this girl at the cave party: reckless and brave. It doesn't seem like she's changed much.

Pandora holds my gaze and we're locked in a moment of mutual need. Now it seems both our lives depend upon each other. Then Pandora straightens her shoulders and says, "Just one more time, Lukas."

Before Dylan can stop her—and because I won't stop her—Pandora leans over me and places her cool lips on mine. A hot stream of precious nectar flows into my throat, down into my chest, and swirls inside my belly like the most delicious golden rum.

Instantly, my heart light glows, all my senses heightened. My brain explodes with electricity and complete clarity. I can see my past and present—and can almost see the future. It's as if my brain is creating a thousand new synapses. Everything is possible. Everything has a purpose. I can see that now.

How could I ever dream of living without this *manna*? It's the most delicate yet intoxicating sensation: hot, liquid pleasure. And a rush of pure power. It's how athletes must feel on steroids, bigger and stronger, indestructible.

As Pandora lifts her exquisite face from mine, I notice that her eyes are dilated and luminous, like an azure sky without a hint of clouds. I realize that the *manna* she gives me also intoxicates and empowers her. Now Pandora's cheeks are rosy again, her skin glowing and supple, her lips full, moist. I'm shocked that our sharing of *manna* also has such a potent effect on Pandora. Her vitality and power is restored. But for how long?

I touch the last drop of nectar on Pandora's mesmerizing lips. There is just a moment when we are both bound in this timeless ecstasy, as if we belong together. Always.

"So ... Pandora says with a satisfied smile, "shift, Lukas!"

In perfect pitch, I sing out the soaring tenor arpeggio of my Signature Song. My tail flukes tremble and twitch as the *manna* throbs through my body. I feel utterly invincible, my muscles zinging, energy surging.

My tail flukes split apart and scales scatter everywhere. I'm shocked. No pain. It's the first time I've ever shifted without that deep ache in my legs. Within minutes, I can jump up and balance on my own two feet again. I'm barefoot and nobody has any shoes for me. But who cares? Super-charged, I can run and leap and finally escape. Freedom is as exhilarating as *manna*—well, almost.

"Thank you, Pandora," I say and wrap my arms around her.

She allows my embrace for an unexpected minute. This is the first time I've caught Pandora's alluring, warm scent. Always before Pandora and I were underwater. But now I can deeply breathe in the musky jasmine fragrance of her hair. Pandora's shapely body sways against mine, moving with velvety, voluptuous grace. My hands re-member the slope of her hips, our salsa dance.

"Let's go," Dylan says, his lip curled in disgust. He cocks his head and listens for any sound that the watchman might be waking up from being stunned by their sonar. "It's almost dawn. We don't have much time."

Pandora is already climbing down the steel ladder above the tank's glass ceiling. Dylan is right behind her. I grab hold of the rungs and begin to descend.

Then I hear it, the bleeps and pleading whistles echoing off the cement walls of the tank. It's Loki.

"Please!" the young dolphin pleads. "Take me with you, Lukas."

"No way," says Pandora. Her expression is not hard; it's just matter-of-fact. Her warrior training allows for little sentiment. "Come on, Lukas."

I hang on the ladder with one arm, my mind spinning. We'd have to carry the dolphin down through many decks of this complex Eco-Ark. Loki would certainly slow down our escape. He might even compromise it. What if we were captured again? And yet I can't stop thinking about my sonar bouncing off these cement walls as I swam round and round this hateful tank. How could I leave Loki to face a lifetime of that misery?

I take a deep breath, closing my eyes. All I can hear are Loki's desperate whistles. If I leave this dolphin, it will haunt me. Forever. I'd never be completely free if I abandon this fellow creature who did everything he could to comfort me. To keep me alive.

I scramble back up the ladder to the top of the tank. "Dylan," I call down. "If we both carry him I think we can make it."

Dylan is beside me instantly. "OK," he says. But when Dylan looks at me, I can see there is a new glimmer of respect in his eyes.

"Can you leap through this hatch?" I call down to Loki, who is swimming fast circles in the pool.

"Can I?" Loki whistles once, and then with a burst of speed, he circles the cement tank. His tail flukes propel his sleek silver body upwards—straight through the open hatch. In fact, Loki leaps so high he almost disappears into the ceiling lights above the tank. "Catch me!" Loki shouts as if we're playing a game.

As Loki falls downward, Dylan and I brace our arms together to catch him. It's a good thing I'm so pumped up with *manna*. The falling weight of the dolphin almost topples us. But Dylan and I hold steady, catching Loki safely between us.

"That's quite a leap," Dylan tells Loki with a wry smile.

I realize it's the first time I've seen Dylan smile at anybody except Marina. His expression is unexpectedly warm, not aloof and condescending like Dylan's usual manner. Maybe I shouldn't have dismissed him as just another uppity Aquantan aristocrat.

"I've been practicing that leap all my life!" whistles Loki joyfully.

Somehow Dylan and I manage to carry the dolphin down the steel ladder. As we're struggling to navigate the descent, Dylan catches my eye. Gone now is his smile. He's intensely serious. Our escape isn't going to be easy.

"As soon as we get off this Eco-Ark," Dylan says, "you've got to help me find Marina."

"Is that Pandora's plan?" I surprise myself by asking.

Dylan cast me a critical look and I come to my senses.

What does it matter if it's Pandora's plan? Of course, Dylan is right. We've got to find Marina. The *manna* is confusing me. Marina's well being must be my priority. Who knows what Jake has done with her? Marina could be imprisoned in a lab or in another aquarium.

It unsettles me that my first thought is about Pandora's wishes. Did her *manna* carry with it a kind of emotional enslavement as well as physical addiction? Could Pandora compel me to do something against my will? Like abandon any search for Marina? After all, there is no love lost between the two sisters. And I have a feeling, one day I will have to choose one sister over the other. I believe I'll choose Marina. In my heart, I feel we belong together. Yet my body might have other plans—or needs.

I can't think of this now. It's all too complicated. Besides, the *manna*'s power is surging through my body like bolts of adrenaline. We need to get out of here while it lasts, while I feel unstoppable.

We carefully creep by the old watchman slumped over in his chair and steal past the coral reef and kelp forest exhibits, past the moon jellies and starfish and octopus tanks. I can hear an octopus crying out to us, "Help me, too!"

But we can't stop. Out of the corner of my eye, I see the floating octopus fold her many arms around herself, turning bright red. Then she simply closes her square blue eye in despair, sinking to the bottom of her tank. My heart sinks with her—I wish we could take every creature with us.

But Dylan and I have our hands full carrying Loki. He's so excited to escape his lifelong imprisonment that his slippery body wiggles. It's hard to hold onto the sleek dolphin. Maybe someday I can come back and rescue the other animals.

We race around the last corridor of the aquarium and run toward the back door. I can smell the salt of the ocean. My Aqua-Lungs breathe in the sea air gratefully as Pandora swings open the heavy exit door.

"Oh my god ... you?" It's Courtney carrying her early morning buckets of fish. Feeding time.

Courtney's wide eyes travel down to my legs. "Oh," she exclaims. "I always hoped you were telling the truth, Lukas."

Pandora raises her trident to knock Courtney away from the door. "No!" I shout. "Don't hurt her."

"Oh, she's your girlfriend, now that my sister dumped you?" Pandora asks. She begins humming her stunning spell.

"You don't need to stun her, Pandora. She's a friend."

"Not to us." Pandora's voice is firm. She increases the volume of her hum.

Courtney looks at me in confusion and fear as she starts to sink slowly to the ground. Both buckets of fish spill all over the asphalt. I can't go to her without dropping Loki.

"Sorry, I'm so sorry," I tell Courtney. "I hope you don't get in trouble. You'll be okay soon. You're just stunned."

Courtney smiles, her expression dazed, but still conscious. Go, Lukas," she says. "Get free." She turns to Loki with a tender look. "Be wild." Then in slow motion, Courtney finally falls down on the pavement. But her eyes follow us.

As Dylan and I carry Loki past Courtney's limp body, I glance down. I wish I could linger a moment longer. Courtney looks so vulnerable lying there. I reach down and touch her shoulder lightly. "Thank you," I tell her.

She blinks her understanding like a blessing. Then Courtney passes out.

Suddenly, the morning gong sounds. Everybody on this Eco-Ark will be up and we'll soon be discovered if we don't get out of here.

"Hurry!" Pandora telepaths. "We've got to get down to the lower decks."

Dylan and I carry Loki in our arms like a sling. The young dolphin tries not to whistle and bleep with exhilaration. But his sleek body trembles and his brown eyes are huge.

This is what hope looks like.

Running sideways with Loki between us, Dylan and I follow Pandora's lead. Ducking under steel pipes and dodging whirring generators, we take the exit stairs down several decks. So far no one has spotted us. But that could change at any moment in this floating city. No one ever escapes this Eco-Ark; that's what Loki told me when I was first tossed into the tank with him. Security is too tight and the swim to shore too far. The authorities say the Eco-Ark confinement is for the refugees' own protection. Pirates are everywhere in these waters. But maybe they have ulterior motives for imprisoning animals and people here.

When I was captured and carried to this floating city by the soldiers, they blindfolded me. This mandatory dwelling for so many thousands of refugees is also a work camp. Kind of like having to live on a giant round cruise ship and slave away as a deckhand all your life.

"Over here," Pandora telepaths. "There's an exit on deck one that leads to the open sea. Quick, you two!" She scowls at how slowly Dylan and I have to move while we carry Loki between us. "We can't get caught." I detect a hint of fear in Pandora's typically haughty expression. This surprises me. But then I realize she must be imagining her own captivity in an Eco-Ark aquarium. What good would Pandora's seductive, Warrior wiles be to her if she were trapped inside a tank?

"Move it!' Pandora orders. "Drop the dolphin if you have to."

"No." Dylan says. His voice is flat.

"Please ..." Loki cries and whistles.

I feel a moment's guilt. I should have been the one to protest Pandora's command. "We got you, buddy." I reassure Loki and lift him a little higher.

"Listen!" Dylan says urgently.

We all tune in, and then I hear it: footsteps hitting stairs. Fast. And then the shrill blast of alarm bells. "Break-in on deck nine ... aquarium level," a mechanical voice shrieks. "All guards to the exits!"

"Only one more deck to go!" Dylan shouts.

Pandora is taking the steps three at a time, flying downstairs. Dylan and I take each step carefully so we don't drop Loki. The dolphin has gone completely still, his eyes now wide with terror.

"You can leave me," Loki telepaths. He's looking at Dylan, not at me.

"No way!" Dylan shakes his head. "You belong with us."

I'm struck at how decent Dylan is. I'm not quite as noble—my mind is filled with fears that they'll recapture us and drag me back to that aquarium—even with my legs. If push comes to shove, will I leave Loki behind?

I stumble on the steel crosshatching, and we almost drop the dolphin. But Dylan is strong. He doesn't need *manna*. He comes by his power naturally. He's earned it. Marina belongs with someone like him.

"Open the door!" Dylan shouts to Pandora who is far ahead of us at the bottom of the stairs.

Pandora wastes no time protesting the fact that Dylan is now giving the orders. She throws open the door, not even lingering to hold it for us. She's determined to escape, with or without us. Pandora's normally enchanting blue eyes are now stricken with terror. I don't see the trained stoicism of a Warrior. She looks like a frightened girl running for her life.

For an instant, my body wants to bolt after Pandora and stay near her. Who knows how long her *manna* transfusion will last?

Sprinting across the open deck, Pandora leaps over the railing without a backward glance. Far below, she splashes into the safety of the waves.

My eyes meet Dylan's, and I see that he's reading my mind. "Go after Pandora," he says very calmly. "I can handle this. I can carry Loki by myself. Go!"

"Okay," I shout, feeling a combination of guilt and relief. I start to move, but my feet won't budge. It's as if they're connected to my conscience, when every other part of my body wants to drop my burden and run for safety. Escape the heavy boots I hear thudding down the stairs to deck one. To us!

Dylan and I stare at each other as we hold a helpless dolphin between us. It's as though we're holding the whole world in our hands. This world and ours.

"Both of you save yourselves." Loki looks up at us intensely, and then he simply closes his eyes. "Run!"

His flanks are quiet. I realize that the dolphin is choosing to stop breathing, to die right here, rather than be captured again and imprisoned in that aquarium. I can't let him do that.

"Breathe!" I tell the dolphin "Dammit, keep breathing, Loki."

Dylan heaves open the door. And then we race out onto the deck, still carrying Loki. I can smell the open ocean and the dolphin gasps. He breathes in great draughts of sea air. His whistles are exuberant trills.

"Stop!" A gaggle of guards in black uniforms is closing in on us. "Both of you stop and put your hands above your heads."

"Can't!" Dylan turns almost casually to face the three guards. "We've got precious cargo."

"That dolphin is our property you're stealing," the lead guard says, advancing toward us.

"None of us are your property!" I shout back.

Dylan and I move as one mind now. He doesn't even have to telepath for me to know what we must do. Dylan and I rush across the deck to the railing. One, two, three!

"Biggest leap of your life, Loki!" Dylan shouts as we hurl the dolphin up into the air.

Loki shoots out of our arms and straight up in a beautiful arc over our heads. His Signature Whistle is so loud the guards clap their hands to their ears. It stuns them for a moment as they watch the silvery body soar up into the sky and then dive down into the waves. There isn't even a splash as Loki dives into the ocean—for the first time in his life. Free.

But we're not. One of the guards has pinned my arms behind me. The other two are grappling with Dylan.

"Remember your Marine Arts, Lukas," Dylan telepaths to me. There is the faintest suggestion of a smile on his face.

He's strangely calm. Or maybe it's just his years of training. *Manna* surges powerfully through me. I wiggle my body until my arms are free and then I spring up and punch the guard, just like I hit Dylan during the Temple Tests. And it works. The lead guard falls to the deck, one hand cradling his chin.

As I'm running over to help Dylan he shouts. "No, Lukas. I got this. I'm right behind you. Dive!"

My body makes the decision for me. I jump over a fallen guard and with two hands on the railing I propel myself overboard to freedom. My leap is not as spectacular as Loki's, but it's as sure. It feels like I'm poised midair, head tucked down, arms straight out, feet pointed. I hit the water with a huge splash. The moment my legs feel seawater, they easily shift into tail flukes. Amazing. As if I belong in the sea more than on land.

"Where's Dylan?" Pandora demands floating in the waves. "Why'd you leave him?"

"Dylan's right behind me," I cough, sputtering seawater. "Isn't he?"

I don't ask her why she abandoned us both on deck. Pandora's wild eyes, her cheeks flushed with shame say it all. She's a Warrior who has done the unthinkable: deserted the battle and her companions. It's every true Warrior's nightmare. Instead of feeling any triumph over Pandora's failure, I feel sorry for her. The fact that Dylan and I have witnessed her cowardice will weigh very heavily on Pandora. I want to comfort her and say, "You're only human." But she isn't.

I twirl around, treading water, looking up at the Eco-Ark. It's so huge. There are hundreds of people leaning over the decks, shouting and clapping. For us. They're cheering our escape. I wish we could help them find freedom, too.

But where is Dylan?

I feel a pang of regret and guilt. I never should have left Dylan to fight off those two guards by himself. I'm a coward, too. Pandora says nothing, floating alongside me with her constant, Lak. Pandora's eyes are focused above on the first deck. "We've got to get out of here. Patrol boats are everywhere."

"No!" I say quietly. "We have to wait for Dylan."

"You're right," Pandora says, a catch in her voice. "We'll wait for him."

"Look," Loki whistles.

And there's Dylan, his perfect body in a perfect dive. Dylan in the sky is as aerodynamic and skilled as any dolphin in the waves. The Aquantan aristocrat seems to float in the blue sky before he stretches out to his full length and dives toward us. Then he twirls and shifts midair into his tail flukes. His grace and strength are a sight to behold in any world. A roar of amazement and approval surges up from the Eco-Ark refugees.

Crack! The sharp ricochet of a bullet. Like a magnificent bird, Dylan's body collapses, arms falling, tail flukes tucking protectively. Somersaulting crazily through the sky, he hits the water with a heart-wrenching splat. The guards didn't have to shoot Dylan when he was soaring free. It wasn't self-defense; there was no hope of capturing him mid-air. The reality that these guys gunned Dylan down makes me realize how cruel my kind really are. They shot Dylan out of meanness, like it was some kind of sport.

By the time Loki and I can dive down under the waves to retrieve Dylan, he's almost unconscious. Blood is streaming into the water from a gaping wound to his chest. Dylan's heart light is dimming.

"No!" I shout.

Loki and I hold Dylan up in the waves. Eyes fluttering, he can barely breathe. The scales from his tail flukes are scattering—it's a sure sign of a fatal wound for any Aquantan.

"You can't die!" Pandora is also holding Dylan now.

I never thought I'd see this Warrior weep. But she is. And then Dylan's Constant, the octopus Zwo, joins us. He wraps his tentacles around Dylan as if that can staunch the gush of blood from his body. Zwo makes a keening sound, half-scream and half-snarl.

"Lukas ..." Dylan grabs my arm, and his eyes hold mine fiercely. "Find ... Marina ... promise me ..."

"I will," I assure him. And I mean it.

"I leave her in your ... your care," Dylan says.

Those are his last words. A blue echo shimmers up from his lifeless body. And his spirit slips away.

Zwo lets out a howl and pulls Dylan away from our arms. The octopus is now ghostly pale. Will he die, too? Wrapping his tentacles around Dylan's limp body, Zwo begins a slow pirouette in the waves.

My own heart constricts with pain as I watch the octopus swim in circles, carrying Dylan' body. Zwo's many arms can't protect Dylan from death. Now Zwo must endure the tragedy of any Constant who loses his twin soul: For the first time and forever after, he is truly, achingly alone. And he will probably end up like all solitary Constants—dying of grief.

My eyes blur and I struggle to keep tears from spilling over.

As Zwo woefully carries Dylan in his arms, Pandora sings the honorary Aquantan death blessing. "In another world ... Dylan, in another world ... " Pandora's voice is raw with pain. Her eyes are bloodshot, her beautiful face swollen.

"This is your fault, Lukas Barrios Rodriguez," Zwo says, his voice breaking. "I will hold you accountable if you ever dare come back to our world."

I don't protest. My whole body is in shock, and suddenly it's hard to breathe, like my lungs are filling up with grief. Then without a farewell, Zwo casts his square eye on me—and dives.

"Where's he going?" I ask Pandora.

"He's taking Dylan back to Aquantis for burial at sea," she murmurs. Pandora is no longer crying. She's straight-backed, her expression stern as she pulls herself upright, her eyes hooded and hidden now by her Warrior training. "Dylan will be honored as a hero ... which is more than I can say for you."

Or you, I want to tell Pandora. I want to shout at her that she's not my Constant. That I can leave her any time I want and go search for Marina.

But I say nothing. We float together in the waves, eyeing each other warily. Who knows what will happen next? All I know is that I need Pandora way too much. She may be all that I have left in this world. ~

The End

Coming in 2013, the next adventure in the Aquantis Series

The stunning sequel to *The Drowning World* follows Lukas, Pandora, Marina, and Jake to Cuba—a sinking paradise. Here they encounter the mysterious Aquantan, Master Tara, who has survived SkyeWorld sickness through her magical skills. Master Tara reveals Lukas's shocking heritage and Marina's destiny. But will Pandora and Jake prove to be loyal? Or will they betray those they've sworn to protect?

The next book features a variety of voices: Pandora, Jake, Marina, and Lukas, including some of their Constants and Aquantan Masters. They face dangerous allies and explore many other worlds as the volatile WaveHole carries them to strange, forbidden realms. Dive in with them!

If you'd like to read the first chapter of the sequel to *The Drowning World*, please send your email to:

drowningworld@gmail.com

A PDF of the new novel's first chapter will be sent to you. Get a head start on the sequel. And offer suggestions for the title of the new novel. Also get updates from the author on her blog:

www.BrendaPetersonBooks.com

Acknowledgments

Every book has a community behind it—and this new novel, more than any of my books, is buoyed by what I think of as my "Publishing Pod." And it is informed and inspired by my two decades spent studying whales and dolphins, who are masters in their own water world.

Though I chose to turn down a publisher's offer and enjoy complete artistic control to bring *The Drowning World* out as an indie publication, I didn't leave traditional publishing behind. Professional editors and designers were with me every step of the way, as well as readers and other authors who have lent me their good eyes and great insights.

Since 2003, my film agent, Mary Alice Kier and her partner, Anna Cottle, of CineLit, have read, advised, dreamed, and delighted in this underwater cosmos. When it becomes a film, we'll all stroll arm-in-arm down the red carpet. My long-time literary agent, Sarah Jane Frey-mann, has spent the past year lending me her storytelling brilliance in an exacting content edit. "Cave Dancing" was her idea and Sarah Jane is my WaveMate in all things ocean. My *Animal Heart* book designer, Elizabeth Watson, created this glorious cover. Sherry Wachter elegantly designed the paperback book's interior. Fine artist, Christine Lamb's, animal icons graced an early cover design.

My *Animal Heart* editor, Linda Gunnarson, offered precious advice and great encouragement as I swam through what seemed like many WaveHoles of revision. *Living by Water* editor, Marlene Blessing, blessed this book with a thoughtful final edit, as did Meredith Bailey, whose final line editing was astute and rigorous. My editorial assistant and Young Adult ace reader, Mira Skladany, asked complex questions I'd never considered and has an uncanny gift for marketing. Natasha Lucal drew fabulous sketches of the main characters that sat on my desk as I wrote. Tracey Conway gave the book a close and timely final proofing. I'm always so grateful for the editorial guidance and sister-hood of my *Singing to the Sound* editor, Maureen Michelson. Thanks also to my gifted *Leopard and Silkie* editor, Christy Ottaviano at Henry Holt for Young Readers, who offered excellent advice and direction in early drafts of this novel. And gratitude to my *Leopard and Silkie* co-author, the luminous photographer, Robin Lindsey, whose work always gives me hope for our seas and marine mammals.

To visionary Jungian analyst, Anne DeVore, I give lifelong thanks for her literary scholarship, musical artistry, and intuitive perceptions. She travels many worlds. I am so grateful for my sister author, the amazing Sy Montgomery, who read early and final drafts. She is a true PodMate in this drowning world. Respected book critic and Tufts University professor, Marion Copeland, read the finished book and gave the book an early review. She also caught a few typos!

When it came time to publish this new novel, I turned to the wide world for support with a Kickstarter.com campaign. And the book was fully funded—lifted on the high tide of almost 62 generous backers, including my wonderful students, old friends, family, and even good-souled strangers who helped to publish this book. I am so grateful to all my Kickstarter backers, especially my inspiring elder, Mary Matsuda Gruenwald and my wise memoir editor, Merloyd Lawrence.

Much gratitude to Diane Johnson, Joy Harjo, Terri Windling, Janet Smith, Donna Highfill, Jean Sward, Clare Meeker, Sally Richardson, Kip Greenthal, Sarah Jane Freymann, Laura Foreman, Christine Lamb, Andrew Federspiel, Laurel Liefert, Andrea Adams, Janice Harper, Pamela Warren, Nancy Leimbacher, Pamela Leptich, Patricia Monaghan, Melinda Simon, Dori Jones Yang, Joe Olsen, Sensei Kimberly Richardson, Wendy Noritake, Maureen Michelson, Lizbeth Adams, Catherine Johnson, Lindsay Pyfer, Yuri Shvets, Courtney and Charlotte Peterson, and my brother and sister-in-law, Dana Mark and Renee Peterson, who were the ones who put me over the top at over 102% Kickstarter funding. And thanks so very much to the other 30-plus Kickstarter.com backers whose support makes this book possible, including Thomas Geraghty, Lori Pignatelli, Elani Henry, Lena McCullough, Suky Hutton, Brian Tucker, Meredith Baily, Alexis Henry, Heather Galusha Ripley, Mary Anne Mercer, Susan Bloch, Rubiee

Tallyn Hayes, Kristin Paystrup, Pamela Sage Dodson, the Simons Family, Linda Yapp, Rebecca Dare & Bill Opfermann, Amanda Mander, Steven Markusfeld, Anna Lazar-Johnson, Leslie Helm, Suzanne Montagne, Margaret Schulze, and Barbara Berger. I can hardly wait to send you all your rewards.

Finally, I'd like to thank my dear students who also teach me every week and inspire me with their courage to tell their own stories. My 12th House Club—Jerry Halsey, Taoist healer, Jim Dowling, and Lu Leeland—who meditate and read poetry with me here by the Salish Sea. My neighborhood pals and true sister, Tracey Conway, and her sublime Siberian husky, Lulu, for nourishing walks; my feline ascended masters, Loki and Tao; my travel companion and dear ally, Vanessa Adams; my musical inspiration, Diana Shvets, who also keeps me healthy with her Russian cuisine; gratitude for the harmonies of artistic director John Gulhaugen and all the community singers of my Metropolitan chorale. To my lifelong friend, Susan Biskeborn, who helps keep me sane; and the family, who nourishes my work and sustains my soul: Dana Mark, Renee, Charlotte, Courtney, Christina, and Katy Peterson. Thank you all for accompanying me on this otherworldly journey. It takes a Pod!

Please check out other books by Brenda Peterson at
www.BrendaPetersonBooks.com

CPSIA information can be obtained at www.ICGtesting.com
Printed in the USA
LVOW08s1229060114

368268LV00002B/436/P